Thomas Amory

The Life of John Buncle

Thomas Amory

The Life of John Buncle

ISBN/EAN: 9783744711333

Printed in Europe, USA, Canada, Australia, Japan

Cover: Foto ©Raphael Reischuk / pixelio.de

More available books at **www.hansebooks.com**

THE
LIFE
OF
John Buncle, Efq;

CONTAINING

Various OBSERVATIONS and REFLECTIONS,

made in feveral Parts of the WORLD,

AND

Many extraordinary RELATIONS.

Μέμνησο, ὅτι ὑποκριτὴς εἶ δράματος, οἴου ἂν θέλη
ὁ διδάσκαλος· ἂν βραχὺ, βραχέος· ἂν μακρὸν,
μακρῦ.—Ἔςι γάρ τις καὶ ἐνθάδ᾽ οἰκοδεσπότης,
ἑκαςα διατάσσων· &c.
Arr. Epict. L. III. C. 22. Enchirid. C. 23.

IN FOUR VOLUMES.

VOL. III.

A NEW EDITION.

ADVERTISEMENT.

IN a book publiſhed in the year 1756, I related the principal tranſactions of my life, from my entrance into the univerſity to the day of my marriage, in the year 1725; and endeavoured, by the way, to entertain my Readers with a variety of notions and remarks.

I now proceed to tell the remainder of my ſtory, and to lay before the Public ſome more of my obſervations and hints: This ſecond part is chiefly a further vindication of myſelf; and the obſervations I add on ſubjects and matters of various kinds, are ſuch reflections as reſulted from the reaſon and

and nature of things, and were formed by a judgment free, and unbiaſſed
by any authority. My own apology
is the principal thing, interſperſed
with real characters of ſeveral ſorts;
and the additions to it, are as many
ſolid, natural, and delicate adventi-
tious things as came in my way.
This is my book. I write with mo-
deſty, and I purpoſe to do good.. I
imagine then, that all *Critics* (except
the *Critical Reviewers*) will wink at
the blemiſhes of a laudable writing.
Scholars and men of ſenſe (who are
above malevolence and the ſuperci-
lious temper,) can bear deformities
in a long work, and juſtly lay them
on the imperfection of human nature. They know it is incapable
of faultleſs productions.

FELICES.

CONTENTS

OF THE

THIRD VOLUME.

CONTENTS.

28 Some

CONTENTS.

41 De-

CONTENTS.

CONTENTS.

67 An

CONTENTS.

87 De-

CONTENTS.

THE

THE

LIFE

OF

JOHN BUNCLE, Efq;

PART II.

SECTION I.

Felices homines! quos ftricto fœdere jungit,
Et focios natura facit! fic cura levatur!
Sic augentur opes! fic mutua gaudia crefcunt!
Thompfon's Tuphlo-pero-gamia *.

That is,

Go, happy pair! in ftricteft bonds ally'd!
Whom nature joins, and can, alone, divide:
'Tis thus their riches and their joys increafe,
Their cares grow lighter, and they fmile in peace.

§. I. WHEN I confider how happy I have been in the married ftate, and in a fucceffion of feven wives, never had one uneafy hour; that even a Paradife

An apology for the married ftate.

---

* The author of *Tuphlo-pero-gamia* is the Rev. Mr. *William Thompfon*; a junior Fellow of Trinity Col-

Paradife without an *Eve*, would-have been a wildernefs to me; that the woods, the groves, the walks, the profpects, the flowers, the fruits, the day, the night, all would have wanted a relifh, without that dear, delightful companion, a wife; it amazes me to hear many fenfible people fpeak with abhorrence of matrimony, and infift upon it, that wedlock produces fo many troubles, even where the pair have affection, and forrows fo very great, when they have no love for each other, or begin to fail in the kind and obliging offices, that it is contrary to reafon to contract, if we have a juft regard to peace and fatisfaction of mind, and would avoid, as much as poffible, the woes and bewailings of this turbid period. If you have acquired the divine habits, marriage may unhinge them. It often forces even the pious into immoralities. True, unhappy are many a wedded pair: years of calamity this engagement has produced to thoufands of mor-

---

lege, *Dublin*, when I was a member of that univerfity. He was a man of the fineft parts and learning, and was remarkable for a temper fo vaftly happy, that he was always called *Benign Billy*. His paraphrafe on *Job*, in blank verfe, is an admirable thing. It is, in my opinion, far preferable to the ingenious *Broome*'s paraphrafe on this facred book.

tals:

tals: it has made the most pious divines become very cruel, as I could relate: it has caused the most generous, sensible men, to murder the women they adored before they were their wives.

The History of Orlando and Bellinda.

§. 2. This story has been told before by the *Tatler*, in his 172d paper; but as he has related only by hear say, and was mistaken in several particulars, the account I give of this extraordinary affair, may be grateful to the reader.

When I was a little boy in *Dublin*, between seven and eight, Mr. *Eustace* and his Lady lived next door to my father, in *Smithfield*, and the two families were intimate. Being a lively prating thing, Mrs. *Eustace* was fond of me, and by tarts and fruit, encouraged me to run into her parlour as often as I could. This made me well acquainted in the house; and, as I was a remarker so early in my life, I had an opportunity of making the following observations.

Orlando Eustace was a tall, thin, strong man, well made, and a very genteel person.

fon. His face was pale, and marked with
the fmall-pox: his features were good, and
yet there was fomething fierce in his look,
even when he was not difpleafed. He had
fenfe and learning, and, with a large fortune, was a generous man; but paffionate
to an amazing degree, for his underftanding; and a trifle would throw him into a
rage. He had been humoured in every
thing from his cradle, on account of his
fine eftate; from his infancy to his man-
hood, had been continually flattered, and
in every thing obeyed. This made him
opinionated and proud, obftinate, and incapable of bearing the leaft contradiction.

Bellinda Coot, his Lady, with whom he
had been paffionately in love, was as fine a
figure as could be feen among the daughters of men. Her perfon was charming;
her face was beautiful, and had a fweetnefs in it that was pleafing to look at.
Her vivacity was great, and her underftanding extraordinary; but fhe had a fati-
rical wit, and a vanity, which made her
delight in fhewing the weaknefs of other
minds, and the clearnefs of her own conception. She was too good, however, to
have the leaft malice in fuch procedure. It
was human weaknefs, and a defire to make
her neighbours wifer. Unfortunately for
                                    her,

her, she was married to a man, who, of all men in the world, was the unfittest subject for her quick fancy to act on.

But, notwithstanding this, *Eustace* and *Bellinda* were, for the most of their time, very fond. As she was formed in a prodigality of nature, to shew mankind a finished composition, and had wit and charms enough to fire the dullest and most insensible heart; a man of *Orlando's* taste for the sex, could not be without an inflamed heart, when so near the transporting object of desire. She was his delight for almost a year, the dear support of his life. He seemed to value her esteem, her respect, her love; and endeavoured to merit them by the virtues which fortify love: and therefore, when by his being short, positive, and unreasonable in his dictates, as was too often his wont; and on her being intemperate in the strong sentiments her imagination produced upon the occasion, which was too frequently the case; when they seemed to forget the Apostle's advice for a while, *that ye love one another with a pure heart, fervently;* 1 *Pet.* i. 22. and had strifes and debates, which shewed, for the time they lasted, that they were far from being perfect and entire, wanting nothing; then would her throwing her face into

smiles,

smiles, with some tender expression, prove
a reconciling method at once. Till the
fatal night, this always had a power to
soften pain, to ease and calm the raging
man.

But poor at best is the condition of human life here below; and, when to weak
and imperfect faculties, we add inconsist-
encies, and do not act up to the eternal
law of *reason*, and of God; when love of
fame, curiosity, resentment, or any of our
particular propensities; when humour, vanity, or any of our inferior powers, are
permitted to act against justice and veraci-
ty, and instead of reflecting on the *reason
of the thing*, or the *right of the case*, that
by the influence this has on the mind, we
may be constituted virtuous, and attached
to truth; we go down with the current of
the passions, and let bent and humour determine us, in opposition to what is decent
and fit: if in a state so unfriendly as this
is to the heavenly and divine life, where
folly and vice are for ever striving to introduce disorder into our frame, and it is difficult indeed, to preserve, in any degree,
an integrity of character, and peace within:—if, in such a situation, instead of labouring to destroy all the seeds of envy,
pride, ill-will, and impatience, and endea-
vouring

vouring to eſtabliſh and maintain a due inward œconomy and harmony, by paying a perpetual regard to truth, that is, to the real circumſtances and relation of things in which we ſtand,—to the practice of reaſon in its juſt extent, according to the capacities and natures of every being; we do, on the contrary, diſregard the *moral faculty*, and become a mere ſyſtem of paſſions and affections, without any thing at the head of them to govern them;—what then can be expected, but deficiency and deformity, degeneracy and guilty practice? This was the caſe of *Euſtace* and *Bellinda*. *Paſſion* and *own-will* were ſo near and intimate to him, that he ſeemed to live under a deliberate reſolution not to be governed by reaſon. He would wink at the light he had, ſtruggle to evade conviction, and make his mind a *chaos* and a *hell*. *Bellinda*, at the ſame time, was too *quick*, too *vain*, and too often forgot to take into her idea of a good character, a *continual ſubordination* of the *lower powers* of our nature to the *faculty of reaſon*. This produced the following ſcene.

Maria (ſiſter to *Bellinda*) returned one evening with a five-guinea fan ſhe had bought that afternoon, and was tedious in praiſing ſome *Indian* figures that were

B 4   painted

painted in it. Mrs. *Euftace*, who had a tafte for pictures, faid, the colours were fine, but the images were ridiculous and defpicable ; and her fifter muft certainly be a little *Indian-mad*, or her fondnefs for every thing from that fide of the globe could not be fo exceffive and extravagant as it always appeared to be.

To this *Maria* replied with fome heat, and *Euftace* very peremptorily infifted upon it, that fhe was right. With pofitivenefs and paffion, he magnified the beauties of the figures in the fan, and with violence reflected fo feverely on the good judgment *Bellinda*, upon all occafions, pretended to, (as he expreffed it) that at laft, her imagination was fired, and, with too much eagernefs, fhe not only ridiculed the opinion of her fifter, in refpect of fuch things, but fpoke with too much warmth againft the defpotic tempers of felf-fufficient hufbands.

To reverence and obey (fhe faid) was not required by any obligation, when men were unreafonable, and paid no regard to a wife's domeftic and perfonal felicity ; nor would fhe give up her underftanding to his weak determination, fince cuftom cannot confer an authority which nature has denied : It cannot licenfe a hufband to be unjuft, nor give right to treat her as a flave. If this

was

was to be the case in matrimony, and women were to suffer under conjugal vexa-
tions, as she did, by his senseless argu-
ments every day, they had better bear the
reproach and solitude of antiquated virginity, and be treated as the refuse of the
world, in the character of old maids.

This too lively, though just speech, enraged *Eustace* to the last degree, and from
a fury, he sunk in a few minutes into a
total sullen silence, and sat for half an
hour, while I stayed, cruelly determining,
I suppose, her sad doom. *Bellinda* soon
saw she had gone too far, and did all that
could be done to recover him from the fit
he was in. She smiled, cried, asked pardon; but 'twas all in vain. Every charm
had lost its power, and he seemed no longer man. When this beauty stood weep-
ing by his chair, and said, My love, for-
give me, as it was in raillery only I spoke,
and let our pleasures and pains be hereafter honestly shared; I remember the
tears burst from my eyes, and in that condition I went away. It was frightful to
look at *Eustace*, as he shook, started, and
wildly stared; and the distress his Lady
appeared in, was enough to make the
most stony heart bleed: it was a dismal
scene.

This

This happened at nine at night, and at
ten *Orlando* withdrew to bed, without
speaking one word, as I was informed.
Soon after he lay down, he pretended to
be fast asleep, and his wife rejoicing to
find him so, as she believed, in hopes that
nature's soft nurse would lull the active in-
struments of motion, and calm the raging
operations of his mind; she resigned herself to slumbers, and thought to abolish
for that night every disagreeable sensation
of pain: but no sooner did this furious
man find that his charming wife was really
asleep, than he plunged a dagger into her
breast. The monster repeated the strokes,
while she had life to speak to him, in the
tenderest manner, and conjured him, in regard to his own happiness, to let her live,
and not sink himself into perdition here
and hereafter, by her death. In vain she
prayed; he gave her a thousand wounds,
and I saw her the next morning a bloody,
mangled corpse, in the great house in
Smithfield, which stood at a distance from
the street, with a wall before it, and an
avenue of high trees up to the door; and
not in the country, as the *Tatler* says.

Euftace fled, when he thought she was
expiring, (though she lived for an hour
after, to relate the case to her maid, who
                                    heard

heard her groan, and came into her room) and went from *Dublin* to a little lodge he had in the country, about twenty miles from town. The magiſtrates; in a ſhort time; had information where he was; and one *John Manſel*; a conſtable, a bold and ſtrong man, undertook, for a reward, to apprehend him. To this purpoſe, he ſet out immediately, with a caſe of piſtols, and a hanger, and lurked ſeveral days and nights in the fields, before he could find an opportunity of coming at him; for *Euſtace* lived by himſelf in the houſe, well ſecured by ſtrong doors and bars, and only went out now and then, to an alehouſe, the maſter of which was his friend. Near it, at laſt, about break of day, *Manſel* chanced to find him, and, upon his refuſing to be made a priſoner, and cocking a piſtol to ſhoot the officer of juſtice, both their piſtols were diſcharged at once; and they both dropt down dead men. *Euſtace* was ſhot in the heart, and the conſtable in the brain. They were both brought to *Dublin* on one of the little low-back'd cars there uſed; and I was one of the boys that followed the car, from the beginning of *James-ſtreet*, the out-ſide of the city, all thro' the town. *Euſtace's* head hung dangling near the ground, with his face upwards, and his torn bloody breaſt bare;

and

and of all the faces of the dead I have feen, none ever looked like his. There was an anxiety, a rage, a horror, and a defpair to be feen in it, that no pencil could exprefs.

§. 3. Thus fell *Euftace* in the 29th year of his age, and by his hand his virtuous, beauJ tiful, and ingenious wife : and what are we to learn from thence? Is it, that on fuch accounts, we ought to dread wedlock, and never be concerned with a wife? No, furely; but to be from thence convinced, that it is neceffary, in order to a happy marriage, to bring the will to the obedience of reafon, and acquire an equanimity in the general tenour of life. Of all things in this world, *moral dominion,* or the *empire over ourfelves,* is not only the moft glorious, as reafon is the fuperior nature of man, but the moft valuable, in refpect of real human happinefs. A conformity to reafon, or good fenfe, and to the inclination of our neighbours, with very little money, may produce great and lafting felicity; but without this fubfervience to our own reafon, complaifance to company, and foftnefs and benevolence to all around us, the greateft

The apology for the married ftate continued.

mifery

misery does frequently sprout from the largest stock of fortunes.

It was by ungoverned passions, that *Eustace* murdered his wife, and died himself the most miserable and wretched of all human beings. He might have been the happiest of mortals, if he had conformed to the dictates of reason, and softened his passions, as well for his own ease, as in compliance to a creature formed with a mind of a quite different make from his own. There is a sort of sex in souls; and, exclusive of that love and patience which our religion requires, every couple should remember, that there are things which grow out of their very natures, that are pardonable, when considered as such. Let them not, therefore, be spying out faults, nor find a satisfaction in reproaching; but let them examine to what consequences their ideas tend, and resolve to cease from cherishing them, when they lead to contention and mischief. Let them both endeavour to amend what is wrong in each other, and act as becomes their character, in practising the social duties of married persons, which are so frequently and strongly inculcated by revelation and natural reason; and then, instead of matrimony's being a burthen, and hanging a weight upon our very beings, there

there will be no appearance of evil in it, but harmony and joy will shed unmixed felicities on them: they will live in no low degree of beatitude in the suburbs of heaven.

This was my case: wedlock to me became the greatest blessing: a scene of the most refined friendship, and a condition to which nothing can be added to complete the sum of human felicity. So I found the holy and sublime relation, and in the wilds of *Westmoreland*, enjoyed a happiness as great as human nature is capable of, on this planet. Sensible to all the ties of social truth and honor, my partner and I lived in perfect felicity, on the products of our solitary farm. The amiable dispositions of her mind, chearfulness, good nature, discretion, and diligence, gave a perpetual dignity and lustre to the grace and loveliness of her person; and as I did all that love and fidelity could do, by practising every rule of caution, prudence, and justice, to prevent variance, soften cares, and preserve affection undiminished, the harmony of our state was unmixed and divine. Since the primitive institution of the relation, it never existed in a more delightful manner. Devoted to each other's heart, we desired no other happiness in this world, than

than to pafs life away together in the folitude we were in. We lived, hoped, and
feared but for each other; and made it
our daily ftudy to be what revealed religion prefcribes, and the concurrent voice
of nature requires, in the facred tie. Do
fo likewife, ye mortals, who intend to
marry, and ye may, like us, be happy.
As the inftincts and paffions were wifely
and kindly given us, to fubferve many purpofes of our prefent ftate, let them have
their proper, fubaltern fhare of action; but
let reafon ever have the fovereignty, (the
divine law of reafon and truth) and be, as
it were, fail and wind to the veffel of life.

§. 4. Two years, almoft, *Our manner*
this fine fcene lafted, and dur- *of living at*
ing that period, the bufinefs and Orton-
diverfions of our lone retreat Lodge.
appeared fo various and pleafing, that it waf
not poffible to think a hundred years fo
fpent, in the leaft degree dull and tedious.
Exclufive of books and gardening, and the
improvement of the farm, we had, during
the fine feafon, a thoufand charming amufements on the mountains, and in the glens
and vallies of that fweet filent place.
Whole days we would fpend in fifhing, and
dine in fome cool grot by the water-fide; or
under an aged tree; on the margin of fome
beauti-

beautiful ftream. We generally ufed the fly and rod ; but, if in hafte, had recourfe to one of the little water-falls, and, by fixing a net under one of them, would take a dozen or two of very large trouts, in a few minutes time.

By a little water-fall, I mean one of thofe that are formed by fome fmall river, which tumbles there in various places, from rock to rock, about four feet each fall, and makes a moft beautiful view from top to bottom of a fall. There are many of thefe falling waters among the vaft mountains of *Weftmoreland*. I have feen them likewife in the *Highlands* of *Scotland*.

Glencrow water-falls.   At *Glencrow*, half way between *Dumbarton* and *Inverary*, there are fome very fine ones, and juft by them one *Campbell* keeps a poor inn. There we were entertained with water and whifky, oat-cakes, milk, butter, and trouts he took by the net, at one of the little falls of a river that defcends a prodigious mountain near his lone houfe, and forms, like what we have at *Orton-Lodge*, a moft beautiful fcene. Several happy days I paffed at this place, with a dear creature, who is now a faint in heaven.

At

At other times we had the diverfion of taking as much carp and tench as we pleafed, in a large, ftanding, fenny water, that lies about two miles from the lodge, in a glen, and always found the fifh of this water of an enormous fize, three feet long, though the general length of fifh of this fpecies is eleven inches in our ponds : this vaft bignefs muft be owing to the great age of thefe fifh ; I may fuppofe, at leaft, an hundred years ; for it is certain, that in garden-ponds, which have, for experiment's fake, been left undifturbed for many years, the carp and tench have been found alive, and grown to a furprifing bignefs.

The great age and fize of carp and tench, in a fenny water near Orton-Lodge.

A gentleman, my near rela-tion, who lived to a very long age, put fome fifh of thefe fpe-cies into a pond, the day that Colonel *Ewer*, at the head of feven other officers, prefented to the Commons that fatal remonftrance, which in fact took off the head of *Charles*, that is, *November* 20, 1648 ; and in the year 1727, fe-venty-nine years after, on his return to that feat, he found them all alive, and near two feet and a half in length. This demon-ftrates

The ftate of carp and tench put into a pond by a gen-tleman of my acquaintance.

ftrates that fifh may live to a very great age. It likewife proves that they continue to grow till they are an hundred years old, and then they are the fineft eating.

Another of our amufements, during the fummer's bright day, was the pointer and gun, for the *black cock*, the *moor cock*, and the *cock of the wood*, which are in great plenty on thofe vaft hills. *Charlotte* was fond of this fport, and would walk with me for hours, to fee me knock down the game; till, late in the evening, we would wander over the fells, and then return to our clean, peaceful, little houfe, to fup as elegantly on our birds (1), as the great could do, and with a harmony and unmixed joy they are

for

Defcription of the black cock. (1) The *black cock* is as large as our game cocks, and flies very fwift and ftrong. The head and eyes are large, and round the eyes is a beautiful circle of red. The beak is ftrong, and black as the body; the legs robuft and red. It is very high eating; more fo than any native in *England* except the fen-ortolan; but in one particular it exceeds the fen birds, for it has two taftes; it being brown and white meat: under a lay of brown is a lay of white meat; both delicious: the brown is higher than the black moor cock, and the white much richer than the pheafant.

The moor-cock. The *moor cock* is likewife very rare, but is to be had fometimes in *London*, as the fportfmen meet with it now and then on the hilly heaths, not very far from town; particularly

on

for ever ſtrangers to. After ſupper, over
ſome little nectared-bowl, we ſweetly
chatted, till it was bed-time ; or I played on
my flute, and *Charlotte* divinely ſung. It
was a happy life ; all the riches and honours of the world cannot produce ſuch
ſcenes of bliſs as we experienced in a cottage, in the Wilds of *Weſtmoreland*. Even
the winter, which is ever boiſterous and extreme cold in that part of the world, was no
ſeverity to us. As we had moſt excellent
proviſions of every kind in abundance, and
plenty of firing from the ancient woods,
which cover many of thoſe high hills ; and
two men ſervants, and two maids, to do whatever tended to being and to well-being, to
ſupply our wants, and to complete our happineſs ;

---

on *Hindhead-heath*, in the way to *Portſmouth*. It is as
large as a good *Darking* fowl, and the colour is a deep
iron-grey. Its eyes are large and fine as the black
cock's ; hut, inſtead of the red circle round them, it
has bright and beautiful ſcarlet eye-brows.

The *cock-of the wood*, (as unknown *The cock of the*
in *London* as the black cock) is almoſt *wood.*
as large as a turkey, but flies well.
The back is a mixture of black, grey, and a reddiſh
brown ; the belly grey, and the breaſt a pale brown,
with tranſverſe lines of black, and a little white at the
tips of the feathers. It has a large round head, of
the pureſt black, and over its fine hazle eyes, there is
a naked ſpace, that looks like an eye-brow of bright
ſcarlet. It is delicious eating, but far inferior to the
black cock.

pinefs; this foftened the hard rough
fcene, and the roaring waters, and the howl-
ing winds, appeared pleafing founds.   In
fhort, every feafon, and all our hours, were
quite charming, and full of delight.   Good
Tom Fleming, our friend, did likewife enhance our felicity, by coming once or twice
a week to fee us, and ftaying fometimes
two or three days.   In the fummer time we
alfo went now and then to vifit him; and,
if one was inclined to melancholy, yet it
was impoffible to be dull while he was by;
his humour, and his fongs, over a bowl of
punch, were enough to charm the moft
fplenetic, and make even rancour throw its
face into fmiles.

The death of
Charlotte,
my friend
Tom Flem-
ing, and
others. 1727.
ætat. 24.

§. 5.   Two years, as I have
faid, this fine fcene lafted;
and during that foft, tranf-
porting period, I was the happieft man on earth.   But in
came *Death*, when we leaft expected him, fnatched my charming partner
from me, and melted all my happinefs into
air, into thin air.   A fever, in a few days,
fnapt off the thread of her life, and made
me the child of affliction, when I had not a
thought of the mourner.   Language cannot paint the diftrefs this calamity reduced
me to; nor give an idea of what I fuffered,
                                                                    when

when I faw her eyes fwimming in death, and the throws of her departing fpirit. Bleft as fhe was, in the exercife of every virtue that adorns a woman, how inconfol- able muft her hufband be! and to add to my diftrefs, by the fame fever fell my friend *Tom Fleming*, who came the day before my wife fickened to fee us. One of my lads likewife died, and the two fervant maids. They all lay dead around me, and I fat like one inanimate by the *corps* of *Charlotte*, till Fryer *Fleming*, (the brother of *Tom*,) brought coffins and buried them all. Thus did felicity vanifh from my fight, and I re- mained like a traveller in *Greenland*, who had loft the fun.

§. 6. *O eloquent, juft, and mighty death!* (fays *Raleigh*) *A reflection on death.*

It is thou alone puts wifdom into the human heart, and fuddenly makes man to know himfelf. It is *death* that makes the *conqueror* afhamed of his fame, and wifh he had rather ftolen out of the world, than purchafed the report of his actions, by ra- pine, oppreffion, and cruelty; by giving in fpoil the innocent and labouring foul to the idle and infolent; by emptying the ci- ties of the world of their ancient inhabitants, and filling them again with fo many, and fo variable forts of forrows. It is *death* tells

tells the *proud* and *infolent*, that they are but *abjects*, and humbles them at the inftant; makes them cry, complain, and repent; yea, even to hate their former happinefs. It is *death* takes the account of the *rich*, and proves him a *beggar*, a naked beggar, which hath intereft in nothing but the gravel which fills his mouth. It is *death* holds a glafs before the eyes of the moft *beautiful*, and makes them fee therein their *deformity* and *rottennefs*, and they acknowledge it.

Whom none could advife, thou haft perfuaded: what none have dared, thou haft done: and whom all the world hath flattered, thou only haft caft out of the world, and defpifed. Thou haft drawn together all the far-ftretched greatnefs, all the pride, cruelty, and ambition, of man; all the powerful charms of beauty; and covered it all over with thefe two narrow words, *Hic jacet*.

Nor is this all, *mighty death!* It is thou that leadeft to the refurrection of the dead; the diffolution of the world; the judgment day; and the eternal ftate of men. It is thou that finifhes the trial of men, and feals their characters, for happinefs or mifery for ever.

Be

Be thou then, *death*, our morning and evening meditation: let us learn from thee the vanity of all human things; and that it is the moſt amazing folly to melt away time, and miſapply talents, as the generality of reaſonable beings do: that we were not made men, thinking, rational beings, capable of the nobleſt contemplations, to ſpend all our thoughts and time in ſenſe and pleaſure, in dreſſing, feeding, and ſporting; or, in purchaſes, building, and planting; but to prepare for a *dying hour*; that, when at the call of God, we go out of the body, *not knowing whither we go*, we may, like *Abraham*, travel by faith, and truſt to the conduct of the Lord of all countries. Since we muſt die, and thy power, O *death*, we ſee, is uncontrolable: ſince to the duſt we muſt return, and take our trial at the bar of Almighty God, as *intelligent and free agents*; (for *under moral government*, and God is a perfectly wiſe and righteous governor, the *wickedneſs of the wicked will be upon him*, and the *righteouſneſs of the righteous will be upon him*;)—ſince we muſt be numbered with the *dead*, and our *circumſtances* and *condition* indicate a *future judgment*, ſurely we ought to remove our chief concern from this world to the other, and transfer our principal regard to the immor-

tal fpirit; that in the *hour of agony*, *a virtuous mind*, *purity of confcience*, and *good
actions*, may procure us the favour of God,
and the guidance of his good fpirit to the
manfions of the bleffed, where new pleafures are for ever fpringing up, and the
happinefs of the heavenly inhabitants is perpetually increafing. This is the one thing
needful. *Death* demonftrates, that this
world of darknefs and error, changes and
chances, is not worth fixing our heart on.
To fecure our paffage into the regions of
perfect and eternal day, fhould be the employment of immortal mortals.

§. 7. Thus did I reflect as I fat among
the *dead*, with my eyes faftened on the breath-
lefs corps of *Charlotte*, and I wifhed, if it
was poffible, to have leave to depart, and in
the hofpitable grave lie down from toil and
pain, to take my laft repofe; for I knew
not what to do, nor where to go. I was
not qualified for the world; nor had I a
friend, or even an acquaintance in it, that I
knew where to find. But in vain I prayed;
it was otherwife decreed: I muft go on, or
continue a folitary in the wild I was in.
The latter it was not poffible for me to do,
in the ftate of mind I was in; overwhelmed
with forrow, and without a companion of
any kind; and therefore, I muft of ne-
cefſity

ceffity go to fome other place. I fold all the living things I had to Fryar *Fleming*, and locked up my doors. My furniture, linen, clothes, books, liquors, and fome falt provifions, inftruments of various kinds, and fuch like things, I left in their feveral places. There was no one to take them, or probability that any one would come there to difturb them; and perhaps, fome time or other, the fates might bring me back again to the lone place. Though it was then a defolate, filent habitation, a ftriking memento of the vanity and precarious exiftence of all human good things; yet it was poffible, that hearty friendfhip, feftivity, and focial life, might once more be feen there. The force and operation of cafualties did wonders e-very day, and time might give me even a relifh for the folitude in a few years more. Thus did I fettle affairs in that remote place; and, taking leave of my friend the fryar with my lad *O Finn*, rode off.

S E C T. II.

Collect thy powers divine, and then drive off
That *evil thing* call'd *fear*, that *flavifh fiend*.
Let *hope*, let *joy*, thy *bofom inmates* be,
Through life ftill cherifh'd, and in death held faft.
A gracious God, loud-fpeaking to thy heart,
Through all his works, this truth inculcates ftill,
Nature's thy *nurfe*, and *providence* thy *friend*.
Integrity, with *fearlefs* heart, ride on :
Undaunted tread the various path through life.

Day Thoughts.

Auguft 4.
1727.
*The author's
departure
from* Orton-
Lodge, *to
try his for-
tune once
more.*

§. 1. THE fun was rifing, when we mounted our horfes, and I again went out to try my fortune in the world; not like the Chevalier of *La Mancha*, in hopes of conquering a kingdom, or marrying fome great Princefs; but to fee if I could find another good country girl for a wife, and get a little more money; as they were the only two things united, that could fecure me from melancholy, and confer real happinefs. To this purpofe, as the day was extremely fine, and *Finn* had fomething cold, and a couple of bottles at the end of his wallet, I gave my horfe the rein, and let
him

him take what way his fancy chose. For some time, he gently trotted the path he had often gone, and over many a mountain made his road: but at laſt, he brought me to a place I was quite a ſtranger to, and made a full ſtop at a deep and rapid water, which ran by the bottom of a very high hill I had not been up before. Over this river I made him go, though it was far from being ſafe, and in an hour's ride from that flood, came to a fine rural ſcene.

§. 2. It was paſture-ground, of a large extent, and in many places covered with groves of trees, of various kinds; walnuts, cheſnuts, and oaks; the poplar, the plane-tree, the mulberry, and maple. *A delightful ſpot of earth among the fells of* Weſtmoreland. There was likewiſe the *Phœnician* cedar, the larix, the large-leafed laurel, and the cytiſſus of *Virgil.* In the middle of this place were the ruins of an old ſeat, over-run with ſhrubby plants; the *Virginia* creeper, the box-thorn, the jeſſamine, the honey-ſuckle, the periwinkle, the birdweed, the ivy, and the climber; and near the door was a flowing ſpring of water, which formed a beautiful ſtream, and babbled to the river we came from. Charming ſcene! ſo ſilent, ſweet,

and

and pretty, that I was highly pleafed with the difcovery.

§. 3. On the margin of the brook, under a mulberry tree, I dined, on fomething which *Finn* produced from his wallet, tongue and ham, and potted *black cock*; and having drank a pint of cyder, fet out again, to try what land lay right onwards. In an hour, we came to a large and dangerous watery moor, which we croffed over with great difficulty, and then arrived at a range of mountains, through which there was a narrow pafs, wet and ftony, a long and tedious ride, which ended on the border of a fine country: at four in the afternoon, we arrived on the confines of a plain, about a hundred acres, which was ftrewed with various flowers of the earth's natural produce, that rendered the glebe delightful to behold, and was furrounded with groves. The place had all the charms that verdure, foreft, and vale, can give a country. In the centre of this ground was a handfome fquare building, and behind it a large and beautiful garden, which had a low, thick, holly-hedge, that encompaffed it. As the door of this houfe was not locked, but opened by a filver fpring turner,

A defcrip-tion of Bafil Groves, *the feat of* Charles Henley, Efq;

er, I went in, and found it was one fine fpacious room, filled on every fide with books, bound in an extraordinary manner. Globes, telefcopes, and other inftruments of various kinds, were placed on ftands, and there were two fine writing-tables, one at each end of the library, which had paper, ink, and pens. In the middle of the room there was a reading-defk, which had a fhort infcription, and on it leaned the fkeleton of a man. The legend faid, — *This fkeleton was once Charles Henley, Efq*;

Amazed I ftood, looking on thefe things, and wondered much at the figure of the bones, tack'd together with wires; once, to be fure, the mafter of this grand collection of books and manufcripts, and this fine room, fo fweetly fituated in the centre of diftant groves : this fkeleton had a ftriking effect on my mind; and the more fo, as it held a fcroll of parchment, on which was beautifully written in the *court-hand*, (to appear more remarkable, I fuppofe) the following lines :

" Fellow-mortal, whoever thou art, whom the fates fhall conduct into this chamber, remember, that before many years are paffed, thou muft be laid in the bed of corruption, in the dark caverns

of

of death, among the lifeleſs duſt, and
rotten bones of others, and from the
grave proceed to the general reſurrection
of all. To new life and vigour thou
wilt moſt certainly be raiſed, to be brought
to a great account. Naked and defence-
leſs thou muſt ſtand before the awful tri-
bunal of the great God, and from him receive a final ſentence, which ſhall determine and fix thee in an eternal ſtate of
happineſs or miſery.

What an alarm ſhould this be! Ponder,
my fellow-mortal, and remember, God
now commandeth men every where to repent, becauſe he hath appointed a day, in
which he will judge the world in righteouſneſs, by that man, whom he hath ordained; whereof he hath given aſſurance unto
all men, in that he hath raiſed him from the
dead.—— *Judge the world!* — *judgment!*
—the very ſound is ſolemn. Should it
not deaden ſome part, at leaſt, of your concern for things temporal, and quicken your
care and induſtry for the future life ;—ought
it not to make us condemn, before the dying hour, our vanity, and devotedneſs to
bodily things, and make us employ the
greateſt part of our time in the acquiſition
of wiſdom, and an improvement in virtue,
that when we appear at the ſeſſions of righteouſneſs, a ſacred knowledge, a heavenly
piety,

piety, and an angelic goodnefs, may fecure us from eternal punifhment, and entitle us to a glorious eternity? Since a
future judgment is moft certainly the cafe,
and the confequence eternal damnation or
falvation, how contemptible a thing is a
long bufy life, fpent in raking through the
mire of trade and bufinefs, in purfuit of
riches and a large eftate; or in fweating
up the fteep hill of ambition, after fame
and ambition; or in living and dreffing
as if we were *all body*, and 'fent into time
for no other purpofe, than to adorn like
idols, gratify like brutes, and wafte life in
· fenfuality and vanity: — how contemptible and unreafonable is this kind of exiftence for beings, who were created to no
other end, than to be partakers of a divine
life with God, and fing hallelujahs to all
eternity; to feparate the creature from error, fiction, impurity, and corruption, and
acquire that purity and holinefs, which a-
lone can fee God. Away then with a
worldly heart: away with all thofe follies,
which engage us like fools and madmen;
and let the principal thing be, to follow
the fteps of our great mafter, by patience
and refignation, by a charity and contempt
of the world; and by keeping a confcience
void of offence, amidft the changes and
chances of this mortal life; that at *his fe-*

cond

cond coming, to judge the world, we may be found *acceptable* in his fight.

What a fcene muft this fecond coming be! I faw, (fays an apoftle) a great white throne, and him that fat on it; from whofe face the earth and the heavens fled away, and there was no place found for them; and I faw the dead fmall and great ftand before God; and the books were opened, and the dead were judged out of thofe things which were written in the books: and the fea gave up her dead, and death and hell delivered up their dead which were in them, and they were judged every man, according to their works. The *fecret wic-kednefs* of men will be brought to light; and *concealed piety* and *perfecuted virtue* be acknowledged and honoured. While innocence and piety are fet at the right hand of the judge, and the righteous fhall fhine forth as the fun in the kingdom of their father for ever and ever, fhame and con-fufion muft fit upon the faces of the finner and the ungodly. *Damnation* will ftand before the brethren in iniquity, and when the intolerable fentence is executed, what inexpreffible agonies will they fall into? what amazement and exceffes of horror muft feize upon them?

Ponder

Ponder then, in time, fellow-mortal, and chufe to be good, rather than to be great: prefer your baptifmal vows to the pomps and vanities of this world; and value the fecret whifpers of a good confcience more than the noife of popular applaufe.

Since you muft appear before the judgment-feat of Chrift; that every one may receive the things done in his body, according to that he hath done, whether it be good or bad, let it be your work, from morning till night, to keep Jefus in your hearts; and long for nothing, defire nothing, hope for nothing, but to have all that is within you changed into the fpirit and temper of the *holy Jefus*. Wherever you go, whatever you do, do all in imitation of his temper and inclination; and look upon all as nothing, but that which exercifes and increafes the fpirit and life of Chrift in your fouls. — Let this be your Chriftianity, your church, and your religion, and the judgment-day will be a charming fcene. If in this world, the will of the creature, as an offspring of the divine will, *wills* and *works* with the *will* of *God*, and labours, without ceafing, to come as near as mortals can, to the purity and perfection of the divine nature; then will the *day of the Lord* be a day of great joy,

and

and with unutterable pleafure you fhall
hear that tremendous voice: *Awake, ye
dead, and come to judgment.* In tranfports,
and full of honour and glory, the wife and
righteous, will hear the happy fentence,
*Come, ye bleffed of my father, inherit the
kingdom prepared for you from the foundation
of the world.*"

This, and the fkeleton, aftonifhed me not
a little; and my wonder at the whole increafed, as I could find no human creature
living, nor difcover any houfe or cottage
for an inhabitant. This I thought exceeded
all the ftrange things I had feen in this
wonderful country. But perhaps, (it oc-
curred at-laft,) there might be a manfion
in the woods before me, or fomewhere in
the groves on either fide; and therefore,
leaving the library, after I had fpent an
hour in it, I walked onwards, and came to
a wood, which had private walks cut
through it; and ftrewed with fand. They
fhewed only light enough to diftinguifh
the blaze of day from evening fhade, and
had feats difperfed, to fit and liften to the
chorus of the birds, which added to the
pleafures of the foft filent place. For a-
bout three hundred yards the walk I was
in extended, and then terminated in meadows, which formed an oval of twenty
acres,

acres, furrounded by groves, like the large plain I came from. Exactly in the middle of thefe fields, part of which were turned into gardens, there ftood a very hahdfome ftone houfe, and not far from the door of it, a fountain played. On either fide of the water was a garden-chair, of a very extraordinary make, curious and beautiful; and each of them ftood under an ever-green oak, the broad-leaved Ilex, a charming fhade.

§. 4. In one of thefe chairs fat an ancient gentleman, a venerable man, whofe hair was white as filver, and his coun- *A defcription of John Henley, Efq;* tenance had dignity and goodnefs. His drefs and manner fhewed him to be a perfon of fortune and diftinction, and by a fervant in waiting, it appeared, he was Lord of the feigneurie I was arrived at. He was tall and graceful, and had not the leaft ftoop, tho' he wanted but a year of an hundred. I could not but admire the fine old gentleman.

§. 5. On the fame chair, next to him, fat a young Lady, who was at this time juft turned of twenty, and had fuch *Defcription of Statia Henley, the granddaughter of* diffufive

John Hen-
ley, *Efq*;

diffufive charms as foon new fired my heart, and gave my foul a foftnefs even beyond what it had felt before. She was a little taller than the middle fize, and had a face that was perfectly beautiful. Her eyes were extremely fine; full, black, fparkling; and her converfation was as charming as her perfon; both eafy, unconftrained, and fprightly.

*A converfa-
tion between.
John Hen-
ley, Efq; and
the author.*

§. 6. When I came near two fuch perfonages, I bowed low to the ground, and afked pardon for intruding into their fine retirement. But the ftars had led me, a wanderer, to this delightful folitude, without the leaft idea of there being fuch a place in our ifland, and as their malignant rays had forced me to offend, without intending it, I hoped they would pardon my breaking in upon them.

To this the old Gentleman replied, You have not offended, Sir, I affure you, but are welcome to the *Groves of Bafil*. It gives me pleafure to fee you here; for it is very feldom we are favoured with any one's company. It is hard to difcover or make out a road to this place, as we are furrounded

rounded almoft by impaffable mountains, and a very dangerous morafs: Nor can I conceive how you found the way here without a guide, or ventured to travel this country, as there are no towns in this part of the country. There muft be fomething very extraordinary in your cafe, and as you mentioned your being a wanderer, I fhould be glad to hear the caufe of your journeying in this uninhabited region. But firft (Mr. *Henley* faid) as it is now near eight at night, and you muft want refrefhment, having met with no inn the whole day, we will go in to fupper. He then arofe, and brought me to an elegant parlour, where a table was foon covered with the beft cold things, and we immediately fat down. Every eatable was excellent, and the wine and other liquors in perfection. Mifs *Henley* fat at the head of the table, her grand-father over-againft her, and placed me at her right-hand between them both. The young lady behaved in a very eafy genteel manner; and the old gentleman, with freedom, chearfulnefs, and good manners. 'Till nine this fcene lafted, and then Mr. *Henley* again requefted I would oblige him with an account of my travels in that part of the world. This I faid I would do in the beft manner I could; and while he leaned back in his eafy chair, and the beautiful
ful

ful *Statia* faſtened her glorious eyes upon me, I went on in the following words.

§. 7.   I am an Engliſhman, Sir, but have paſſed the greateſt part of my life in *Ireland*, and from the weſtern extremity of it I came.   My father is one of the rich men in that kingdom, and was, for many years, the tendereſt and moſt generous parent that ever ſon was bleſſed with.   He ſpared no coſt on my education, and gave me leave to draw upon him, while I reſided in the univerſity of *Dublin* five years, for what I pleaſed.   Extravagant as I was in ſeveral articles, he never ſet any bounds to my demands, nor aſked me what I did with the large ſums I had yearly from him.   My happineſs was his felicity, and the glory of his life to have me appear to the greateſt advantage, and in the moſt reſpected character, that money can gain a man.

A ſummary of the author's hiſtory, from the beginning of his 17th year till his arrival at the Groves of Ba-ſil in 1727, in the 25th year of his age.

But at laſt, he married his ſervant-maid, an artful cruel woman, who obtained by her wit and charms ſo great an aſcendant over him, that he abandoned me, to raiſe a young nephew this ſtepmother had, to

what

what splendor and power she pleased. He
had every thing he could name that money
could procure, and was absolute master of
the house and land. Not a shilling at this
time could I get, nor obtain the least thing
I asked for; and because I refused to become preceptor to this young man, and
had made some alteration in my religion,
(having renounced that creed, which was
composed, nobody knows by whom, and
introduced into the church in the darkest
ages of popish ignorance; a symbol, which
strongly participates of the true nature and
spirit of popery, in those severe denuncia-
tions of God's wrath, which it pours so
plentifully forth against all those whose
heads are not turned to believe it), my father was so enraged that he would not even
admit me to his table any longer, but bid
me be gone. My mother-in-law likewise
for ever abused me, and her nephew, the
lad, insulted me when I came in his way.

Being thus compelled to withdraw, I set
sail for *England* as soon as it was in my
power, and arrived in *Cumberland* by the
force of a storm. I proceeded from thence
to the mountains of *Stanemore*, to look for
a gentleman, my friend, who lived among
those hills; and as I journeyed over them,
and missed him, I chanced to meet with a
fine

fine northern girl, and a habitation to my
purpofe. I married her, and for almoft
two years paft was the happieft of the human race, till the fable curtain fell between
us, and the angel of death tranflated her
glorious foul to the fields of paradife. Not
able to bear the place of our refidence, after
I had loft my heart's fond idol, I left the
charming fpot and manfion, where unmixed felicity had been for fome time my
portion, and I was travelling on towards
London, to fee what is ordained there in re-
ferve for me; when by accident I loft my
way, and the fates conducted me to the
Groves of *Bafil*. Curiofity led me into the
library I found in the plain, without this
wood, from whence, in fearch for fome
human creatures, I proceeded to the fountain, where I had the pleafure of feeing
you, Sir, and this young lady. This is a
fummary of my paft life; what is before
me heaven only knows. My fortune I
truft with the Preferver of men, and the
Father of fpirits. One thing I am certain
of by obfervation, few as the days of the
years of my pilgrimage have been, that
the emptinefs and unfatisfying nature of
this world's enjoyments, are enough to
prevent my having any fondnefs to ftay in
this region of darknefs and forrow. I
fhall never leap over the bars of life, let
what

what will happen: but the fooner I have leave to depart, I fhall think it the better for me.

§. 8. The old gentleman feemed furprized at my ftory, and after fome moments filence, when I had done, he said, Your meafure, Sir, is hard, and as it was, in part, for declaring againft a falfe religion at your years, you pleafe me fo much, that if you will give me leave, I will be your friend, and as a fubaltern providence, recompence your lofs as to fortune in this world. In what manner you fhall know to-morrow, when we breakfaft at eight. It is now time to finifh our bottle, that we may, according to our cuftom, betimes retire.

The old gentleman's reply to the ftory.

§. 9. At the time appointed I met the old gentleman in the parlour, and juft as we had done faluting each other, *Statia* entered, bright and charming as *Aurora*. She was in a rich drefs, and her bright victorious eyes flafhed a celeftial fire. She made our tea, and gave me fome of her coffee. She afked me a few civil queftions, and faid two or three good things on

The hiftory of Ch. Henley, Efq; and his beautiful daughter Statia.

on the beauties of the morning, and the charms of the country. She left us the moment we had done breakfaſt, and then the old gentleman addreſſed himſelf to me in the following words.

I do not forget the promiſe I made you, but muſt firſt relate the hiſtory of my family. I do it with the more pleaſure, as I find you are of our religion, and I cannot help having a regard for you, on your daring to throw up a fortune for truth; for bravely daring to renounce thoſe ſyſtems, which have an *outward orthodox roundneſs* given to them by their eloquent defenders, and *within* are *mere corruption and apoſtacy*.

The *ſkeleton* you ſaw in the library was once my ſon, *Charles Henley*, a moſt extraordinary man. He had great abilities, and underſtood every thing a mortal is capable of knowing, of things human and divine.—When he was in his nineteenth year, I took him to *France* and other countries, to ſee the world, and, on our return to *England*, married him into a noble family, to a very valuable young woman, of a large fortune, and by her he had the young lady you ſaw ſitting on the chair near the table by me. This ſon I
loſt,

loft, three years after his marriage, and with him all relifh for the world: and being naturally inclined to retirement and a fpeculative life, never ftirred fince from this country-houfe. Here my fon devoted himfelf entirely to ftudy, and amufed himfelf with inftructing his beloved *Statia*, the young lady you have feen. At his death he configned her to my care; and as her underftanding is very great, and her difpofition fweet and charming, I have not only taken great pains in educating her, but have been delighted with my employment. Young as fhe is, but in the fecond month of her one and twentieth year, fhe not only knows more than women of diftinction generally do, but would be the admiration of learned men, if her knowledge in languages, mathematics, and philofophy, were known to them: and as her father taught her mufic and painting, perhaps there is not a young woman of finer accomplifhments in the kingdom. ·

Aug. 14. 1727.

Her father died towards the end of the year 1723, in the 39th year of his age, when fhe was not quite fixteen, and, by his will, left her ten thoufand pounds, and *Bafil-Houfe* and eftate; but fhe is not to inherit it, or marry, till fhe is two and twenty.

twenty. This was her father's will. As to the *skeleton* in the library, it was my son's exprefs order it fhould be fo, and that the figure fhould not be removed from the place it ftands in, while the library remained in that room; but continue a folemn memorial in his family, to perpetuate his memory, and be a *memento mori* to the living.

§. 10. This is the hiftory of *Bafil Groves*, and the late owner of this feat, and his daughter *Statia*. We live a happy, religious life here, and enjoy every bleffing that can be defired in this lower hemifphere. But as I am not very far from a hundred years, having paffed that *ninety-two* which Sir *William Temple* fays, he never knew any one he was acquainted with arrive at, I muft be on the brink of the grave, and expect every day to drop into it. What may become of *Statia*, then, gives me fome trouble to think; as all her relations, except myfelf, are in the other world. To fpend her life here in this folitude, as feems to be her inclination, is not proper; and to go into the world by herfelf, when I am dead, without knowing any mortal in it, may involve her in troubles and diftreffes.

Old Mr. Henley offers me his granddaughter in marriage.

Hear

Hear then, my son, what I propose to you. You are a young man, but serious. You have got some wisdom in the school of affliction, and you have no aversion to matrimony, as you have just buried, you say, a glorious woman, your wife. If you will stay with us here, till *Statia* is two and twenty, and in that time render yourself agreeable to her, I promise you, she shall be yours the day she enters the three and twentieth year of her age, and you shall have with her fortune all that I am owner of, which is no small sum. What do you say to this proposal?

§. 11. Sir, I replied, you do me vast honour, much *My reply.* more I am sure than my merits can pretend to. I am infinitely obliged to you, and must be blind and insensible, if I refused such a woman as Miss *Henley*, were she far from being the fortune she is: But I have not vanity enough to imagine, I can gain her affections; especially in my circumstances; and to get her by your authority, or power of disposing of her, is what I cannot think of. I will stay however, a few months here, since you so generously invite me, and let Miss *Henley* know, I will be her humble servant, if she will allow me the honour

of

of bearing that title. This made the old gentleman laugh, and he took me by the hand, faying, This is right. Come, let us go and take a walk before dinner.

§. 12. There I paſſed the winter, and part of the ſpring, and lived in a delightful manner. The mornings I generally ſpent in the library, reading, or writing extracts from ſome curious MSS. or ſcarce books; and in the afternoons Miſs *Henley* and I walked in the lawns and woods, or ſat down to cards. She was a fine creature indeed in body and ſoul, had a beautiful underſtanding, and charmed me to a high degree. Her converſation was rational and eaſy, without the leaſt affectation from the books ſhe had read; and ſhe would enliven it ſometimes by ſinging, in which kind of muſic ſhe was as great a miſtreſs as I have heard. As to her heart, I found it was to be gained; but an accident happened that put a ſtop to the amour.

My reſidence at Baſil Groves for ſeven months, and manner of living.

The death of old Mr. Henley, and Statia's behaviour thereupon.

§. 13. In the beginning of March, the old gentleman, the excellent Mr. *Henley*, *Statia*'s grandfather and guardian, and my great friend, died, and by his

his death a great alteration enfued in my
affair. I thought to have had Mifs *Henley*
immediately, as there was no one to plead
her father's will againft the marriage, and
intended to fend *O Finn* for Fryar *Fleming*;
but when *Statia* faw herfelf her own mif-
trefs, without any fuperior, or controul,
and in poffeffion of large fortunes, money,
and an eftate, that fhe might do as fhe
pleafed; this had an effect on her mind,
and made a change. She told me, when I
addreffed myfelf to her, after her grand-
father was interred, that what fhe intended
to do, in obedience to him, had he lived,
fhe thought required very ferious confi-
deration now fhe was left to herfelf: That,
exclufive of this, her inclination really
was for a fingle life; and had it been o-
therwife, yet it was not proper, fince her
guardian was dead, that I fhould live with
her till the time limited by her father's will
for her to marry was come; but that, as
fhe had too good an opinion of me, to imagine her fortune was what chiefly urged
my application, and muft own fhe had a
regard for me, fhe would be glad to hear
from me fometimes, if I could think her
worth remembering, after I had left the
Groves of Bafil. This fhe faid with great
ferioufnefs, and feemed by her manner to
forbid my urging the thing any further.

§. 14. I

§. 14. I affured her, however, that time only could
wear out her charming image
from my mind, and that I had
reafon to fear, fhe would long
remain the torment of my
heart. She had a right to be
fure to difmifs me from her
fervice; but in refpect of her
inclination to live a fingle life,
I begged leave to obferve, that it was certainly quite wrong, and what fhe could not
anfwer to the wife and bountiful Father of
the Univerfe, as fhe was a Chriftian, and
by being fo, muft believe, that *baptifm*
was a *memorial* of the *covenant of grace*.

My reply to Mifs Hen-ley; being an apology for matrimony, as it is by the gofpel made a memorial of the covenant of grace.

The *Catholics* and the *Vifion-mongers* of
the proteftant fide, (the Rev. Mr. *Wm.
Law*, and others of his row) may magnify
the excellence of *celibacy* as high as they
pleafe, and work it into Chriftian perfection, by founding words and eloquent
pens; but moft furely, *revelation* was directly againft them, and required the
faithful to *produce* in a *regular way*.

Confider, illuftrious *Statia*, that when
the Moft High gave the *Abrahamic ccve-
nant* in thefe words, *I will be a God unto
thee, and to thy feed after thee, and in thy
feed fhall all the families, or nations of the*

4

earth

earth be bleffed; which includes an intereft in God, as a God, father and friend for ever, and a fhare in all the bleffings wherewith the *Meffiah*, in the gofpel, hath inriched the world; thefe ineftimable bleffings and promifes of life and favour, were defigned by the divine munificence for rifing generations of mankind; and it was moft certainly intended, not only that they fhould be received with the higheft gratitude and duty, but that they fhould be ftrongly inculcated upon the thoughts of fucceeding generations, by an inftituted fign or memorial, to the end of the world.

Circumcifion was the firft appointed token or memorial, and at the fame time, an inftruction in that moral rectitude to which the grace of God obliges: and when the New Teftament fucceeded the Law, then was the *covenant intereft of infants*, or their *right* to the *covenant of grace*, to be confirmed by the *token* or *fign* called *baptifm*; that action being appointed to give the expected rifing generation an intereft in the love of God, the grace of Chrift, and the fellowfhip of the Holy Spirit, that is, in all covenant bleffings. But what becomes of this great charter of heaven, if Chriftian women, out of an idle notion of perfection, will refolve to lead fingle lives, and thereby hinder rifing generations from sharing in the honours and privileges of the church of Jesus Christ. Millions of the faithful must thereby be deprived of the token instituted by God to convey to them those covenant blessings, which his love and goodness designed for the rising generations of his people. Have a care then what you do, illustrious *Statia*, in this particular. It must be a great crime to hinder the regular propagation of a species, which God hath declared to be under his particular inspection and blessing, and by circumcision and baptism, hath made the special object of divine attention and care. Away then with all thoughts of a virgin life, whatever becomes of me. As God |hath appointed matrimony and baptism, let it be your pious endeavour to bear sons and daughters, that may be related to God, their Father; to Jesus, their Redeemer, and first born in the family; and to all the excellent, who are to enjoy, through him, the blessings of the glorious world above. Marry, then, illustrious *Statia*, marry, and let the blessing of *Abraham* come upon us gentiles. Oppose not the gospel covenant; that covenant which was made with that patriarch; but mind the comfortable promises; *I will circumcise thy heart, and the heart of thy seed. I will pour out my spirit upon thy seed, and my blessing upon thine offspring. The seed of the righteous is blessed.*

ed. They are the seed of the blessed of the Lord, and their offspring with them. Such is the magna charta of our existence and future happiness; and as infants descending from *Abraham,* in the line of election, to the end of the world, have as good a right and claim as we to the blessings of this covenant, and immense promise, *I will be a God unto thee, and to thy seed after thee, in their generations;* it must be a great crime, to deprive children of this intailed, heavenly inheritance, by our resolving to live in a state of virginity. In my opinion, it is a sin greater than murder. What is murder, but forcing one from his post against the will of providence; and if the virgin hinders a being or beings from coming on the post, against the will of providence, must she not be culpable; and must she not be doubly criminal, if the being or beings she hinders from coming on the stage, or into this first state, were to be a part of the *perpetual generations,* who have a right to the *inheritance,* the *blessing,* and were to be *heirs* according to the *promise* made to *Abraham?* Ponder, illustrious *Statia,* on the important point. Consider what it is to die a maid, when you may, in a regular way, produce heirs to that inestimable blessing of life and favour, which the munificence of the Most

High

High was pleafed freely to beftow, and which the great Chriftian mediator, agent, and negociator, republifhed, confirmed, and fealed with his blood. Marry then in regard to the gofpel, and let it be the fine employment of your life, to open gradually the treafures of revelation to the underftandings of the little Chriftians you produce.

This I am fure your holy religion requires from you: and if from the facred oracles we turn to the book of nature, is it not in this volume written, that there muft be a malignity in the hearts of thofe mortals, who can remain unconcerned at the deftruction and extirpation of the reft of mankind; and who want even fo much good will as is requifite to propagate a creature, (in a regular and hallowed way) tho' they received their own *being* from the mere benevolence of their divine Mafter? What do you fay, illuftrious *Statia?* Shall it be a *fucceffion*, as you are an upright Chriftian? And may I hope to have the high honour of fharing in the mutual fatisfaction that muft attend the difcharge of fo momentous a duty? (2)

§. 15.

Of celibacy and marriage.

(2) If *fucceffion* be the main thing, and to prevent the extirpation of the reft

§. 15. All the smiles sat on the face of *Statia*, while I was haranguing in this devout manner, and her countenance became a constellation of wonders.

Miss Henley's answer.

When I

rest of mankind by *junction*, why may it not be carried on as well without marriage, as in that confined way? I answer, that as the author and founder of marriage, was the *Ancient of Days*, God himself, and at the creation he appointed the *institution* : as *Christ*, who was veiled with authority to abrogate any laws, or supersede any custom, in which were found any flaw or obliquity, or had not an intrinsic goodness and rectitude in them, confirmed the *ordinance*, by reforming the abuses that had crept into it, and restoring it to its original boundary: as he gave a *sanction* to this amicable covenant, and statuted that men should maintain the dignity of the conjugal state, and by virtue of this primordial and most intimate bond of society, convey down the race of mankind, and maintain its succession to the final dissolution; it is not therefore to be neglected or disregarded. We must not dare to follow our fancies, and in unhallowed mixtures, or an illegal method, have any posterity. As the great God appointed and blessed this institution only, for the continuance of mankind, the race is not to be preserved in another way. We must *marry in the Lord*, to promote his glory, as the *apostle* says, 1 *Cor.* vii. 39. The earth is not to be replenished by licentious junction, or the promiscuous use of women. Dreadful hereafter must be the case of all who slight an *institution of God*.

I am sensible, the libertine who depreciates and vilifies the dignity of the married state, will laugh at
this

I had done, this beauty said; I thank you, Sir, for the information you have given me. I am a Chriſtian. There is no ma-lignity in my heart. You have altered
my

this aſſertion: The fop and debauchee will hiſs it, and ſtill do their beſt to render wedlock the ſubject of contempt and ridicule. The *Roman* clergy will likewiſe decry it, and injuriouſly treat it as an im-pediment to devotion, a cramp upon the ſpiritual ſerving of God, and call it an inſtrument of pollu-tion and defilement, in reſpect of their heavenly *ce-libacy.*

But as God thought marriage was ſuitable to a pa-radiſaical ſtate, and the ſcriptures declare it *honour-able in all:* as this is the way appointed by heaven to people the earth; and the *inſtitution* is *neceſſary,* in the reaſon and nature of things, conſidering the cir-cumſtances in which mankind is placed; to prevent confuſion, and promote the general happineſs; as the bond of ſociety, and the foundation of all hu-man government; ſure I am, the *rake* and the *maſs-prieſt,* muſt be in a dreadful ſituation at the ſeſſions of righteouſneſs; when the one is charged with li-bertiniſm and gallantries, with madneſs and folly, and with all the evils and miſchief they have done by illicit gratification, contrary to reaſon, and in di-rect oppoſition to the *inſtitutes* of God;——and when the other, the miſerable *maſs-prieſts,* are called to an account, for vilifying the honour and dignity of the married ſtate, and for ſtriving to ſeduce mankind into the ſolitary retirements of celibacy, in violation of the laws of God; and more eſpecially of the pri-mary law or ordinance of heaven. *Wretched prieſts!* Your inſtitutions are breaches in revealed religion, treſpaſſes upon the common rights of nature, and ſuch oppreſſive yokes as it is not able to bear. Your
celibacy

my way of thinking, and I now declare for
a *succession.*——Let Father *Flemming* be
sent for, and without waiting for my being
two-and-twenty, or minding my father's
will,

celibacy has not a grain of piety in it. It is *policy* and
impiety.

Hear me then, ye *libertines* and *mass-priests:* I call
upon you of the first row, ye *rakes of genius,* to consider what you are doing, and in time turn from
your iniquities: Be no longer profligate and licentious, blind to your true interest and happiness, but
become virtuous and honourable lovers, and in regard to the advantages of this *solemn institution,* called
wedlock, as well to the general state of the world, as
to individuals, *marry in the Lord*; so will you avoid
that dreadful sentence, *Fornicators and adulterers God
will judge,* that is, punish; and in this life, you may
make things *very agreeable,* if you please; though it
is in the heavenly world alone, where there shall be
all joy and no sorrow. Let there be true beauty
and gracefulness in the mind and manners, and these
with discretion, and other things in your power,
will furnish a fund of happiness commensurate with
your lives. It is possible, I am sure, to make marriage productive of as much happiness as falls to our
share in this lower hemisphere, as the nature of man
can reach to in his present condition. For, as to joy
flowing in with a full, constant, and equal tide,
without interruption and without allay, there is no
such thing. Human nature doth not admit of this.
" The sum of the matter is this: To the public the
advantages of marriage are certain, whether the parties will or no; but to the parties engaging, not so:
to them *it is a fountain that sendeth forth both sweet
and bitter waters.* To those who mind their duty

and.

will, as there's no one to oblige me to it,
I will give you my hand. Charming
news! I difpatched my lad for the Fryar.
The prieft arrived the next day, and at
night we were married. Three days after, we fet out for *Orton-Lodge*, at my
wife's requeft, as fhe longed to fee the
place. For two years more I refided
there; it being more agreeable to *Statia*
than the improved *Groves of Bafil*. We
lived there in as much happinefs as it is
poffible to have in this lower hemifphere,
and much in the fame manner as I did with
Charlotte my firft wife. *Statia* had all the
good qualities and perfections which rendered *Charlotte* fo dear and valuable to

and obligations *fweet ones*; to thofe who neglect
them, *bitter ones.*"
. In the next place, ye *monks*, I would perfuade you,
if I could, to labour no longer in ftriving to cancel
the obligations to marriage by the pretence of religion. The voice of heaven, and the whifpers of
found and uncorrupted reafon are againft it. It is
will-worfhip in oppofition to revelation. It is fuch a
prefumption for a creature againft the author of our
nature, as muft draw down uncommon wrath upon
the head of every *mafs-prieft*, who does not repent
their preaching fuch wicked doctrine. Indeed I do
not know any part of popery that can be called chriftianity: but this in particular is fo horrible and
diabolical, that I can confider the preachers for celibacy in no other light than as fo many *devils*.
May you ponder in time on this horrible affair.

me;

me; like her she studied to increase the delights of every day, and by art, good humour, and love, rendered the married state such a system of joys as might incline one to wish it could last a thousand years: But it was too sublime and desireable to have a long existence here. *Statia* was taken ill, of the small-pox, the morning we intended to return to *Basil-Groves*; she died the 7th day, and I laid her by *Charlotte*'s side. Thus did I become again a *mourner*. I sat with my eyes shut for three days: But at last, called for my horse, to try what air, exercise, and a variety of objects, could do.

D 5   SECTION

SECTION III.

'Twas when the faithful herald of the day,
  The village-cock crows loud with trumpet fhrill,
The warbling lark foars high, and morning grey
  Lifts her glad forehead o'er the cloud-wrapt hill;
Nature's wild mufic fills the vocal vale ;
  The bleating flocks that bite the dewy ground;
The lowing herds that graze the woodland dale,
  And cavern'd echo, fwell the chearful found.

April 1. 1729, we leave Orton-Lodge *again, and fet out for* Harrigate Spaw. *A defcription of the country we rid over.* Ætat. 27.

§. 1. VERY early, as foon as I could fee day, the firft of *April*, 1729, I left *Orton-Lodge*, and went to *Bafil-Groves*, to order matters there. From thence I fet out for *Harrigate*, to amufe myfelf in that agreeable place; but I did not go the way I came to Mr. *Henley*'s houfe. To avoid the dangerous morafs I had paff-ed, at the hazard of my life, we went over a wilder and more romantic country than I had before feen. We had higher moun-tains to afcend than I had ever paffed be-fore; and fome vallies fo very deep to ride thro', that they feemed as it were defcents to hell. The patriarch *Bermudez*, in jour-

4   neying

neying over *Abyssinia*, never travelled in more frightful Glins*. And yet, we often came to plains and vales which had all the charms a paradise could have. Such is the nature of this country.

* *Relation de l'Ambassade, dediée a Don Sebastien, roy. de Portugal.*

Through these scenes, an amazing mixture of the terrible and the beautiful, we proceeded from five in the morning till one in the afternoon, when we arrived at a vast water-fall, which descended from a precipice near two hundred yards high, into a deep lake, that emptied itself into a swallow fifty yards from the catadure or fall, and went I suppose to the abyss. The land from this head-long river, for half a mile in length and breadth, till it ended at vast mountains again, was a fine piece of ground, beautifully flowered with various perennials, the acanthus, the aconus, the adonis or pheasant's eye, the purple biltorta, the blue borago, the yellow bupthalmum, the white cacalia, the blue campanula, and the sweet-smelling caffia, the pretty double daify, the crimson dianthus, the white dictamnus, the red fruximella, and many other wild flowers. They make the green valley look charming; and as here and there stood two or three ever-

green

green trees, the cypress, the larix, the balm of *Gilead*, and the *Swedish* juniper, the whole spot has a fine and delightful effect. On my arrival here, I was at a loss which way to turn.

§. 2. I could not however be long in suspense how to proceed, as I saw near the water-fall a pretty thatched mansion, and several inhabitants in it. I found they were a religious society of married people, ten friars and their ten wives, who had agreed to retire to this still retreat, and form a holy house on the plan of the famous *Ivon*, the disciple of *Labadie*, so celebrated on account of his connection with Mrs. *Schurman*, and his many fanatical writings *. A book called the *Marriage Chretien*, written by this *Ivon*, was their directory, and from it they formed a protestant *La Trappe*; with this difference from the Catholic religious men, that the friars of the reformed monastery were to have wives in their convent; the better to enable them to obtain Christian perfection in the religious life. These Regulars, men and

The inhabitants of this fine valley, a society of married friars.

* *See my second volume, where you will find a particular account of Labadie and Ivon.*

and women, were a moſt induſtrious people, never idle, but between their hours
of prayer always at work: the men were
employed in a garden of ten acres, to pro-
vide vegetables and fruit, on which they
chiefly lived ; or in cutting down old
trees, and fitting them for their fire: and
the women were knitting, ſpinning, or
twiſting what they had ſpun into thread,
which they ſold for three ſhillings a
pound : they were all together in a large,
handſome room : they ſat quite ſilent,
kept their eyes on their work, and ſeemed
more attentive to ſome inward medita-
tions, than to any thing that appeared, or
paſſed by them. They looked as if they
were contented and happy. They were
all extremely handſome, and quite clean :
their linen fine and white ; their gowns a
black ſtuff. The women dined at one
table, the men at another ; but all ſat in
the ſame room. The whole houſe was in
bed by ten, and up by four in the morning, winter and ſummer. What they ſaid
at their table I could not hear, as they
ſpoke low and little, and were at a diſtance from me, in a large apartment : but
the converſation of the men, at table, was
very agreeable, rational and improving.
I obſerved they had a great many children, and kept four women ſervants to
attend

attend them, and do the work of the
houfe. The whole pleafed me very greatly. I thought it a happy inftitution.

§. 3. As to the *marriage*
Some thoughts of the *friars* in this cloyftral
on the inftitu- houfe, their founder, *Ivon*, in
tion of mar- my opinion, was quite right
ried regulars. in this notion. *Chafte junction*
cannot have the leaft imperfection in it,
as it is the appointment of God, and the
inclination to a *coit* is fo ftrongly impreffed
on the machine by the author of it; and
fince it is quite pure and perfect; fince it
was wifely intended as the only beft expe-
dient to keep man for ever innocent, it
muft certainly be much better for a *regular* or *retreating prieft,* to have a lawful
female companion with him; and fo the
woman, who chufes a convent, and diflikes
the fafhions of the world, to have her good
and lawful monk every night in her arms;
to love and procreate legally, when they
have performed all the holy offices of the
day; and then, from love and holy generation, return again to prayer, and all the
heavenly duties of the cloyftered life; than
to live, againft the inftitution of nature
and providence, a *burning, tortured nun,*
and a *burning, tortured friar*; locked up
in walls they can never pafs, and under the
govern-

government of some old, crofs, impotent superior. There is fome fenfe in fuch a *marriage chretien* in a convent. *Ivon's* convent is well enough. A cloyfter may do upon his plan, with the dear creature by one's fide, after the daily labours of the *monk* are over. It had been better, if that *infallible* man, the *Pope*, had come into this fcheme. How comfortable has *Ivon* made it to the human race, who renounce the drefs and pageantry, and all the vanities of time. Their days are fpent in piety and ufefulnefs; and at night, after the *completorium*, they lie down together in the moft heavenly charity, and according to the firft great hail, endeavour to increafe and multiply. This is a divine life. I am for a cloyfter on thefe terms. It pleafed me fo much to fee thefe *monks* march off with their fmiling partners, after the laft pfalm, that I could not help wifhing for a charmer there, that I might commence the *Married Regular*, and add to the ftock of children in this holy houfe. It is really a fine thing to *monk* it on this plan. It is a divine inftitution: gentle and generous, ufeful and pious.

On the contrary, how *cruel* is the *Roman church*, to make *perfection* confift in *celibacy*, and caufe fo many millions of men

and

and women to live at an eternal diftance
from each other, without the leaft regard
to the given points of contact! How unfriendly to fociety! This is abufing Chriftianity, and perverting it to the moft per-
nicious purpofes; under a pretence of
raifing piety, by giving more time and lei-
fure for devotion. For it never can be
pious, either in defign or practice, to cancel any moral obligation, or to make void
any command of God: and as to prayer,
it may go along with every other duty, and
be performed in every ftate. All ftates
have their intermiffions; and if it fhould
be otherwife fometimes, I can then, while
difcharging any duty, or performing any
office, pray as well in my heart, *O God be
merciful to me a finner, and blefs me with
the blefsing of thy grace and providence*, as if
I was proftrate before an altar. What
Martha was reproved for, was on account
of her being too folicitous about the
things of this life. Where this is not the
cafe, *bufinefs* and the *world* are far from
being a hindrance to piety. God is as
really glorified in the difcharge of relative
duties, as in the difcharge of thofe which
more immediately relate to himfelf. He is
in truth more actively glorified by our difcharging well the *relative duties*, and we
thereby may become more *extenfively ufeful* in
the

the church and in the world, may be more *public bleffings*, than it is poffible to be in a *fingle pious* ftate. In fhort, this one thing, *celibacy*, (were there nothing elfe) the making the unmarried ftate a more holy ftate than marriage, fhews the prodigious *nonfenfe* and *impiety* of the *Church* of *Rome*, and is reafon enough to flee that communion, if we had no other reafons for protefting againft it. The tenet is fo fuperftitious and dangerous, that it may well be efteemed a doctrine of thofe *devils*, who are the feducers and deftroyers of mankind: but it is (fays *Wallace* *) fuitable to the views and defigns of a church, which has difcovered fuch an enormous ambition, and made fuch havock of the human race, in order to raife, eftablifh, and preferve an ufurped and tyrannical power.

* *Differtation on the numbers of mankind.*

§. 4. But as to the *Married Regulars* I have mentioned, they were very glad to fee me, and entertained me with great civility and goodnefs. I lived a week with them, and was not only well fed with vegetables and puddings on their lean days, Wednefdays and Fridays,

A further account of the Married Regulars I met with among the fells of Weftmoreland.

Fridays, and with plain meat, and good
malt drink, on the other days; but was
greatly delighted with their manner and
piety, their fenfe and knowledge. I will
give my pious readers a fample of their
prayers, as I imagine it may be to edifica-
tion. Thefe friars officiate in their turns,
changing every day; and the morning and
evening prayers of one of them were in the
words following. I took them off in my
fhort-hand.

A Prayer for Morning.

ALMIGHTY and everlafting God,
the creator and preferver of all
things, our law-giver, faviour, and judge;
we adore thee the author of our beings,
and the father of our fpirits. We prefent
ourfelves, our acknowledgments, and our
homage, at the foot of thy throne, and
yield thee the thanks of the moft grateful
hearts for all the inftances of thy favour
which we have experienced. We thank
thee for ever, O Lord God Almighty, for
all thy mercies and bleffings vouchfafed
us; for defending us the paft night from
evil, and for that kind provifion which
thou haft made for our comfortable fub-
fiftence in this world.

But

But above all, moſt glorious Eternal, adored be thy goodneſs, for repeating and reinforcing the laws and the religion of thy creation, by ſupernatural revelation, and for giving us that reaſon of mind, which unites us to thee, and makes us implore thy communications of righteouſneſs, to create us again unto good works in Chriſt Jeſus.

We confeſs, O Lord, that we have done violence to our principles, and alienated ourſelves from the natural uſe we were fitted for: we have revolted from thee into a ſtate of ſin, and by the operation of ſenſe and paſſion, have been moved to ſuch practices as are exorbitant and irregular: but we are heartily ſorry for all our miſdoings: to thee in Chriſt we now make our addreſs, and beſeech thee to inform our underſtandings, and refine our ſpirits, that we may reform our lives by repentance, redeem our time by righteouſneſs, and live as the glorious goſpel of thy Son requires. Let the divine ſpirit aſſiſt and enable us to over-rule, conduct, and employ, the ſubordinate and inferior powers, in the exerciſe of virtue, and the ſervice of our creator, and as far as the imperfections of our preſent ſtate will admit, help us ſo to live by the meaſures and laws of heaven,

heaven, that we may have the humility and meeknefs, the mortification and felf-denial of the holy Jefus, his love of thee, his defire of doing thy will, and feeking only thy honour. Let us not come covered before thee under a *form* of godlinefs, a *cloke* of creeds, obfervances and inftitutions of religion; but with that *inward falvation* and *vital fanctity*, which renounces the fpirit, wifdom, and honours of this world, dethrones felf-love and pride, fubdues fenfuality and covetoufnefs, and *opens a kingdom of heaven within* by the fpirit of God. O let thy Chrift be our Saviour in this world; and before we die, make us fit to live for ever with thee in the regions of purity and perfection.

Since it is the peculiar privilege of our nature, through thy mercy and goodnefs, that we are made for an eternal entertainment in thofe glorious manfions, where the bleffed fociety of faints and angels fhall keep an everlafting fabbath, and adore and glorify thee for ever, let thy infpiring fpirit raife our apprehenfions and defires above all things that are here below, and alienate our minds from the cuftoms and principles of this mad, degenerate, and apoftate world: mind us of the fhortnefs and uncertainty of time, of the boundlefs duration,

ration, and the vaft importance of eternity; and fo enable us to imitate the example
of the holy Jefus in this world, that we
may hereafter afcend, with the greateft ar-
dour of divine love, to thofe realms of holinefs, where our hearts will be filled with
raptures of gladnefs and joy, and we fhall
remain in the higheft glory for ever and
ever.

We live, O Lord, in reconciliation and
friendfhip, in love and good-will, with thy
whole creation, with every thing that de-
rives from thee, holds of thee, is owned
by thee; and under the power of this affection, we pray for all mankind; that
they may be partakers of all the bleffings
which we enjoy or want, and that we may
all be happy in the world to come, and
glorify thee together in eternity. To this
end bring all the human race to the knowledge of thy glorious gofpel, and let its
influence transform them into the likenefs
of Chrift.

But efpecially, we pray for all who fuffer
for truth and righteoufnefs fake, and befeech thee to profper thofe that love thee.
Defend, O Lord, the juft rights and liberties of mankind, and refcue thy religion
from the corruptions which have been in-

troduced

troduced upon it, by length of time, and
by decay of piety.   Infatuate the counfels,
and fruftrate the endeavours of the priefts
of *Rome*, and againft all the defigns of
thofe, who are enemies to the purity of
the gofpel, and fubftitute human inventions in the place of revealed religion; profper the pious labours of thofe who teach
mankind to worfhip one, eternal, and omniprefent being; in whofe underftanding,
there is the perfection of wifdom; in whofe
will, there is the perfection of goodnefs; in
whofe actions, there is the perfection of
power; a God without caufe, the great
creator, benefactor, and faviour of men:
— And that the duty of man is to obey, in
thought, word, and deed, the precepts of
godlinefs and righteoufnefs, without regard
to pleafure, gain, or honour; to pain,
lofs, or difgrace; diligently imitating the
life of the holy Jefus, and ftedfaftly con-
fiding in his mediation.

In the laft place, O Lord God Almighty,
we befeech thee to continue us under thy
protection, guidance, and bleffing this day,
as the followers and difciples of thy Chrift,
through whom we recommend our fouls
and our bodies into thy hands, and according to the doctrine of his religion, fay,
Our Father, &c.

In

In this manner, did thefe pious *Ivonites* begin their every day; and when the fun was fet, and they had finifhed their fupper, they worfhipped God again in thefe words.

A Prayer for Night.

MOST bleffed, glorious, and holy Lord God Almighty, who art from everlafting to everlafting, God over all, magnified and adored for ever! we, thy unworthy creatures, humble our fouls in thy prefence, and confefs ourfelves miferable finners. We acknowledge our mifcarriages and faults, and condemn ourfelves for having done amifs. We deprecate thy juft offence and difpleafure. We cry thee mercy. We afk thee pardon: and as we are quite fenfible of our weaknefs and inability, and know thou loveft the fouls of men, when they turn and repent, we befeech thee to give us true repentance, and endue us with the grace of thy fanctifying fpirit, that we may be delivered from the bondage and flavery of iniquity, and have the law of the fpirit of life which is in Chrift Jefus. Upon thee our God, we call for that help which is never wanting, and befeech thee to give us thy heavenly affiftance, that we may

recover

recover our reasonable nature, refine our
spirits by goodness, and purify ourselves
even as the Lord Jesus is.pure. O thou
Father of Lights, and the God of all comforts, inform our understandings with
truth, and give us one ray of that divine
wisdom which fitteth on the right hand of
thy throne. O let us be always under thy
communication and influence, and enable
us, through the recommendation of thy
Son, our mediator and redeemer, to lay
aside all passion, prejudice, and vice, to
receive thy truth in the love of it, and to
serve thee with ingenuity of mind, and
freedom of spirit: that we may pass thro'
a religious life to a blessed immortality,
and come to that eternal rest, where we
shall behold thy face in righteousness, and
adore and bless thee to eternity, for our
salvation through him who hath redeemed
us by his blood.

We praise and magnify thy goodness,
O Lord God Almighty, for our mainte-
nance and preservation, by thy constant
providence over us, and we beseech thee
to take us into thy special care and protection this night. Defend us from all the
powers of darkness, and from evil men and
evil things, and raise us in health and safety. Do thou, most great and good God,
protect

protect us and bless us this night, and when we awake in the morning, let our hearts be with thee, and thy hand with us. And the same mercies we beg for all mankind; that thy goodness and power may preserve them, and thy direction and influence secure their eternal salvation, thro' Jesus Christ our Lord, by whom thou hast taught us to call upon thee as our Father, &c.

§. 5. By the way, I cannot help observing, that these disciples of *Ivon* are much reformed in respect of what his cloystered followers were in *An observation on the prayers of the Ivon recluses.* his time. It appears from *Ivon*'s books, that he was as great a *visionary* and *tritheist* as his master *Labadie*, or any of our modern mystics now are. But these *Regulars* I found among the fells, though on *Ivon*'s plan, are as rational Christians as ever adorned the religion of our Master by a purity of faith. You see by their prayers, that their devotions are quite reasonable and calm. There is no rant, nor words without meaning: no feeling instead of seeing the truth; nor expectation of covenant mercy on the belief of a point repugnant not only to the reason and nature of things, but to the plain repeated declarations of

VOL. III.   E   God

God in the Chriſtian religion. Their
prayer is a calm addreſs to the great *Maker*,
Governor, and *Benefactor* of the univerſe;
and honour and obedience to Chriſt as *Mediator*, according to the will and appointment of God *the Father*.

*An anſwer to
a queſtion I
aſked one of
theſe* Ivon-
ites.

§. 6. Upon my aſking one
of theſe gentlemen, how they
came to differ ſo much from
Ivon, their founder, and ceaſe
to be the patrons of viſion,
and an implicit incomprehen-
ſible faith? He told me, they had read
all the books on both ſides of the queſtion, that had been written of late years,
and could not reſiſt the force of the evidence in favour of reaſon and the divine
unity. They ſaw it go againſt mechanical
impulſe, and ſtrong perſuaſion without
grounds, and therefore they diſmiſſed *I-
von*'s notions of believing without ideas, as
they became ſenſible it was the ſame thing
as ſeeing without light or objects. Without dealing any longer in a miſt of words,
or ſhewing themſelves orthodox, by empty,
inſignificant ſounds, they reſolved, that
the object of their worſhip, for the time to
come, ſhould be, that one ſupreme ſelf-
exiſtent Being, of abſolute, infinite perfection, who is the firſt cauſe of all things,

2   and

and whofe numerical identity and infinite perfections are demonftrable from certain principles of reafon, antecedent to any peculiar revelation;—and confeffed, that the *bleffing*, with which *Jefus Chrift* was *fent* by *God* to blefs the world, confifts in *turning men from their iniquities*. They now perceived what the *creed-makers*, and *Ivon*, their founder, could not fee, to wit, that it is againft the *facred texts*, to afcribe to Each Perfon of Three the nature and all effential attributes and properties of the One only true God, and yet make the Three the One true God only, when confidered conjunctly; for if Each has all poffible perfections and attributes, then *Each* muft be the *fame true God* as if and when *conjoined*; and of confequence, there muft then be *Three One true Gods*, or *One Three true Gods*; Three One Supreme Beings, or One Three Supreme Beings, fince to *each* of the three muft be afcribed (as the orthodox fay) *any thing* and *every thing*, that is moft *peculiar* and *appropriated* to the *divine nature*, without any difference. In fhort, by conjobbling matters of faith in this manner, they faw, we had *three diftinct felfs*, or intelligent agents, equal in power and all poffible perfections, agreeing in one common effence, one fort of fpecies, (like a fupreme magiftracy of diftinct perfons, acting by a joint

exercife

exercife of the fame power) and fo the *three* are *one*, not by a *numerical* but *fpecific* identity; *three Omnipotents* and *one Almighty*, in a collective fenfe. This, (continued this gentleman) on fearching the fcriptures, we found was far from being the truth of the cafe. We difcovered, upon a fair examination, and laying afide our old prejudices, that there was nothing like this in the New Teftament. It appeared to us to be the confufed talk of weak heads. In the Bible we got a juft idea of One Eternal Caufe, God the Father, *almighty, all-wife, unchangeable, infinite*; and are there taught how to worfhip and ferve him. The greateft care is there taken to guard againft the ill effects of *imagination* and *fuperftition*; and in the plaineft language, we are ordered to pray to this *bleffed and only potentate, the King of kings, and Lord of lords, who only,* (or *alone*) *hath immortality*; and this in imitation of *Jefus,* who *in the morning very early went out into a folitary place, and there prayed**. Who *difmiffing his difciples, departed into a mountain to pray* †. And *he continued all night in prayer to GOD*‡: We are ordered to *glorify and blefs this only wife God for ever* §.

---

* Mark i. 35. † Mark vi. 46. ‡ Luke vi. 12.
§ Rom. xvi. 27.

Bleffed

Bleſſed be the God and Father of oar Lord Jeſus Chriſt *. *To God and our Father be glory for ever* †. — And to *love him truly by keeping the commandments.* Cui Jeſus ſic reſpondit : primum omnium præceptorum eſt : audi Iſraelita. Dominus Deus veſter dominus unus eſt. Itaque dominum Deum tuum toto corde, toto animo, tota mente, totiſque viribus amato. Hoc primum eſt præceptum. *Hear, O Iſrael, the Lord our God is one Lord. And thou ſhalt love the Lord thy God with all thy heart, and with all thy ſoul, and with all thy ſtrength. This is the firſt Commandment* ‡.

Et voicy le ſecond. Vous aimerez voſtre prochain comme vous même. And the ſecond is like the firſt. Hunc ſimile eſt alterum, alterum ut teipſum amato. His majus aliud præceptum nullum eſt. *Thou ſhalt love thy neighbour as thyſelf. There is none other commandment greater than theſe.*

To ſay it ; — we became fully ſatisfied, that the *ſupreme God* and *Governor of the world*, who exiſts by a *prior neceſſity*, and

---

* 2 Cor. i 3. † Phil. iv. 20. ‡ Mark xii. xii. 29, 30, 31.

therefore

therefore muſt be *one*, a perfect moral a-
gent, and poſſeſſed of all moral perfections, is the *ſole object* of *religious worſhip*:
that *Jeſus Chriſt* was a *temporary miniſter*,
with a legatarian power, to publiſh and
declare the *ſpiritual laws* of this *Great God*:
and that it is incumbent on mankind to
yield a perfect obedience to theſe ſpiritual
laws of this *Supreme Being*: that is, the
duty of all, to make the object propoſed
by Chriſt, his God and our God, his Father and our Father, the ſole object of
faith; and to expect happineſs or ſalvation
on the term of being turned from all our
iniquities. This ſeemed a matter worthy
of the Son of God's appearing in the
world. Every thing elſe muſt be *enthuſiaſm*
and *uſurpation*.

§. 7. Here the *Ivoniſt* had
A reflection on done, and I was greatly pleaſ-
true and falſe ed with his ſenſe and piety.
religion. What a heavenly Chriſtianity
ſhould we profeſs (I ſaid) if
the notions of our modern enthuſiaſts were
as conſiſtent with *Chriſt's great deſign and
profeſſion!* We ſhould then ſet up the
Kingdom of God among men, and be di-
ligent and active in promoting the laws of
that kingdom. We ſhould then believe, like
Jeſus Chriſt and his apoſtles, that there is
but

but *One* God, the *Father Almighty.* *There is no one good* (so commonly called) *but one, that is God*; or *only the one God* *. Nullus eſt bonus niſi unus Deus. *Caſtalio.* (And. Cant. MS. Clem. Alex. adds, —— *My Father who is in Heaven.*) *This is life eternal, to acknowledge thee, O Father, to be the only true* GOD †. *It is one God who will juſtify* ‡. *We know that there is none other Gods but one.* *For to us there is one* GOD *the Father* ‖. *There is one* GOD *and Father of all, who is over all, and through all, and in you all* §. And we ſhould confeſs *one Mediator, —— the man Chriſt Jeſus* **. We ſhould be conſiſtent, and not throw off thoſe principles upon which chriſtianity was founded, and alone could be firſt built. We ſhould invite men into our religion, by repreſenting to them the *perfection* of that *primary law* of God, *reaſon* or *natural religion*; by declaring the plainneſs and clearneſs of it to all attentive and well-diſpoſed minds; and then ſhew them how worthy it was of the Supreme Governor to give ſuch creatures as he has made us the goſpel: that by the religion of favour, he has, with glory to

---

* Mark x. 18. † John xvii. throughout. ‡ Rom. iii. 30.   ‖ 1 Cor. viii. 4. 6.   § Eph. iv. 6. ** 2 Tim. ii. 5.

himſelf,

himſelf, diſplayed his paternal regard for us, by doing much more than what is *ſtrictly neceſſary* for our eternal good. God, on a principle of love, ſends his *Chriſt*, to adviſe us and awaken us to a ſenſe of our danger in paſſing through this world, in caſe (which he ſaw would be the thing) we ſhould not conſtantly attend to the light we might ſtrike out ourſelves with ſome trouble. He calls us in an *extraordinary* manner to forſake vice and idolatry, and practiſe the whole ſyſtem of morality. We might expect, that a good God would, once at leaſt, interpoſe by ſuch an *extraordinary* method as *revelation*, to turn and incline his reaſonable creatures to the ſtudy and practice of the *religion of nature*. This was acting like the Father of the Univerſe, conſidering the negligence and corruption of the bulk of mankind. The *reaſon* he gave us, the *law of nature*, was giving us all that was *abſolutely neceſſary*. The *goſpel* was an addition of what is *excellently uſeful*. What, my beloved, (might a rational divine ſay) can be more paternal, and worthy of the almighty Creator, than to *reveal plainly the motive of a judgment to come*, in order to ſecure all obedience to the religion of nature? Reaſon may, to be ſure, be ſufficient to ſhew men their duty, and to encourage their performance of it with
the

the assurance of obtaining a reward, if they would duly attend to its dictates, and suffer them to have their due effect upon them: it may guide mankind to virtue, and happiness consequent to it, as God must be a rewarder of all those who diligently seek him, and was enough to bring them to the knowledge, and engage them in the practice of true religion and righteousness, if they had not shut their eyes to its light, and wilfully rejected the rule written in their hearts. But as this was what mankind really did, and now do; as errors and impieties, owing to an undue use or neglect of reason, became universal; (just as the case of Christians is, by disregarding the New Testament; and reason, through men's faults, was rendered *ineffectual*, though still *sufficient*, (which justifies both the *wisdom* and *goodness* of God, in leaving man for so many ages to his natural will, and so great a part of the globe to this day with no other light than the law of nature); and reason, I say, was rendered *ineffectual*, though still *sufficient* to teach men to worship God with pious hearts and sincere affections, and to do his will by the practice of moral duties; to expect his favour for their good deeds, and his condemnation of their evil works; then was *revelation* a more *powerful means* of

E 5　　　promoting

promoting true religion and godlineſs. The goſpel is a *more effectual* light. It is a clearer and more powerful guide: a brighter motive and ſtronger obligation to univerſal obedience than reaſon can with certainty propoſe. And therefore, though there was not a neceſſity for God to give a *new rule* in vindication of his providence, and in order to render men accountable to him for their actions; yet the divine goodneſs was pleaſed to enforce the principles of reaſon and morality more powerfully by an expreſs ſanction of future rewards and puniſhments, and by the goſpel reſtore religious worſhip to the original uncorrupted rational ſervice of the Deity. This diſplays his paternal regard to his children, with glory to himſelf. Love was the moving principle of his ſending Chriſt into the world, to reform the corruptions of reaſon, to reſtore it to its purity, and moſt effectually to promote the practice of the rules of it. The goſpel-revelation conſidered in this manner appears to be the pure effect of the divine goodneſs. It is a conduct accompanied with the greateſt propriety and glory.

If this repreſentation of Chriſtianity was as much the doctrine of the church as it is of the *Ivonites* I have mentioned, we might

might then, with hopes of fuccefs, call.
upon the rational infidels to come in.
They could hardly refufe the invitation,
when we told them, our religion was the
eternal law of *reafon* and of God reftored,.
with a few excellently ufeful additions:
that the gofpel makes the very *religion of*
nature, a main part of what it requires,
and fubmits all that it reveals to the teft
of the law of reafon: that the fplendor of
God's *original light*, the light of nature,
and the revelation of Jefus, are the fame;.
both made to deliver mankind from *evils*
and *madnefs* of *fuperftition*, and make their
religion worthy of God, and worthy of
men; to enable them, by the voice of
reafon in conjunction with the words of the
gofpel, to know and worfhip *One God*, the
Maker, the *Governor*, the *Judge*, of the
world; and to practife all that is good and
praife-worthy: that we may be bleffed as
we turn from iniquity to virtue; and by
entering cordially into the fpirit of the
meritoricus example or *exemplary merits* of
Chrift, be determined dead to fin, and a-
live to righteoufnefs: in fhort, my brethren, in the fuffering and death of Jefus,
his patient, pious, and meek, his benevolent and compaffionate behaviour, under
the moft fhocking infult, indignity, and
torture, we have what we could not learn

from the religion of nature, a deportment that well deserves both our admiration and imitation. We learn from the *perfect example* of *Jesus*, recommended in his gospel, to bear patiently ill-usage, and to desire the welfare of our most unreasonable and malicious enemies. This is improving by religion to the best purpose; and as we resemble the Son of God, the *man Christ Jesus*, in *patience, piety,* and *benevolence,* we become the approved children of the Most High, who is kind and good to the unthankful and to the evil. In this view of the *gospel,* all is fine, reasonable, and heavenly. The gentile can have nothing to object. We have the religion of nature in its original perfection, in the doctrine of the New Testament, enforced by pains and pleasures everlasting; and we learn from the *death* of the *Mediator,* not only an unprecedented patience, in bearing our sins in his own body on the tree; but the divine compassion and piety with which he bore them. We have in this the noblest example to follow, whenever called to suffer for well-doing, or for righteousness-sake; and by the imitation, we manifest such a command of temper and spirit, as can only be the result of the greatest piety and virtue. This added to keeping the commandments must render men the blessed of the Father,

and

and entitle them to the kingdom prepared for the wife, the honeft, and the excellent.

But, alas! inftead of giving fuch an account of Chriftianity, the cry of the doctors is, for the moft part, Difcard reafon, and proftrate your underftanding before the adorable myfteries. Inftead of a Supreme Independent Firft Caufe of all things to believe in and worfhip, they give Three true Gods in number, Three infinite independent Beings, to be called One, as agreeing in one common abftract effence, or fpecies; as all mankind are one, in one common rational nature, or abftract idea of humanity. Amazing account! A triune, no infidel or gentile of fenfe will ever worfhip.

Inftead of fixing falvation on moral rectitude, and our preferring the will of God, as delineated in the words of the gofpel, before all other confiderations, we are told of an innocent, meritorious, propitiating blood, fpilt by wicked hands, and fo made an acceptable facrifice, to a Being who is of purer eyes than to behold iniquity. This, we are affured, fatisfies all the demands of the law. Here is infinite fatisfaction: — and moft certainly, I add, a

cool

cool indifference as to perfonal rectitude. When fuch a faith or credulity becomes the principal pillar of truft and dependence, then mere reliance on fuch fatisfaction to divine juftice, may be a ftupifying opiate, and make many remifs in the labours of a penitential piety, and that exact rectitude of mind and life, which even reafon requires, to render us acceptable to the Deity. Many an appetite and paffion are indulged under this fubterfuge ; and with little fervency or zeal for good works, men expect to partake of the heavenly joys, by trufting to the merits of their Saviour, in their laft will and teftament. Deplorable cafe ! Alas ! how has Chriftianity fuffered by its doctors ! The infidel laughs at it as thus preached. It becomes a by-word, and a hiffing to them that pafs by.

Some remarks on a paffage in Binius; *and a few thoughts in relation to the invocation of faints.* §. 8. As to the library of my friends, the *Ivonites,* it was far from being a grand one, but I faw many curious books in it which had not come in my way before. From them I made feveral extracts, and to gratify my reader's curiofity a little, I will here favour him with one of them.

The

The firſt book I chanced to open in this library, was the ſecond volume of *Severin Bini*'s edition of the Councils (3), (edit.

---

(3) *Severin Bini*, or *Binius*, as he is commonly called, was a doctor of divinity at *Cologne*, in the circle of the *Lower Rhine* in *Germany*, and canon of that archiepiſcopal cathedral. He *Of councils, and the editors of them.* publiſhed in that city, in the year 1606, an elegant edition of all the councils, in four very large volumes, folio, and by this work, made the editions or collections of *James Merlin*, *Peter Crabb*, and *Lawrence Surius*, of no value: but the 2d edition, publiſhed by *Binius* in the year 1618, in nine volumes ſmaller folio, is far preferable to the firſt: and the Paris Edition of *Bini's Councils* in 1638, in ten large volumes, folio, is enlarged, more correct, and of conſequence ſtill better than the 2d edition of *Binius*. This is not however the beſt edition to buy, if you love to read that *theological ſtuff* called Councils. The *Louvre* edition des Conciles en 1644, in 37 volumes in folio, is what you ſhould purchaſe; or, that of 1672, *Paris*, by the Jeſuits *Labbé* and *Coſſart*, in 18 large volumes in folio. This laſt is what I prefer, on account of the additions, correctneſs, and beauty of the impreſſion. *Pere Hardouin* did likewiſe print a later very fine edition of the *Councils*, with explications and free remarks; an extraordinary and curious work I have been told: but I could not even ſee it in *France*, as the parliament of *Paris* had ordered the work to be ſecreted, on account of the remarks.

N. B. *Binius*, whom I have mentioned, was born in the year 1543, and died 1620, æt. 77.

N. B. *James Merlin*, the firſt editor of the Councils, was a doctor of divinity, and chanoine of *Notre-*

(edit. *Paris*, 1630) and over-againſt a very
remarkable paſſage from *Cyril*, (p. 548.)
I found ſeveral written leaves, bound up
in the volume, and theſe leaves referred to
by

---

tre-dame de Paris. Beſides the Councils, two large
volumes in folio, he publiſhed the works, of *Richard
de St. Victor*, *Paris*, 1518. — the works of *Peter de
Blois*, *Paris*, 1519. — and the works of *Durand de
St. Pourçain*, *Paris*, 1515. His own works are, *A
Defence of Origen*, in 4to. a good thing; and, *Six
Homilies on Gabriel's being ſent to the Virgin Mary*, in
8vo; which homilies are not worth half a farthing.
——*Merlin* was born in the year 1472, and died
1541, aged 69.

N. B. *Peter Crabb*, the 2d editor of the councils,
was a Franciſcan friar. He publiſhed two volumes
in folio of Councils, at *Cologne*, in 1538; and a third
volume in 1550. — Was born 1470; died 1553;
æt. 83.

N. B. *Lawrence Surius*, the third editor of the
Councils, a monk of the *Chartreux*, publiſhed his
edition of them, in four large volumes in folio,
1560; and a few years after printed his Lives of the
Saints, in ſix tomes. He writ likewiſe a ſhort *Hiſtory
of his own Time*; and, *An Apology for the Maſſacre of
St. Barthelemi*. He was the moſt outrageous, abu-
ſive bigot that ever writ againſt the Proteſtants. The
great men of his own church deſpiſed him; and
Cardinal *Perron*, in particular, calls him *bête* and
l'ignorant. He was born 1522; died 1578, æt. 56.

N. B. *Philip Labbé*, the *Jeſuit*, the 5th editor of
the councils, and the next after *Binius*, was born in
1607; died 1667, æt. 60. He lived only to publiſh
11 vols. of the Councils, the 11th came out the year
he died; and the other ſeven were done by *Coſſart*.
Labbé was a man of learning, and beſides his collection

by an afterifk. The paffage I call *remark-able*, is part of a *homily* pronounced by the *Alexandrian Patriarch* before the *council* of *Ephefus*

---

lection of *Councils*, writ feveral other pieces. The best of them are, *Bibliotheca bibliothecarum : Concordia chronologica : Bellarmini philologica :* and *The Life of Galen.*

Gabriel Coffart, the continuator, publifhed the other feven volumes in 1672, and died at *Paris* the 18th of *December* 1674, æt. 59.

N. B. 1. *Richard de St. Victor*, (whofe works I faid were publifhed by *Merlin*, at *Paris*, 1518) was a *Scotchman*, and *prior* of the *abbey* of *St. Victor* in *Paris*. He died the 10th of *March*, 1173, æt. 91. — He was the author of *Three critical and hiftorical differtations on the Tabernacle*; *two on the Temple*; *three on the harmony of the chronology of the kings of Judea and Ifrael*; *Commentaries on the Pfalms, Canticles, the Epiftles of St. Paul, and the Revelation*; *Some treatifes in divinity*; and *Several difquifitions relating to fpiritual life*. There have been four editions of thefe pieces, and the beft of them is that of *Rouen* in 1650, in two volumes, by *Father John de Touloufe*, who writ the life of *Richard*, and added it to his edition. The three other editions are that of *Paris*, 1518; of *Venice*, 1592; of *Cologne*, 1621. *Richard de Victor* has been highly commended by feveral celebrated writers, by *Henri de Grand*, *Trithem*, *Bellarmine*, and *Sixte de Sienne*. There are many curious and fine things in his writings, it muft be allowed: but in general, he is too fubtil, too diffufe, and too full of digreffions. His commentaries, for the moft part, are weak. I am fure he did not underftand *St. Paul*. But, for the 12th century, he was an extraordinary man.

But

Ephesus on St. *John*'s day, in a church dedicated to his name. In rehearsing his discourse to the *Holy Fathers*, the *Saint* cites *Heb*.

But who was *St. Victor*, to whom the *abbey* of *Chanoines Reguliers* in *Paris*, and the greater *abbaye* of *Chanoines* in *Marseilles*, are dedicated? He was a *Frenchman*, who fought under the Emperors *Dioclesian* and *Maximian* with great applause, in the most honourable post; but in the year 302, suffered martyrdom for refusing to sacrifice to the idols. He was executed on the spot where the abbey of *St. Victor* in *Marseilles* now stands, and there they have his reliques, *a la reserve du pié*, that is, except his foot, which lies in the *Abbaye de St. Victor de Paris*. *William Grimaud, abbot* of *St. Victor de Marseille*, on his being made *Pope Urban* the 5th, A. D. 1362, took the foot of *St. Victor* from his abbey, when he left it, and made a present of it to *John*, Duke of *Berry*, (one of the sons of *John* the first, king of *France*, who was taken prisoner by *Edward* the Black Prince, in the battle of *Poitiers*, *Sept*. 19. 1356): and this *duke* of *Berry* gave the *inestimable foot* to the *monks* of *St. Victor* in *Paris*. There it remains to this day; and tho' so small a part of the blessed *Victor*, sheds immense benefits on the pious Catholics who adore it. Happy Catholics!

2. As to *Peter de Blois*, he was archdeacon of *Bath* in the reign of *Henry* the second, and died in *London*, in the year 1200, æt. 71. His works are 183 letters on various subjects, 20 sermons, and 17 tracts of several kinds. They were first printed at *Mayence* in 1500.—Then by *Merlin*, *Paris*, 1519, as before mentioned.—Afterwards, *John Busée*, the *Jesuit*, gave an edition of them in 1600, which is far preferable to that of *Merlin*. But the most valuable edition is

that

Heb. i. 6. and then addreſſes himſelf to the *apoſtle.*

"Οταν

---

that of *Peter de Gouſſainville*, in folio, *Paris,* 1667: To this edition is prefixed the *life* of *Peter de Blois,* and very learned remarks on *Peter's writings,* and the ſubjeĉts he writ on, are added, by *Gouſſainville.* *De Blois's* works contain many excellent things, and his life is a curious piece. Some of his notions relating to the ſcriptures are very good, and he writes well againſt vice. He is a good author for the age he lived in. His letters are well worth reading; eſpecially ſuch of them as relate to his own time. King *Henry* the ſecond ordered him to make a collection of them for his (the king's) uſe.

3. *Durand de St. Pourçain,* was *biſhop* of *Meaux,* in 1326, and died the 13th of *September* 1333, in the 89th year of his age. His works are, *Liber de origine juriſdiĉtionum,* (a learned piece); and *Commentaries on the four books of Sentences.* (The book called, *The Sentences,* was written by the famous *Peter Lombard,* biſhop of *Paris,* who died in the year 1164, æt. 82. In the *Sentences,* one of the propoſitions argued on is this: *Chriſtus ſecundum quod eſt homo, non eſt aliquod.* Some call theſe *Sentences* excellent, which is what I cannot think them: But in *Durand's Commentary* on them, there are ſeveral excellent things.)

As to the *Jeſuit, Jean Buſée,* (who publiſhed the 3d edition of *Peter de Blois*) he died at *Mayence* the 30th of *May* 1611, aged 64, and was the author of many books not worth mentioning.

The learned *Gouſſainville* (who printed the laſt edition of *De Blois,* with notes, and the life) died in the year 1683, extremely poor and miſerable. He likewiſe publiſhed the works of *St. Gregory,* the firſt pope of that name, with many valuable remarks and notes.

῞Οταν δὲ πάλιν εἰσαγάγῃ τὸν πρωτότοκον
εἰς τὴν οἰκυμένην, λέγει, καὶ προσκυνησάτωσαν
αὐτῷ πάντες ῎Αγγελοι Θεῦ. ----- " *When he*
bringeth

---

notes. There are four editions of this pope's works;
that of *Tuffiniani*, bifhop of Venice, by order of pope
Sixtus the 5th: the *Paris* edition, 1640: *Gouffain-*
ville's edition: and the late *Benedictine* edition: but
Gouffainville's is, in my opinion, the moſt valuable.

N. B. The *Sermons* in the firſt and fecond editions
of *Peter de Blois'* works, are not his, but *Peter Come-*
ſtor's. *De Blois'* fermons are only to be found in
Gouffainville's edition of this arch-deacon's works.
Note, *Peter Comeſtor* was a regular canon of *St. Vic-*
tor's in *Paris*, and died in the year 1198, æt. 65.—
Befides the fermons publiſhed by miſtake as the
work of *De Blois*, he writ a large *fcholaſtic hiſtory*,
which comprehends the facred hiſtory from *Geneſis*
to the end of the *Acts*. This is reckoned a good
thing; and has been abridged by one *Hunter*, an
Engliſhman.

But as to *Councils*; we have the fol-
Of Councils. lowing account of the eighteen general
ones in the *Vatican* library, and are
told, that the feveral *inſcriptions* affixed to them were
made by pope *Sixtus* the 5th; the famous *Felix Pe-*
retti, who was born the 13th of *December* 1521, and
died the 27th of *Auguſt* 1590, in the 69th year of his
age.

1ſt *Council*, which is that of *Nice* in 325. St. *Syl-*
veſter being *pope*, and *Conſtantine* the great *emperor*,
Jefus Chriſt the Son of God is declared confubſtan-
tial with his Father; the impiety of *Arius* is condemned; and the emperor, in obedience to a decree
of the council, ordered all the books of the *Arians* to
be burnt.

2d

bringeth in the first-begotten into the world,
he saith, Let all the angels of God worship
him." ------ Μυϛαγώγεσον Ἐυαγγελιϛὰ, ἐπὶ
xαὶ Νυν, ὦ Μαxάριε Ἰωάννε, &c. —O blessed

2d *Council*, which is that of *Constantinople* in 381.
The holy *Damasus* being *pope*, and *Theodosius* the elder
emperor, the divinity of the Holy Ghost is defended
against the impious *Macedonius*, and his false doctrine
is anathematized.

3d *Council*, which is that of *Ephesus* in 431. St.
Celestin being *pope*, and *Theodosius* the younger *emperor*,
Nestorius, who divided *Jesus Christ* into two persons,
is condemned; and the Holy Virgin is decreed to be
the mother of God.

4th *Council*, which is that of *Chalcedonia* in 451.
St. *Leo* being *pope*, and *Marcian* emperor, the unhap-
py *Eutychius* is anathematized, for maintaining that
Jesus Christ had but one nature.

5th *Council*, which is the *second* of *Constantinople* in
553. *Vigilius* being *pope*, and *Justinian, emperor*, the
debates relating to the doctrine of *Theodore*, bishop of
Mopsueste, *Ibas*, bishop of *Edessa*, and *Theodoret*, bishop of *Cyr*, are suppressed, and the errors of *Origen*
are separated from the holy doctrine.

6th *Council*, which is the *third* of *Constantinople* in
680. St. *Agatho* being *pope*, and *Constantine Pago-
natus, emperor*, the heretics called *Monothelites*, who
admitted but one will in *Jesus Christ*, are condemned.

7th *Council*, which is the *second* of *Nice* in 784. *A-
drian* being *pope*, and *Constantine*, the son of *Irene*,
being *emperor*, the impiety of the image-breakers is
condemned, and the worship of the holy images is
established in the church.

8th

fed *John* the Evangelift, explain this myf-
tery: Who is this firft-begotten — how
came he into the world?   Myfterium hoc
aperi,

8th *Council*, which is the *fourth* of *Conftantinople* in
689.   *Adrian* the fecond being *pope*, and *Bafil*, emperor, *Ignatius*, patriarch of *Conftantinople*, is re-eftablifhed in his fee, and *Photius*, the ufurper, is with
ignominy driven away.

9th *Council*, which is the *firft* of *Lateran* in 1122. *
10th *Council*, which is the *fecond* of *Lateran* in
1139. *

. 11th *Council*, which is the *third* of *Lateran* in 1179.
Alexander the third being *pope*, and *Frederick* the firft
emperor, the errors of the *Vandois* are condemned.

12th *Council*, which is the *fourth* of *Lateran* in 1215.
Innocent the third being *pope*, and *Frederick* the fecond, *emperor*, the falfe opinions of the abbot *Joa-
chim* are condemned ; the holy war, for the recovery
of *Jerufalem*, is refolved ; and the croifades are appointed among chriftians.

13th *Council*, which is the *firft* of *Lyons* in 1245.
Under the pontificate of *Innocent* the 4th, the emperor
Frederick is declared an enemy to the church, and de-
prived of the empire ; they deliberate on the recovery
of the Holy Land ; St. *Lewis*, king of *France*, is declared chief of that expedition.   The cardinals are
honoured with red hats.

14th *Council*, which is the *fecond* of *Lyons* in 1274.
Gregory the tenth being *fovereign pontiff*, the *Greeks*
are reunited to the church of *Rome* ; St. *Bonaventure*
does fignal fervice to the church in this council ;

---

* The canons of thefe two councils are wanting, and they have
no infcription in the Vatican.

Friar

aperi, effare etiam nunc, qui voces habes immortales. Refera nobis puteum vitæ. Da, ut nunc quoque de falutis fontibus hauriamus.

This

Friar *Jerome* brings the king of the *Tartars* to the council, and that prince receives, in the moft folemn manner, the bleffed water of baptifm.

15th *Council*, which is that of *Vienne* in 1311. Under the *pontificate* of *Clement* the fifth, the *Decretals*, called the *Clementines* from the name of this pope, are received and publifhed; the proceffion of the holy facrament is inftituted throughout *Chriftendom*; and profeffors of the oriental languages are e-ftablifhed in the-four moft famous univerfities in *Europe*, for the propagation of the chriftian faith in the *Levant*.

16th *Council*, which is that of *Florence* in 1439. The *Greeks*, the *Armenians*, and the *Ethiopians*, are re-united to the catholic church, under the *pontificate* of *Eugene* the fourth.

17th *Council*, which is the *fifth* of *Lateran*, began in the year 1517. They declared war againft the *Turks*, who had feized the ifland of *Cyprus*, and poffeffed themfelves of *Egypt*, on the death of the fultan: the emperor *Maximilian* the firft, and *Francis* the firft, king of *France*, are appointed generals of this war, under the popes *Julius* the fecond, and *Leo* the tenth.

18th *Council*, which is that of *Trent*, the laft of the œcumenical or general councils: held from the year 1545 to the year 1563. *Paul* the third, *Julius* the third, and *Pius* the fifth, reigning at *Rome*: the *Lutherans* and other heretics are condemned, and the ancient difcipline of the church is re-eftablifhed in her exact and regular practice.

Thefe,

This paſſage of *Cyril* I have heard ſeveral learned Roman Catholic gentlemen call a *prayer*, and affirm it was a *proof* of the *Father's*

Theſe, reader, are the *eighteen famous General Councils*; and if you will turn to the third volume of a work, called, *Notes relating to Men, and Things, and Books,* you will find my obſervations on them; my remarks on the *popes*, the *princes*, and the *fathers*, aſſembled; their *unchriſtian immoralities*, and *ſad acts* againſt the laws of Chriſt, in order to eſtabliſh for ever, that *very ſenſeleſs*, and *very wicked religion*, called *Popery*; that is, *a compoſition of ſin and error* ſo *baſe* and *abominable*, that we might expect ſuch a thing from the *devil*; but it is impoſſible it could come from heavenly-inſpired fathers. In that book, you will find many thoughts on the *religion* delivered to the world by thoſe *Councils*, and by them eſtabliſhed, tho' it is in reality a diſgrace to chriſtianity; a diſhonour to the religion of nature; and a faction againſt the common rights of mankind: what ought to be the *juſt object* of *univerſal contempt* and *abhorrence*; whether we conſider it as a *ſyſtem* of *idolatry, impiety,* and *cruelty*; or, as a *political ſcheme*, to *deſtroy* the *liberties*, and *engroſs* the *properties* of *mankind.* Of theſe things, particularly and largely, in the piece referred to.

Here I have only further to obſerve, that in the large collections of the *Councils*, it is not only the *eighteen œcumenical* the collectors have gathered, but ſo much of all the *councils* as they could find, their *acts, letters, formularies of faith,* and *canons,* from the firſt *council* at *Jeruſalem*, A. D. 49, to the *laſt council* in the 18th century; which was convoked by the *archbiſhop* of *Ambrun* againſt *Jean de Soanem, biſhop* of *Senez.*

ther's Invocation of saints, in the beginning of the 5th century ; for St. *Cyril* succeeded his uncle *Theophilus* in the see of *Alexandria*, *October* 16. 412. But to this it may be answered,——

1. That *Binius*, though a zealous pleader for the *catholic cause*, (as the *monks* of *Rome* miscall it) was of another opinion, for he takes no notice of this passage in his notes (in calce part 3. Concil. Ephesini, tom. 2. p. 665, &c.) and most certainly, he would not have failed to urge it, if he had considered it as a prayer, and believed it did prove the invocation of saints.

Senez. These amount to above 1600 *councils.* Note, Reader, the *condemnation*, the *banishment* of old *John de Soanem* (in the 8oth year of his age) the most learned and excellent prelate in *France*, of his time, by *Firebrand Tartuff*, archbishop of *Ambrun*, and his council, (A. D. 1727, *September* 21.) was on account of the bishop's admirable *pastoral instruction* against the *execrable constitution unigenitus*, and the antichristian *formulary* of pope *Alexander* the seventh ; and because he recommended the reading of *Pere Quesnel*'s very pious and fine *Reflections Morales.*—This famous *Jansenist*, and father of the oratory, *Pasquier Quesnel*, was the author of many books, (some of them very good) and lived to a great age. He was born in 1636, and died at last in prison (if I mistake not) a sufferer for religion. He was severely persecuted for many years.

2. Nor does *Bellarmine*, in his treatife de fanctorum beatitudine, *Henricus Vicus*, de fanctorum invocatione, *Gabriel Vafquez*, de adoratione, or *Gregorius de Valentia*, de oratione, make ufe of this paffage of *Cyril*, though they do, *ex profeſſo*, and datâ operâ, diligently quote all the councils and fathers they can, to prove *invocation of faints*.

3. As *rhetorical apoſtrophes*, or *profopopœias*, are ufual in all authors, facred or civil, this may be one in *Cyril*, and it feems very plain from the paffage, that it was intended for no more. It appears to be a *rhetorical figure*, and not a *prayer*; fuch a figure as the Greek fathers were wont very frequently to ufe in their orations and poems.

Cyril intending, as appears by the fequel, to anfwer his own queſtion with a paffage in St. *John*'s gofpel, makes a long *rhetorical apoſtrophe* to the *apoſtle*, as if he were there prefent, then adds, Annon dicentem audimus, Ὀυκᾶν ἀκᴂομιν λέγοντος? *But do we not hear him faying?* Or, as *Binius* has the reading, Ὀυκᾶν ἀκᴂομιν λέγοντος, *let us hear what St. John faith*, audiamus itaque dicentem, as if they had heard *John* giving his anfwer, and then concludes

concludes with the firſt verſe of the firſt
chapter of his goſpel, 'Εν 'Αρχῆ ἦν ὁ Λόγος,
&c. *In the beginning was the word,* &c.

It is therefore very plain, that this paſſage of *Cyril* is only a part of his homily
or ſermon, and that in a rhetorical manner, he quotes a text from a goſpel written by *John* about 330 years before, in
anſwer to his own queſtion, who the word
was? For *Cyril* to pray to *John* to tell
them what he had told them long before,
were ſenſeleſs and ridiculous ; but to deſire
the apoſtle to do it in a *rhetorical apo-*
ſtrophe, was allowable. It amounts to no
more than the figurative expreſſion in our
liturgy, *Hear what comfortable words our*
Saviour ſaith. Hear what St. Paul ſaith.

But if *Cyril* did in this paſſage truly
pray to St. *John,* that could be no argument for *popiſh invocation* of *ſaints* ; for, if
an *hundred fathers* in the beginning of the
fourth century, had preached up, and prac-
tiſed *invocation of ſaints,* yet that could
not make it lawful and right, ſince we are
taught by the *ſcriptures* to direct our prayers
neither to *ſaint nor angel,* but to *God only,*
and in the name and *mediation of Jeſus*
Chriſt only. We are not only poſitively ordered by the *apoſtles* to make all our ad-

dreſſes

dreſſes and prayers to *God only*, and by the *mediation and interceſſion of Jeſus Chriſt*; but are told, that God is *omniſcient*, and ſo *able to hear all our prayers*; — *all-ſufficient*, and therefore *able to ſupply all our neceſſities*; —and that his *mercies in Jeſus Chriſt are infinite*. This makes *our way ſure* in this particular.

On the contrary, the *papiſts* have no *precept* to *pray* to *ſaints*; nor *any promiſe* that they ſhall be *heard*; nor any *practice* of the primitive church, for 300 years after Chriſt, to *encourage* them; and therefore, ſuch *popiſh invocation* is a *novel, groundleſs*, and *impious error*.

Some remarks on the doctrine of the invocation of ſaints.   We are told by St. Peter, (*Acts* v. 31.) that *God had exalted the Lord Jeſus Chriſt to be a Prince and Saviour*, that is, an *interceſſor*.—By St. *Paul*, (*Heb.* vii. 25.) that *Chriſt is able to ſave to the uttermoſt all that come to God by him, ſeeing he ever liveth to make interceſſion for them*; (chap. ix. 24) that *he is gone to heaven* (for this very end) *to appear in the preſence of God for us*: (1 *Tim.* ii. 5.) that there is no other *mediator betwixt God and men but the man Chriſt Jeſus*, that is, whoſe *prerogative* it is to *intercede*

for

for sinners to the Divine Majesty; being an *honour* and *dignity* God hath exalted him unto, after his sufferings, and as a *reward* thereof: — Thus are we informed by the divine oracles, and yet, notwithstanding this, to make prayers and supplications to the *Virgin Mary*, and a thousand other *saints*, for *aid* or *help*; and to have by their *merit* and *intercession*, the *gifts* and *graces* they pray for *conferred* upon them;— this is a doctrine of such dangerous consequence, as it is a *depriving* of *Christ Jesus* of that grand *dignity* and *prerogative* he is now in heaven exalted to, as much as in men lies, that I should have admired how it ever came to be embraced by such as profess christianity, had not the spirit of God foretold (1 *Tim.* iv. 4.) that *some should depart from the faith, giving heed to seducing spirits,* (that is, seducing men) and *doctrines of devils,* that is to say, doctrines concerning *demons,* or *souls of famous men departed this life*; which the heathens called *demons*; and to whom they gave the worship of prayer or invocation, as intercessors or inferior divinities. This prophecy hinders my wondering at the thing: but then I must call such modern invocation *gentilism christianized*; a *deplorable corruption.*

Ponder

Ponder then, ye *Catholics*, in time, and think not to excufe yourfelves by arguing from the *command Chriftians have here on earth to require each others prayers to God for them :* — For, we have no command to fupplicate any in heaven but only God. (*Mat.* vi. 8.) We have no reafonable af-furance that the *faints in heaven do hear our prayers*, and of confequence have not the fame *reafons* to requeft *their* prayers to God for us that we have to requeft the prayers of *faints on earth :* nor is this all : our *prayers* to each other in this life are only chriftian *requefts* to recommend our conditions to God : *offices* only of *kindnefs* ; no *aĉts of religious. worfhip.*

When St. *Paul* was on earth, had any one on *bended knees*, with *hands* and *eyes lifted up to heaven*, in time of *public prayer*, and amidft the *folemn prayers to God*, be-feeched him for *aid* and *help*, and for the *conference* of *gifts* and *graces*, he would have *rent his cloathes*, and faid, *Why do ye thefe things?* and can we fuppofe, that, now in heaven, the apoftle is lefs careful to preferve entire *God's prerogative*.

Befide, there is a great deal of difference betwixt St. *Paul's* faying, *Brethren, pray for us*, or our requefting the prayers of the
faithful

faithful here on earth for us, and *praying to faints in heaven*, as *practised* in the *Roman church*. Our's, are only *wishes* and *requests*; their's, *solemn prayers* on bended knees, made in the *places* and proper seasons of *divine worship*, and joined with the *prayers* they make to *God*. They use the same *postures* and *expressions* of devotions they use to God himself. They pray to them for *help* and *aid*, and make them *joint petitioners* with Christ; relying on *their merits* as the *merits of Christ*.

In sum, in the *tabernacle of this world*, we are to request the prayers of every good christian for us: but in the *tabernacle* of *heaven*, we are to *call on none* but *Him* in *whom we believe*. As in the *outward court* of the *Jewish tabernacle*, every *priest* was permitted to officiate, to receive and present the devotions of the people to the divine majesty; but in the *holy place, within the vail*, none but the *high-priest* was to do any *office* or *service*: even so in the *tabernacle* of *this world*, every christian being a *priest* to *God*, has this honour conferred upon him; but in the *holy of holies*, in *heaven*, none but *Christ*, our *high-priest*, is to officiate. He only is there to *appear in the presence of God for us*. It is *his prerogative alone* to receive our prayers, and present

them

them to the divine majefty. As none but the *high prieft* was to offer *incenfe* in the *holy of holies*, fo none in heaven but *Chrift* our *high-prieft* is to *offer* our prayers to *God his father*. He alone is that *angel* to whom *much incenfe was given, that he fhould offer it with the prayers of all faints, upon the golden altar that was before the throne.* (Rev. viii. 3.) Which alludes to the *altar* that was before the *mercy-feat*, on which the *high-prieft* only was to offer *incenfe*.

But the *catholic* may fay perhaps, that as on earth, men do not prefently run to *kings* to *prefent* their *requefts*, but obtain his favours by the *mediation* of *courtiers* and *favourites*; even fo, it is fitting we have recourfe to faints, who are *favourites* in heaven, that we may obtain *accefs* to God, and have our *fuits* accepted of him. Thus have I heard fome learned men of the church of *Rome* argue. They fhould confider, in the firft place, that if an *earthly prince* had declared he would have no *follicitor* but his *fon*, and that all *favcurs* and *royal graces* fhould come to his *fubjects* *through his hands*, and by means of his *mediation*; fuch fubjects could deferve no favour, if they make their application to *other favourites*, contrary to their prince's command.——In the next place, if the *follicitor*,

licitor, the *fon*, was out of the queftion, and no fuch one had been declared by the king, yet as we petition earthly princes by fuch as enjoy their prefence, becaufe they cannot give audience to all their fubjects, nor do they know the worthy; but *God* is *omniprefent*, his *ears always open*, and his *head bowed down* to the *prayers* of his people; is no *refpecter* of *perfons*, but gives a like *accefs* to the *beggar* as to the *prince*, and promifes to caft out none that make their application to him; it follows of confequence, that we ought to addrefs ourfelves *immediately* to *God*, and *afk from him*. If an *earthly prince* fhould thus invite his fubjects to petition him for the fupply of their wants, I fhould account the man no better than a *fool* or a *madman*, who would *apply* himfelf to any of the *king's favourites*.

The conclufion is; O thou that heareft prayer, unto thee fhall all flefh come. (*Pf.* xv. 2.) Since *God*, who is infinite in mercy, omniprefent, and omnipotent in wifdom and action, admits every man to the *throne of grace*, bids him afk in the *name* of *Jefus Chrift*, and promifes, whatever we afk in his Son's name, he will do it.——Since the practice of *praying to faints* is *injurious* to *Chrift*, and doth manifeftly *rob* him of his

F 5   *royal*

royal prerogative, which is to be the *one,* and, *only mediator* betwixt God and man; for in this *office,* he hath no *sharers* or *partners,* according to the scripture account: As *God* is but *one,* and there is *no other;* so the *mediator* (by the appointment of God) is but *one,* and there is, there can be *no other* (4)---And since, exclusive of these unalterable things, the *Roman doctors* cannot be certain, *that saints in heaven hear the requests of suppliants on earth,* or *know whether our prayers are fit to be accepted of God* (5); let us reject that *unlawful* practice,

the

----

(4) Quid tam proprium Christi quam advocatum apud deum patrem adstare populorum. (Ambros. in Psal. xxxix)——Pro quo nullus interpellat, sed ipse pro omnibus, hic unus verusque mediator est. (Aug. Cont. Parmen l. 2. c. 8.)

(5) The *Roman doctors* say, the *saints* know the transactions that are done here below, by *revelation* or *intuition.*——To this I answer, if it is by *revelation* that they know our requests and prayers to them, then it must be either *from God* or *from angels;* of which there is not the least assurance or certainty to be any where found; but if we could be sure of it, then, in my opinion, we ought to pray to *God* or *angels* to make known our prayers to *saints;* which would be strange religion.—If it be by *intuition,* as the greatest part of the *doctors* say, and that the *saints see* the requests in the *divine essence,* as men see things in a corporeal glass; then, (exclusive of answering that the scriptures say no such thing) the *saints* must see *all things* in the *divine essence,* or only such things as God

is

the *invocation of faints*, and *pray* for *pardon*
and *grace* (as the *gofpel* directs) to *God the
judge of all*, through *Jefus Chrift the mediator of the new covenant*. This do; and
thou fhalt live.

N. B. Who was the author of thefe good
remarks, thefe friars could not tell me; as
they were in the book when they bought
it. If I miftake not, they are an abftract
from a letter of Bifhop *Barlow* to Mr. *Eve-
lyn*, with feveral additions. I have not
Bifhop *Barlow*'s works by me; but I think
I have feen fomething to this purpofe, written by this prelate about one hundred years
ago.

---

is pleafed to *permit them to fee*: if *all things*, they would
be *omnifcient*: if only the *things permitted to be feen*, how
is it poffible for us to know whether God is pleafed to
permit them to fee therein our prayers, or to know the
requefts we make to them, unlefs he had told us fo.
Let it be *revelation* or *intuition*, it is fad fuff.

SECTION III.

" Say, why was man fo eminently rais'd
" Amid the vaft creation; why ordain'd
" Through life and death to dart his piercing eye,
" With thoughts beyond the limits of his frame;
" But that th' Omnipotent might fend him forth
" In fight of mortal and immortal powers,
" As on a boundlefs theatre, to run
" The great career of juftice; to exalt
" His generous aim to all diviner deeds;
" To fhake each partial purpofe from his breaft;
" And thro' the mifts of paffion and of fenfe,
" And thro' the toffing tide of chance and pain,
" To hold his courfe unfault'ring, while the voice
" Of truth and virtue, up the fteep afcent
" Of nature, calls him to his high reward,
" Th' applauding fmile of heav'n? Elfe wherefore
" burns
" In mortal bofoms this unquenched hope,
" That breathes from day to day fublimer things,
" And mocks poffeffion? Wherefore darts the mind
" With fuch refiftlefs ardor to embrace
" Majeftic forms; impatient to be free,
" Spurning the grofs controul of wilful might;
" Proud of the ftrong contention of her toils;
" Proud to be daring?"

April 8. §. 1. THE eighth of *April*
1729, *we*
leave the re- 1729, I bid the *I-*
ligious, and *vonites* adieu, and by their di-
proceed in the rections walked up a very fteep
journey. and ftony mountain, which
took me two hours, and then arrived at
what

what I had often feen before in this part of
the world, a great lake, the water of which
was black as ink to look at as it ftood,
though very bright in a cup, and muft be
owing, as I fuppofe, to its defcending to the
abyfs. By the fide of this water, under the
fhade of oak-trees, many hundred years
old, we rid for an hour, on even ground,
and then came to a defcent fo very dangerous and dark, through a wood on the
mountain's fide, that we could hardly creep
it down on our feet, nor our horfes keep
their legs as we led them to the bottom.
This declivity was more than a mile, and
ended in a narrow lane between a range of
precipices that almoft met at top. This
pafs was knee-deep in water, from a fpring
in the bottom of the mountain we had come
down, which ran through it, and fo very
ftony, that it took us three hours to walk
the horfes to the end of it, though it was
not more than two miles: but at laft we
came to a fine plain, over which we rid for
an hour and a half, and arrived at a wood,
which feemed very large, and ftood between
two very high unpaffable hills. In this foreft was our way, and the road fo dark, and
obftructed by the branches of trees, that
it was difmal and uneafy to go. On however we went for a long time, and about
the middle of it came to a circular opening
of

of about four acres, in which four very
narrow roads met; that we had travelled,
another before us, and one on each hand.
The way ftrait on we were cautioned by
my friends not to go, as it was a terrible
ride; but whether to turn to the right or
left, we had forgot. I thought to the
right; but my lad was pofitive, he remembered the direction was to take the left-
hand road. This caufed a ftop for fome
time, and as I was a little fatigued, I thought
it beft while we paufed to dine. *Finn* brought
immediately fome meat, bread, and a bottle of cyder, from his valife, and under a
great oak I fat down, while our horfes fed
on the green. One hour we refted, and
then went on again, to the left, as *O Finn*
advifed. For feveral hours we rid, or rather, our horfes walked, till we got out of
the wood, and then arrived at the bottom
of a fteep mountain; one fide of which is
in the northern extremity of *Weftmoreland,*
and the other in the north end of *Stanemore-
Richmondfhire.* This vaft hill we afcended,
and came down the other fide of the fell
into a plain, which extends fouth-eaft for
near half a mile to the river *Teefe,* that di-
vides the north end of *Stanemore* from
Bifhoprick, or the county of *Durham. York-
fhire* here ends in an obtufe angle, between
two mountains, and the angle, for a quarter

4

.of

of a mile, is filled with that beautiful tall ever-green tree, the broad-leaved *alaternus,* intermixed here and there in a charming manner, with the fir tree, the *Norway* spruce, and the balm of *Gilead.* It is as fine a grove as can in any part of the world be seen.

§. 2. Just at the entrance of it, by the side of a plentiful spring, which runs into the *Teese,* there stood the prettiest little house I had ever beheld, and over it crept the pretty rock-rose, the cassine, *A description of a little country-seat, in the northern extremity of Stanemore.*
the sea-green coromilla, and other ever-green shrubs. Before the house, was a large garden, seven or eight acres of land, under fruit-trees, and vegetables of every kind; very beautifully laid out; and watered in a charming manner by the stream that murmured a thousand ways from the spring by the house-door. I have not seen a sweeter thing. It appeared so beautiful and useful, so still and delightful a place, so judiciously cultivated, and happily disposed, that I could not help wishing to be acquainted with the owner of such a lodge.

§. 3.

§. 3. As there was no other fence to this fine spot of ground but a ditch like a *ha* to keep cattle out, I leaped into the gardens, and roamed about for

A description of a sleeping parlour in a grove.

some time, to look at the curious things. I then went up to the house, in hopes of seeing a human creature either high or low. I knocked at the door, but no one could I find, though the mansion did not look like an uninhabited place. I then sauntered into the grove behind, and in a winding way of three hundred yards, that had been cut through the perennial wood, and was made between banks of springing flowers, beautiful exotics, and various aromatic shrubs, crept on till I arrived at a sleeping parlour, which stood in the middle of a circular acre of ground, and was surrounded and shaded with a beautiful grove; the larix, the phœnician cedar, and the upright savin. There was a little falling water near the door, that was pleasing to look at, and charmed the ear. Entering this room, I found the walls painted by some masterly hand, in baskets of flowers and the finest rural scenes. Two handsome couches were on either side the chamber, and between these *lits de repos*, was as curious a table, for wood and workmanship, as could be seen. Pretty stools stood near it,

it, and one arm-chair. It was a sweet
silent place, and in every respect far beyond the sleeping parlour in the gardens at
Stow. (6)

§. 4. On one of the couches,
as it was then evening, and I
knew not what to do, I threw
myself down, and very soon
fell fast asleep. I lay the whole

*Passed the
night in the
sleeping par-
lour in the
wood.*

night without waking, and as soon as I
could perceive any day, went to see what
was become of *Finn* and the horses. The
beasts I found feeding on very good grass in
the green: and my lad still snoaring under
a great tree: but he was soon on his legs,
and gave me the following account.

§. 5. About an hour after
my departure from him, he
saw a poor man pass over the plain, who

Finn's story.

had come down the mountain we descended, and was going to cross the *Teese* in a
small skiff of his own, in order to go to
his cottage on the other side in *Bishoprick*:
that he lived by fishing and fowling, and
sold what he got by land and water to the
quality and gentlefolk, twenty miles round

(6) Lord *Cobham's*, now Earl *Temple's* seat in *Buck-
inghamshire*, 59 miles from *London*.

him.

him. And on afking who lived in the houfe
before us, on the fkirts of the grove, he
faid, it belonged to a young lady of great
fortune, Mifs *Antonia Cranmer*, whofe father had been dead about a year, (died in
the houfe I faw): that fhe was the greateft
beauty in the world, and only nineteen,
and for one fo young, wife to an aftonifhing
degree: that fhe lived moftly at this feat,
with her coufin, *Agnes Vane*, who was almoft as handfome as fhe: that Mifs *Cranmer* had no relifh for the world, being ufed
to ftill life, and feldom ftirred from home,
but to vifit an old lady, her aunt, who lived in *Cumberland:* that fhe was at prefent
there, about twenty miles off, and would
foon return: that fhe kept four young
gentlewomen (who had no fortunes) to attend her and Mifs *Vane*; two old men fervants, a gardener, and a cook; and two
boys: that whenever fhe went from her
houfe, fhe took her whole family with her,
and left every place locked up as I faw.
Finn's account furprifed me. It fet me a-
thinking if it was poffible to get this
charming girl. I paufed with my finger in
my mouth for a few minutes, and then bid
him faddle the horfes.

*The author's
manner of liv-*

§. 6. As foon as it was
poffible, I went over the river
to

to the fisherman's house, determining there to wait, till I
could see the beautiful *Antonia*,
and her fair kinswoman, another *Agnes de Castro*, to be
sure. My curiosity could not pass two such
glorious objects without any acquaintance
with them.

*ing for seve-
ral days, in
the cottage of
a poor fisher-
man in* Bish-
oprick.

The poor fisherman gave me a bed very
readily for money, as he had one to spare
for a traveller, and he provided for me
every thing I could desire. He brought
bread and ale from a village a few miles
distant, and I had plenty of fish and wild-
fowl for my table. Every afternoon I crossed
the water, went to the sleeping parlour, and
there waited for the charming *Antonia*.———
Twenty days I went backwards and for-
wards, but the beauties in that time did
not return. Still however I resolved to
wait; and, to amuse myself till they came,
went a little way off to see an extraordinary
man.

§. 7. While I resided in
this cottage, *Christopher* informed me, that about three
miles from his habitation,
there lived in a wild and beautiful glin, a gentleman well

*A description
of a charming
little country
seat, where a
solitary gen-
tleman lived.*

worth my
knowing,

knowing, not only on account of his pretty lodge, and lone manner of spending his time, but as he was a very extraordinary man. This was enough to excite my curiosity, and as soon as it was light, the first of *May*, I went to look for this solitary. I found him in a vale, romantic indeed, among vast rocks, ill-shaped and rude, and surrounded with trees, as venerable as the forest of *Fontainbleau*. His little house stood on the margin of a fountain, and was encompassed with copses of different trees and greens. The pine, the oak, the ash, the chesnut tree, cypresses, and the acasia, diversified the ground, and the negligent rural air of the whole spot, had charms that could always please. Variety and agreeableness were every where to be seen. Here was an harbour of shrubs, with odoriferous flowers: and there, a copse of trees was crowned with the enamel of a meadow. There was a collection of the most beautiful vegetables in one part; and in another, an assembly of evergreens, to form a perpetual spring. *Pan* had an altar of green turf, under the shade of elms and limes: and a *water-nymph* stood by the spring of a murmuring stream. The whole was a fine imitation of nature; simple and rural to a charming degree.

§. 8.

§. 8. Here lived *Dorick Watſon*, an *Engliſh* gentleman, who had been bred a *catholic* in *France*, and there married a ſiſter of the famous *Abbé le Blanc*. But on returning to his own country, being inclined, by good ſenſe and curioſity, to ſee what the proteſtants had to ſay in deꞏ fence of their *reformation*, he read the beſt books he could get on the ſubject, and ſoon perceived, that *Luther, Melanƈthon, Calvin, Zuinglius, Bucer*, and other miniſters of Chriſt, had ſaid more againſt the Romiſh religion than the *pretended catholics* had been able to give a ſolid anſwer to. He ſaw, that *barbarity, policy*, and *ſophiſtry*, were the main props of *popery*; and that, in doctrine and practice, it was one of the *greateſt viſible enemies* that *Chriſt* has in the world. He found that even *Bellarmine*'s *notes* of his church were ſo far from being a clear and neceſſary proof that the *church of Rome* is the body of Chriſt, or true church, that they proved it to be the *Great Babylon*, or that *great enemy* of God's church; which the *apoſtles* deſcribe.

He ſaw, in the firſt place, that there has not been, ſince the writing of the New Teſtament, any empire, but that of

The hiſtory of Dorick Watſou *the hermit.*

The hermit's obſervations on Bellarmine's *notes of the church.*

the

the *church* of *Rome*, fo univerfal for 1260 years together, as to have all that dwell upon earth, peoples, and multitudes, and nations, and tongues, to worfhip it; which is St. *John's* defcription of the *new power* that prevailed on the inhabitants of the earth to receive his idolatrous conftitutions, and yield obedience to his tyrannical authority. *And all that dwell on the earth fhall worfhip him*, except thofe who are inrolled in the regifters, as heirs of eternal life, according to the promifes of the mediator of acceptance and bleffing. *(Rev.* xiii. 8.) *The waters which thou faweft, where the whore fitteth, are peoples, and multitudes, and nations, and tongues.* (Rev. xvii. 15.) *Bellarmine's Univerfality* then is directly againft him.

The Cardinal's fecond note, (continued *Dorick)* is antiquity, and his *third* a *perpetual and uninterrupted duration.* But on examination, I could find no *ruling power,* except *Rome papal,* fo *ancient,* as to have the blood of prophets, and faints, and of all that were flain upon earth, of that kind for that fpace of time, to be found in it. *(Rev.* xviii. 24.) And what *Rule* but *papal Rome* had ever fo long a duration upon feven hills, fo as to anfwer the whole length of of the time of the *Saracen* and *Turkish* empires.

The Cardinal's *fourth note* is *amplitude*, and it is most certain, that never had any other church such a multitude and variety of believers, as to have all nations drink of the wine of her fornication, and to gain a blasphemous power over all kindreds, and tongues, and nations.

The *fifth note* is the *Succession of its bishops*; and the *sixth*, *Agreement with the doctrine of the ancient church:* Now, it is most true, that none but *Rome* was ever so eminently conspicuous for so long a time for the *succession of its bishops* under one supreme patriarch, as to be the *living image* of all the civil dignities of the empire, where it was under one *supreme church-head exercising all the power* of the civil head: nor did ever any enemy of God's church act for so long a time like the *red dragon* in its *bloody laws* against the followers of the lamb: and yet so far agree with the *primitive church* in fundamental *doctrines*, as to answer the character of a false prophet with the horns of the lamb, that is, Christ, but speaking

ing like the *red dragon* to his followers, as the *church* of *Rome* has done. (7)

The

---

(7) Reader, it is well worth your while to turn to the first volume of that admirable work, the *Salter's-hall Sermons against Popery,* and there see how the *Cardinal's notes* of his church are considered by that learned and excellent man, Dr. *Samuel Chandler.* His consideration of the 6th note more immediately concerns me here, and therefore I give you an abstract of it.

The writings of the apostles are allowed even by our adversaries to be the oldest records of christianity, and therefore to this ancient and infallible rule we ought to appeal, to determine the controversy between us and the *papists,* that is, to see how far this antiquity favours their doctrine and practices, or is in agreement with ours.

1. The protestants renounce the Pope, and acknowledge one law-giver, the Lord *Jesus* Christ, for these reasons,—That the Pope is not mentioned in the New Testament ; that Christ says, *one is your master, even Christ* ; and St. *Paul* says, *there is but one Lord, and one Faith : the whole family in heaven and earth is named of the Lord Jesus Christ.*

2. Protestants do not pay any worship at all to saints and angels, but, as St. *Paul* directs, consider *Jesus Christ* as their *sole mediator* and *advocate* ; for *there is but one God, and one mediator between God and man, the man Jesus Christ.* They say, such veneration and prayer to saints and angels is superstition and will-worship, and only worship God with all their hearts and souls, with the most raised affections, and the highest degrees of love and fear, faith and confidence ; for it is written, *Thou shalt worship the*

Lord

. The *seventh note* of *Bellarmine's holy Ro-man catholic church*, is the *Union of the members among themselves, and with the head:*

Lord God, and him only shalt thou serve : And the angel in the *Revelation* said to *John*, who fell down at his feet to worship him, *See thou do it not, for I am thy fellow-servant.*

3. We affirm, that in the sacrament of the Lord's Supper, after consecration, there is nothing existent but bread and wine; for St. *Paul* says, *Whosoever shall eat this bread and drink this cup*, and *as often as you eat this bread and drink this cup.*

4. We affirm the eucharist is only a memorial of Christ's death; for Christ says, *do this in remembrance of me*; and St. *Paul* assures the *Corinthians* from Christ himself, (1 *Cor.* xi. 24.) that they were to receive the elements with this view only : and in his epistle to the *Hebrews* he tells us, that *by one offering Christ hath for ever perfected those who are sanctified*; and that because there *is remission of sins under the new covenant, there is no more offering for sin*; which proves, the eucharist is not a propitiatory sacrifice.

5. We renounce the doctrine of purgatory, and affirm, that the future state is no state of probation; for at death, *the dust shall return to the earth as it was, and the spirit shall return to God who gave it.* And St. *Paul* declares, that at the judgment-seat of Christ every one *shall receive the things done in the body, according to that he hath done, whether it be good or bad.*

6. Protestants affirm, that the worship of God ought to be performed in a language which all men understand; and that they have a right to search the scriptures : For, *if I speak with tongues* (says the *apostle*) *in such a language as those I speak to cannot understand, what shall I profit you?* *Let all things be done to edi-*

head: And fure it is, that no where elfe 'but in *Rome papal,* has there been fuch an *union of head and members* for that length of time, as to apply the one mind of the ten kings for their *agreement* together, *to give their power, and ftrength, and their* whole *kingdoms* to the beaft.

The *eighth note* produced by Cardinal *Bellarmine,* is *Sanctity*; and *Watfon* faw it fairly proved by the proteftant writers, that no church but *Rome* did ever appear fo long

---

fying. And *Chrift* bids us *fearch the fcriptures:* And how could the word of Chrift dwell richly in us in all wifdom, teaching and admonifhing one another in pfalms, hymns, and fpiritual fongs, if we had not the word of Chrift, and the fcriptures of truth to read and confult for ourfelves.

Thefe are the proteftant doctrines, and we fee they were taught by Chrift and his apoftles. We have the fanction of the moft venerable antiquity on our fide, and this note of the true church of Chrift belongeth to us in the higheft perfection.

When the *papifts* then fcornfully fay, *Where was your church* before *Luther* and *Calvin?* The anfwer is obvious: the doctrine of our church was in the *writings* of the *infpired apoftles,* where the church of *Rome* is never to be found;—the fame that was taught by *Chrift* himfelf, whom they have forfaken, and whofe faith they have corrupted. As to our *predeceffors* and *profeffors,* they were the *perfecuted difciples* of the *crucified Jefus,* thofe *martyrs* and *confeffors,* whofe blood the

long together with such a medley of *sanctity*, in some *doctrines*, and outward appearances of a strict *holiness of life*, joined with the most abominable doctrines, and practices, to qualify it for the horns of the lamb, and the speech of the dragon for the idolatrous and cruel commands of the image; or, for having the form of godliness in the latter times, and yet denying the power thereof.

In short, *Dorick* not only found, on a careful inquiry, that the *system* of the *church of Rome* was *error* and *turpitude, abomination, gain*, and *cruelty*,—and her *great de-*

---

the church of *Rome* hath cruelly spilt. This is the genuine antiquity the *protestants* have to boast of. Their *doctrines* are the *word* of *Christ*, and their *fathers* were *put to death* by *papists* for the *testimony of Jesus*.

But the *papists* on the contrary, exclusive of the example of the *devil*, who was a murderer from the beginning, and *Antiochus Epiphanes, Nero, Domitian*, and other monsters of mankind, who went before them in the measures of persecution, cruelty, and blood; and excepting the *idolatrous nations* of the earth, and the *false prophets* and deceivers among the Jews, by whose authority and example they may vindicate their own idolatries, they have no genuine antiquity to plead. Many of their doctrines were unknown to, or abhorred by the primitive church, and are mere novelties and innovations, that were originally introduced by superstition, and then maintained by cruelty and blood.

sign

fign the *very reverfe* of the gofpel revelation, which came down from heaven to
prepare men, by the practice of univerfal
holinefs and virtue, for eternal life; but
likewife, that even her *Cardinal's notes*
prove, this church cannot be, in any fenfe,
the true church of Chrift; and *Bellarmine*
was perfectly infatuated to make choice of
fuch things for the marks of his church,
as make it the very picture of *Babylon* the
Great. He refolved then to come out of
Rome. He determined to forfake a *church,*
which had *altered* the *inftitutions* of *Chrift,*
and is therefore *guilty* of *herefy* as well as
fchifm.

This change in religion gave *Dorick* the
higheft fatisfaction, (as he told me) and it
was doubled by his being able to convert
his beloved *Adelaïde* from popery to the
church of *Chrift.* But this joy had foon after fome mitigation, by lofing one of the
moft agreeable women in the world. Death
robbed him of his heart's fond idol, and
by that ftroke he was fo wounded, that he
could not heal himfelf for a long time. He
became the real *mourner.* He kept the
reafons of his anguifh continually before
him, and was more intent upon fpending
his fpirits than his forrows. He grew fond
of folitude and filence, that he might indulge

dulge his paffion, and provoke the emo-
tion of that grief that was ready to devour
him. In fhort, he retreated to the filent
place I found him in, which was a part of
his own eftate, and turned *hermit*. He
built the little villa I faw by the water-fide,
and formed the ground into the natural
garden I beheld. *Le Blanc* mentions it in
his letters, as an extraordinary thing, and
very juftly prefers it to the laboured and
expenfive gardens at *Chifwick*, the work of
the late Lord *Burlington*. Here *Watfon*
laid in every thing he had a mind for; and
filled his clofet with books. He amufed
and kept himfelf healthy by working in
his garden, and when he had done abroad,
went in to read. His principal ftudy was
the contemplation of the beft learning,
which is the true chriftian; and from that
he went to know what the *Greeks* and *Ro-*
mans have refolved and taught. In fome
things, I found he was a learned agreeable
man, and wondered greatly at his whim in
turning hermit. I faid a great deal againft
it, as we fat over a bottle of claret; told
him he might employ his time and talents
more ufefully in the world, by mixing and
converfing with his fellow-creatures, and
by a mutual participation and conveyance
of the common bleffings of nature and pro-

G 3   vidence;

vidence; and as he was not forty yet, advised him to go over the *Teese*, and make his addresses to Miss *Cranmer* or Miss *Vane*, both of them being most glorious girls, as I was told, and capable of adding greatly to the delights of philosophy. You have not seen two finer creatures, soul and body, than they are, if I have been rightly informed; and I think, it would be a nobler and more religious act to get one of them with child, in the state of holy wedlock, than to write the best book that was ever printed. For my own part, I had rather marry, and double-rib one of these dear creatures, than die with the character of a father of the deserts. But in vain did I remonstrate to this anchoret. Contemplation was become his *Venus*, from the hour he lost his *Adelaïde*; and he had lived so very happy in his lone state for seven years past, that he could not think of hazarding felicity by a change of life. He had all he desired. If at any time, any thing was wanting, *Christopher* the fisherman, who came to see him once or twice a week, very quickly got him whatever he required. This was *Watson*'s answer to my advice, and seeing it was to no purpose to say any more, I wished my hermit health, and bid him adieu.

§. 9.

§. 9. Having, in the pre- *A few re-* ceding article, mentioned the *marks relat-* famous *Abbé le Blanc*, I think *ing to the* I ought to say something of *Blanc, and* him in this place, by adding a *his letters.* few remarks in relation to this extraordinary man. He was in *England* in the year 1735, and writ two volumes of letters in octavo, which were translated into *English*, and printed for *Brindley* in 1747. In this account of *England*, the *French monk* pretends to describe the natural and political constitution of our country, and the temper and manners of the nation; but, as is evident from his epistles, knew nothing at all of any of them.

Voltaire, however, (that wonderful compound of a man, *half infidel, half papist*; who seems to have no regard for *christianity*, and yet compliments *popery*, at the expence of his understanding (8); who
writes

---

(8) *Voltaire's* words are,——And notwithstanding all the troubles and infamy which the church of *Rome* has had to encounter, she has always preserved a greater decency and gravity in her worship than any of the other churches; and has given proofs, that when in a state of freedom, and under due regulations, she was formed to give lessons to all others.—— Is not this facing the world, and contradicting truth

with

writes the hiſtory of *England* with a *partiality* and *malevolence* almoſt as great as *Smollet's*, and pretends to deſcribe the *Britannic* conſtitution, though it is plain from what he ſays, that he has not one true idea of the *primary inſtitutions* of it, but taking this nation to be juſt ſuch another kingdom of ſlaves as his own country, *rails* at the *Revolution*, and like all the *Jacobite dunces*, prates againſt the *placing* the *Prince of Orange* on the *throne*, and the *eſtabliſhment* of

---

with a bold front ? *Decency* and *gravity* in the church of *Rome !* The *licentious whore.* And *formed to give leſſons.* *Leſſons, Voltaire !*——Is not her *wiſdom,* in every article of it, *earthly, ſenſual, deviliſh*;—and her zeal, that *bitter, fierce,* and *cruel* thing, which for ever produces *confuſion* and *every evil work ?* With a juſt abhorrence, and a manly indignation, we muſt look upon this *myſtery of iniquity,* and never let that *horror* decay, which is neceſſary to guard us againſt the groſs corruptions of the *Roman* church; the *idolatry* of her worſhip,—the abſurdity and impiety of her doctrines,—the *tyranny* and *cruelty* of her principles and practices. Theſe are her leſſons, *Voltaire* ; and you ought to aſk the world pardon for daring to recommend a *church,* whoſe *ſchemes* and *pieties* bid *defiance* to *reaſon,* and are *inconſiſtent* with the *whole tenor of revelation.* This is the more incumbent on you, as you ſay you are a *philoſopher,* and let us know in more places than one in your writings, that by that word, you mean a man who believes nothing at all of any revelation.

the

the *succession* in the *present protestant heirs*; though most certain it be, that *these things* were the *natural fruit and effect of our incomparable constitution*, and are *de jure*: —— In short, that *Zoilus* and *plagiary*,—that *carping superficial critic*, (as a good judge calls him) who abuses the *English nation* in his *letters*, and denies *Shakespear* almost every dramatic excellence; though in his *Mahomet*, he pilfers from *Macbeth* almost every capital scene: (*Shakespear*, who furnishes out more elegant, pleasing, and interesting entertainment in his plays, than all the other dramatic writers, ancient and modern, have been able to do; and, without observing any one unity but that of character, for ever diverts and instructs, by the variety of his incidents, the propriety of his sentiments, the luxuriancy of his fancy, and the purity and strength of his dialogue): *Voltaire*, I say, speaking of this *Abbé le Blanc*, ' wishes he had travelled through all the world, and wrote on all nations, for it becomes only a wise man to travel and write. Had I always such cordials, I would not complain any more of my ills. I support life, when I suffer. I enjoy it, when I read you.'——This is *Voltaire*'s account of the *Abbé*. How true and just it is, we shall see in a few obser-

G 5

vations on what this reverend man fays of our *religion* and *clergy*.

Some obſervations on the Abbé Le Blanc's *fifty-eighth letter to the Preſident* Bouhier, *in which he miſrepreſents and blackens the reformation of* England, *and abuſes the* Engliſh *clergy.*

The ſubſtance of what this *French monk* reports, vol. II. from p. 64. to p. 75. in his letter to the Preſident *Bouhier* (9), is this:

1. That *Cranmer*, and the other doctors, who introduced the reformation into *England*, were downright *enthuſiaſts*, and compaſſed their deſigns by being ſeconded by thoſe, who were animated by a ſpirit of irreligion, and by a greedy deſire of ſeizing the

Of Monſ. Bouhier, *preſident of the* French *academy.*

(9) Reader—*Bouhier*, preſident of the *French* academy, (to whom *Le Blanc* inſcribes his 58th letter) died in 1746. He was a ſcholar. *L'Abbé de Olivet*, (from whom he had the late fine edition of *Cicero* in ſeven volumes 4to) ſpeaks of him in the following manner:——Je me ſuis prêté à ce nouveau travail, & d'autant plus volontiers, que M. le Préſident *Bouhier* a bien voulu le partager avec moi.—On ſera, ſans doute, charmé de voir Cicéron entre les mains d'un traducteur auſſi digne de lui, que Cicéron luimême étoit digne d'avoir pour traducteur un ſavant du premier ordre. *Tuſc. tome* 1. *p.* 13.——And again;—Feu M. le Préſident *Bouhier*, le Varron de notre

the poffeffions of the monks. It was the defire of a change eftablifhed the reformation. The new doctors feduced the people; and the people having miftaken darknefs for light, quitted the road of truth, to walk in the ways of error.

2. As to morals, that this boafted reformation produced no change in that refpect; for the people are not purer than

---

notre fiecle, & l'homme le plus capable de bien rendre les vraies beautez d'un original Grec ou Latin, avoit tellement retouché fes deux Tufculanes, qu'on aura peine à les reconnoître dans cette nouvelle édition. *Tufc. tome 2. p. 1.*

This is *Olivet*'s account of *Bouhier*; and I have heard fome gentlemen who knew him, fay, that he was a very fine genius; but, they added, a popifh bigot to the laft degree, and therefore *Le Blanc* chofe him as the fitteft perfon of his acquaintance, to write an epiftle to, that abufed the reformation, and the *Englifh* divines. Great is the prejudice of education! when fo bright a mind as *Bouhier*'s cannot fee the *deformity* of *Popery*, and the *beauty* of the *reformation*; but, on the contrary, with pleafure reads the *defpicable defamation* in *Le Blanc*'s letter.

N. B. The two *Tufculans*, fo finely tranflated by *Bouhier*, are the 3d, De ægritudine lenienda: and the 5th, Virtutem ad beatè vivendum feipfa effe contentam. De la vertu: Qu'elle fuffit pour vivre heureux. ——See likewife, M. *Bouhier*'s curious and ufeful remarks on the three books, De Natura Deorum; the five *Tufculans*; *Scipio*'s dream; and on the *Catilinares*, or three orations againft *Catiline*. Thefe remarks are the third volume.

they

they were in former times, and the ecclefiaftics are defpifed and hated for the bad-
nefs of their lives.   The bifhops facrifice
every thing to their ambition ; and the clergy of the fecond rank have no refpect for
their office.   They fpend the whole day
in public places in fmoaking and drinking,
and are remarkable for drunkennefs, fo dif-
honourable to ecclefiaftics.   Their talk is
the moft diffolute, and the vice that de-
grades thefe profeffors fets a bad example
to fober people, and makes them the jeft
of libertines.

3. The only remarkable change produced by the reformation was the marriage
of priefts ; and, exclufive of this being a-
gainft the decifions of the catholic church,
it is contrary to found policy and experience. The marriage of priefts diminifhes the
refpect we fhould have for them. The mif-
conduct of a woman makes the clergyman
fall into contempt.   The lewdnefs of the
daughter makes the prieft, her father, the
object of the moft indecent jefts ; and, for
the moft part, the daughters of the clergy
turn whores after the death of their father ;
who, while living, fpent more of his in-
come in maintaining himfelf and children
in pleafure and luxury, than in works of
charity.

charity.　He lived profusely, and dies poor.

Beside, if the *English* clergy were the greatest and most excellent men, yet a great man in the eyes of the world, loses of the respect which is due to him, in proportion as he has any thing in common with the rest of mankind.　A *Madam Newton*, and a *Madam Fontenelle*, would injure the illustrious men whose name they bore.　Nor is this all.　Those who by their disposition cannot fix that secret inclination, which induces us to love, on one person, are more humane and charitable than others.　The unmarried ecclesiastics are more animated with that charitable spirit their function requires, as they have no worldly affections to divert it.　People very rarely (as Lord *Bacon* says) employ themselves in watering plants, when they want water themselves.—In short, the *English* divines are the worst of men, and there is hardly any religion in *England.*——Thus does this *French* Abbé revile the *English* reformation and divines. He misrepresents the whole nation, and with a falsehood and outrage peculiar to *popery* and *mass-priests*, that is, to devils and the most execrable religion, screams against the pure religion of the gospel, and dishonestly blackens some of the finest characters

characters that ever adorned human nature. So very virulent is this reverend *French* papift againft the clergy of *England*, that he is even pofitive there is not a divine in the nation knows how to behave like a gentleman.

In anfwer to the firft article of impeachment, I obferve, that it is fo far from being true, that *Cranmer*, and the other *Englifh* divines, *our reformers*, were enthufiafts, and compaffed their defigns by the affiftance of thofe who were animated by a fpirit of irreligion, and by a greedy defire of feizing the poffeffion of the monks, (as this *mafs-prieft* afferts); that it is moft certain, on the contrary, *Cranmer*, and the other *reformers*, were wife and upright chriftians, who, from a good underftanding of religion, oppofed the *falfe pretenfions* of the *church* of *Rome*. They faw that popery was contrary to the true genius of chriftianity; its fpirit infolent and cruel; and its worfhip, not only a jumble of the moft ridiculous fopperies and extravagancies, borrowed from heathen cuftoms and fuperftitions; but the impureft that ever appeared in the world: that the *defigns* of *popifh Rome* were contrary to all the *principles* of *humanity*; its *doctrines abominable* and *finful*; and its *offices curfed* and *diabolical:*

lical: it was evident, I fay, to the conception of thefe great men, (I mean *Cranmer,* and the other *English reformers)* that the *Romish church* was treacherous and *inhuman,* *blood-thirfty* and *antichriftian;* that her devotions were horrible and impious; her minifters *falfe prophets* and *liars,* covered and decked with the livery of Chrift, but in every thing acting contrary to the falvation wrought by Jefus; and therefore thefe wife and excellent *reformers* renounced *popery,* and bravely declared for that religion, which promotes the good of all mankind, and infpires men to *worfhip the Father only in fpirit* and *in truth.* They threw off the cloak and garments of antichrift: they glorioufly feparated from him, and joined together in *purity* and *fimplicity,* to *pleafe the Lord Jehovah.* There was no enthufiafm in the cafe, (as *Le Blanc,* the *mafs-prieft,* has the front to fay) but when the light of the gofpel was obfcured, and darknefs had overfpread the earth; when ignorance and fuperftition univerfally prevailed, and the *immoralities* of the *Church of Rome* were made to pafs for chriftianity in the world; then did thefe *reformers* call the people out of *Rome,* and preach to them the effential truths of the faith. They called them from an idolatrous religion, and all its train of direful effects;

from

from that fin of the firft rank, which ftrikes
at the being of a God, and ravifhes from
him the greateft honour that is due to him
from his creature, man; they called them
from the horrible fervice of the mafs, from
their addreffes to angels and faints, and
their worfhip of images; to the inward
knowledge of one true God, and the worfhip due to him only; to the fanctification
and honour which is due to him above all
things, and above every name; to the living hope in God thro' Chrift; to regene-
ration, and inward renovation by faith,
hope, and charity; to a holy converfation,
and a faithful performance of all the commandments; to true repentance, perfeve-
rance to the end, and life eternal. To
thefe *truths*, (not to be found in the religion of our travelling *mafs-prieft*) did the
great, the glorious *Englifh* reformers call
mankind. They laboured to eftablifh them
in every thing tending to a pure faith, and
good life. In this, there is not, there cannot be any enthufiafm.

And as to their being affifted by thofe
who were animated by a fpirit of irreligion, and by a greedy defire of feizing the
poffeffions of the monks, it does not appear
to be the truth of the cafe. Suppofing
there were fuch irreligious men, the affiftance

ance the *reformers* had from any great men in *Henry* the eighth's time, when the abbeys were deftroyed, was fo very little, that malice only could mention it as an objection to the reformation. Popery, in that monarch's reign, was ftill the eftablifhed religion of *England*, and both fides blame this king's *perfecutions*. If *papifts* were put to death for denying the *fupremacy* of *Harry*, *proteftants* were no lefs fufferers for oppofing the adoration of the hoft, and other religious impieties. And after the fhort reign of his fon, *Edward* the fixth, what affiftance had the *reformers* under *bloody Mary?* Did fhe not do all that *infernal popery* could fuggeft, to deftroy *Cranmer*, his brethren, and their reformation? And did not they, without any other affiftance than what they received from the fpirit of God, continue to vindicate the *truth as it is in Jefus*, and teach the pure doctrines of the gofpel, in oppofition to the *frauds* and *vile inventions* of *papal Rome*. Without minding the indignities, the torments, and the cruel death prepared for them, the *brave honeft men* went on with their heavenly work, and, till the flames made them filent, endeavoured to deftroy the *Romifh artifices* and *immoralities*, and to fpread the *pure religion and undefiled before God and the Father*. They were zealous, with the truth

of

of religion on their fide, and laboured to convert, out of a pure and friendly regard to the eternal welfare of mankind. They did the work, by the bleffing of God, and therefore the malicious *Le Blanc*, the *mafs-prieft*, reviles and blackens them.

What he fays of *ufurpation*, in refpect of church-lands, does not deferve any notice. The reforming clergy were not the actors in that fcene. It was the king and his council. And as the Pope had fhewed them the way, by granting *bulls for the dif-folution of the leffer monafteries*, they thought, fince the Pope's power was taken away by a general confent of the nation, the king, the church, and the people concurring, they might, with as little *facrilege*, diffolve the reft. The king and parliament (fays Bifhop *Burnet*) could not difcern the difference between greater and leffer as to the point of *facrilege*. And although fome ufes might ceafe by the doctrines of the reformation, as maffes for fouls departed, and monks to pray the dead out of purgatory; yet there were others to employ the church-lands about, as fome of them were in founding *new bifhopricks*. And if in this cafe, the reformers had been guilty of fome wilful errors, that could be no crime of the reformation. The culpable muft

answer

anſwer it. For the ſatisfaction of conſcience about the reformation, there can be but three queſtions fairly propoſed. Was there ſufficient cauſe for it? Was there ſufficient authority? And whether the proceedings of our reformation were juſtifiable by the rule of ſcripture, and the ancient church? Upon theſe points we ought to join iſſue, and I am ſure the concluſion muſt be in the affirmative.

As to *Le Blanc's* ſecond obſervation in relation to the *marriage of prieſts*, which our *reformation* he ſays produced, it may be anſwered, that the doctrine of a *prieſt's marriage being unlawful,* was borrowed by the church of *Rome* from the ancient heretics; eſpecially from the *Manichees*, who allowed marriage to their hearers, as the church of *Rome* doth to laymen; but forbad it to their *elect*, as that church doth to her *prieſts*. St. *Auguſtin* charges the *Manichees* with this error. Hic non dubito vos eſſe clamaturos invidiamque facturos, caſtitatem perfectam vos vehementer commendare atque laudare, non tamen nuptias prohibere; quandoquidem auditores veſtri quorum apud vos ſecundus eſt gradus ducere atque habere non prohibentur uxores. *De moribus Manichæorum, Lib.* 2. *c.* 18.

The

The firſt *pope* we read of that condemned the marriage of *prieſts*, was Syricius, the *Roman*, A. D. 384—398. And upon this account, I wonder *Baronius* had not a regard to his memory: but it has been the misfortune of his *holineſs* ſince his death to fall under the diſpleaſure of the *Cardinal* to that degree, that he has ſtruck him out of his catalogue of his *Romiſh* ſaints. He does not tell us for what reaſon. Perhaps it was becauſe this pope rather diſſuaded prieſts from marriage than peremptorily forbad it, as appears by his letters. (Syr. epiſt. 1. & 4. apud Binium.)

The next *pope*, who diſtinguiſhed himſelf againſt the *marriage of prieſts*, was the ſon of *Bald-head*, count of *Burgundy*, (whoſe grand-daughter was conſort to *Lewis* the 6th, king of *France*); I mean the celebrated *Guy*, archbiſhop of *Vienne*, who ſucceeded *Gelaſius*, A. D. 1119, and had for ſucceſſor in the year 1124, *Lambert* of *Bononia*, commonly called *Honorius* the ſecond. *Calixtus* the ſecond, pope, and prince of *Burgundy*, was the firſt who abſolutely forbad *prieſts marriage*, and in caſe they were married, commanded them to be ſeparated. (Grat. diſt. 27. c. 8.) This was in the beginning of the twelfth century. And towards the end of it, A. D. 1198, the

the renowned son of Count *Trasimund*, I mean *Innocent* the third, the ever memorable Cardinal *Lotharius*, pronounced all the *marriages* of *priests null*. And afterwards came on the *council* of *Trent*, A. D. 1485—1563, which anathematizes those who say such marriages are valid. (Sess. 24. can. 9.)

But one would think, that God sufficiently declared his approbation of such marriages, in that the whole world hath by his appointment been twice peopled by two married priests; first by *Adam*, secondly by *Noah*. And we are sure, the holy *scripture* tells us, *That marriage is honourable in all*; (Heb. xiii. 4.) and places it among the qualifications of a bishop, *That he be the husband of one wife, having faithful children*. (Tit. i. 6.) *This*, saith St. *Chrysostom, the apostle prescribed to this end, that he might stop the mouths of hereticks, who reproached marriage; declaring thereby, that marriage is no unclean thing, but so honourable, that a married man may be exalted to the sacred throne of a bishop*. (Chrysost. hom. 2, in c, 1. ad tit.) What do you say to this, *Le Blanc?* I fancy you never read this *homily of Chrysostome*. —— And well might this saint think it not unbecoming a *bishop* to *marry*, when our *Lord* thought it not

5

not *unbecoming* an *apoſtle*, no not the prince
of the apoſtles (as the *Romaniſts* will have
him), for it is without doubt, that St. *Peter*
was married; in that the ſcripture makes
mention of his wife's mother. (*Mat.* viii.
14.) And *Clemens* of *Alexandria* tells us,
that it was certainly reported, that when he
ſaw his wife led to death, he rejoiced; and
having exhorted her and comforted her, he
called her by her name, and bid her remember the Lord. (*Clemens Alex. Stromat.* l. 7.
p. 736. Lut. 1629.) And that he was not
only married, but begat children, the ſame
Clemens, in another place, affirms, (*Stromat.* l. 3. p. 448.) Yea, that St. *Philip*
and St. *Jude* were alſo married, and had
children, *Euſebius* is witneſs, (*Euſeb.* eccleſ.
hiſt. l. 3. c. 20.—31.) And in like manner we find, that many of the primitive
biſhops were married. *Charemon* biſhop of
Nilus, St. *Spiridion*, St. *Gregory Nazianzen*,
St. *Gregory Nyſſen*, St. *Hilary*, and many
more, were married men.

Nor can it be ſaid, that they took wives
while they were laymen, and after they
took upon them the ſacred miniſtry, were
ſeparated from them; ſince the *canons*,
commonly called the apoſtles, did prohibit
either biſhop, prieſt, or deacon, to put a-
way his wife upon pretence of religion.
I　　　　　　　　　　　(See

(See canon 5.) And if any such shall abstain from marriage, as in itself abominable, command that he be corrected, or deposed, and cast out of the church. (Canon 50.)

Now, supposing these *canons* (notwithstanding all that *Whiston* has said) were not made by them whose name they bear, yet they are allowed by all to be of much greater antiquity than the first *Nicene* council. And when in that council it was moved, that *bishops* and *priests*, *deacons* and *subdeacons*, might not cohabit with their wives, which they had taken before ordination, the *motion* was presently dashed by the famous *Paphnutius*, who was himself a single person. (*Socrat.* ecclef. hist. l. 1. c. 11.) Yea, a long time after this council, we meet with many *popes*, who were *sons* of *bishops* and *priests*.

Pope *Theodorus*, *Silverius*, and *Gelasius* I. were the sons of bishops: pope *Boniface* I. *Felix* II. and *Agapetus* II. were the sons of priests. (*Gratian.* dist. 56. c. 2.) and that we may not think this strange, *Gratian* himself informs us, that the marriage of priests was in those days lawful in the Latin church. (Dist. 56. c. 12.)

Nor is this doctrine to be rejected only as contrary to scripture, and to primitive and
apostolical

apoftolical practice, but becaufe of the a-
bominable fruits produced in the church
of *Rome* by it. For when the clergy might
not have wives, (which God allowed), inftead of them they took whores; and
that wickednefs fo far prevailed in the
church, that the Cardinal of *Cambray* informs us, (De reform. ecclef.) many cler-
gymen were not afhamed publicly, in the
face of the world, to keep concubines.
And the glofs upon *Gratian* fays, A prieft
may not be depofed for fimple fornication,
becaufe there are few priefts to be found
without that fault. This made *Pius* the
fecond fay, that though priefts were by the
weftern church forbid to marry for good
reafon, yet there was ftronger reafon to re-
ftore marriage to them again. (Hift. Council Trent, l. 7. p. 680.) And many in
that council, were fo fenfible of this, that
they alledged the great fcandal given by
incontinent priefts, and that there was want
of continent perfons fit to exercife the mini-
ftry. *(Paoli,* p. 679. &c.) The Emperor
and the Duke of *Bavaria* did therefore require, that the marriage of priefts might be
granted. *(Paoli,* p. 680, &c.) And many bifhops defired that married perfons might
be promoted to holy orders; but this requeft was not granted, becaufe, as the fathers obferved, if the clergy once come to
be

be married, they will no longer depend on the Pope, but on their prince.

To conclude this article, (and I shall do it in the words of a great man, a prelate of the church of *England*, now living); To make war against the very Being of their species, they (the *Romish priests*) devote themselves to a single life, in blasphemous opposition to that first great command and blessing, *increase and multiply.*

As to *Le Blanc's* third observation, relating to the immoralities and bad behaviour of the *English* clergy; I answer, if there are several bad men among so large a body as the protestant divines are, which is not strange, as it is the common case of all societies, yet the majority of them, orthodox and other dox, are as worthy men as can be found among the human race. I am very sure my acquaintance among them has been much larger than *Le Blanc's* could possibly be; and I can affirm from my own knowledge, that there are very many of this order of men, not only as fine gentlemen as I have ever conversed with; but, a clergy holy in heart, superior to pride, to anger, to foolish desires; who walk as *Christ* also walked, and by their *example* and *doctrine*, labour to make the

VOL. III.　　　H　　　　people

people what the *gospel* requires they should
be; that is, pious and useful, pure and
honest, meek and charitable; to walk by
faith, and not by sight; and so pass thro'
things temporal, that they may be sure of
obtaining the things eternal. This I can
say of many *English* divines of my acquaintance: and I may add, that this testimony from me, who am not over-fond.
of the clergy, (as the main of the christianity of too many of them lies in their
opinion, decked with a few, outward ob-
servances, says Mr. *Wesley* very truly, in
his letter to Bishop *Warburton)* and only
upon occasion, endeavour now to do them
justice, is certainly of more weight in their
favour, than the calumny and abuse of a
furious bigot and mass-priest, can be to make
the world have as bad an opinion of them,
as *popery*, and its wretched emissaries, would
have the public entertain. Consider this
then when you read *Le Blanc*'s letters.

On the other hand, I have had a very
large and intimate acquaintance with *mass-
priests* in my time, in many parts of the
world; and, a few excellent ones excepted,
I can affirm, that more wicked and more
worthless men than these *Romish* monks, I
have never seen. If adultery, fornication,
drunkenness, and swearing, are crimes,
                                    then

then the greateſt criminals I could name in
theſe reſpects, are *Roman-Catholic* prieſts,
Let this aſſertion of mine be ſet over-
againſt the character the *Abbé Le Blanc*
gives the *Engliſh* proteſtant miniſters. Conſider all I have ſaid, when you read this
maſs-prieſt's fifty-eighth letter, and then
judge of our reformation and clergy (10).
——But

---

(10) Note, reader, in the fourth
volume of a work, called, *Notes relat-*
ing to Men, and Things, and Books, you
will find ſome more of my remarks on the *Ablé Le*
Blanc's epiſtles. You will ſee, among other obſervations on this *monk,* a vindication of Archbiſhop *Til-*
lotſon. The *Ablé* rails at one of this prelate's fine
ſermons, with great malice and impudence, and has
the vanity to think his *miſerable declamation* an anſwer. This wretched and deſpicable *Romiſh apoſtate*
has the impudence and impiety to defend the worſhip
of his *God of dough,* and would, if it were in his
power, perſuade the readers of his letters, to adore the
tiny cake he proſtrates himſelf before. For this the
reader will find the *maſs-prieſt* well chaſtiſed in the
work I have referred to; and ſee the doctrine of the
Lord's Supper ſet in a true light. You will find there
a curious hiſtory of the *maſs,* from the time the *popiſh*
doctors firſt drew it out of the *bottomleſs pit*; and ſee it
made quite evident, that in this abominable article of
their faith, as well as in every other part of their execrable religion, *they make void the law of God,* and
ſink the human race into the *vileſt ſlavery* and *idolatry.*
Beware then, Chriſtians, of *popery.* Still bravely
dare to *proteſt* againſt her *infernal ſchemes* and *inven-*

A word or two
relating to tran-
ſubſtantiation.

H 2   *tions,*

———But it is time to return to the cottage of *Chriftopher* the fifherman, and fee what happened to *Antonia* and *Agnes.*

The beginning of my acquaintance with Mifs Cranmer, and how it ended in a marriage.

§. 10. When I came back to the poor man's cottage, he told me the ladies were come home; and as he had given Mifs *Cranmer* fome account of me, as a traveller who had journied into that remote corner of the world, in fearch of antiquities and curiofities, he did not think this lady would be averfe to feeing me and hearing me too, if I contrived any plaufible pretence to throw myfelf in her way.

———

tions, and draw your religion from the *book of God,* that holy volume of ineftimable treafure. It is our light in darkiefs,—our comfort under affliction,—our direction to heaven,—and let us die in defence of it, if ever there fhould be occafion, rather than fuffer the *blood-thirfty papifts,* the *red-handed idolaters,* to fnatch it out of our hands. They will give us for it the defpicable legends of fictitious faints and falfe miracles; —a hiftory of difeafes cured inftantly by relicks;— accounts of fpeaking images;—ftories of travelling chapels;—wonders done by a *Madona*;—and the devil knows what he has crowded into their wretched heads. Down with *popery* then, the *religion of hell,* and may that happy ftate be erected, when *truth* and *love* fhall embrace and reign. *Come, Lord Jefus, come quickly.*

Immediately

Immediately then I croffed the water, went up to the houfe, and as I faw her and the fair *Agnes* her coufin walking in the garden, near the *ha*, leaped it over immediately, broad as it was, and with my hat in my hand, made her a low bow, began an apology for prefuming to introduce myfelf to her prefence in fuch a manner, and concluded with my being in love with her charming character, before I had the honour and happinefs of feeing her. What a condition then muft I be in, when a heaven-born maid, like her, appeared! Strange pleafures filled my foul, unloofed my tongue, and my firft talk could not be any thing but love. A deal I faid on the fubject, not worth repeating to the reader; and the iffue of the matter was, that I became fo well acquainted with this *innocent beauty*, that, on taking my leave, I had an invitation to breakfaft with her the next morning. I was there by eight, and really and truly quite charmed with her. She was pretty as it was poffible for flefh and blood to be, had a beautiful underftanding; and as fhe had very little notion of men, having feen very few, except the two old fervants who lived with her, fhe had not a notion of any danger that could come from converfing freely with a man fhe knew no-

H 3   thing

thing of, and who might be an enemy in difguife.

After breakfaft, I offered to go, but fhe afked me to ftay and dine ; and to fum up the matter, I did dine, fup, and breakfaft with her every day, for a month, till my good prieft, *Friar Fleming*, arrived, on a letter I had fent him, and we were married before the end of fix weeks.   We loved to excefs, and did enhance human happinefs to a high degree.   She was good as an angel ; and for two years we lived in un-fpeakable felicity.   For the greateft part of that time, we were at *Orton-Lodge*, as fhe liked the wild place.   There fhe like-wife died of the fmall-pox, in the firft month of the third year, and left me the moft difconfolate of men.   Four days I fat with my eyes fhut, on account of this lofs, and then left the *Lodge* once more, to live if I could, fince my religion ordered me fo to do, and fee what I was next to meet with in the world.   As grief fat powerfully on my fpirits, and if not diflodged, would have drank them all up very foon, I re-folved to haften to *Harrogate*, and in the feftivities of that place forget my departed partner as foon as I could.   I laid my *Antonia* by my *Charlotte* and my *Statia*, and then rode off.   What happened at the
Wells,

Wells, and all the obfervations I made there, and thereabout, the reader will find in my fifth fection.

N. B. As I mention nothing of any children by fo many wives, fome readers may perhaps wonder at this, and therefore, to give a general anfwer, once for all, I think it fufficient to obferve, that I had a great many, to carry on the *fucceffion*; but as they never were concerned in any extraordinary affairs, nor ever did any remarkable things, that I heard of;—only rife and breakfaft, read and faunter, drink and eat, it would not be fair, in my opinion, to make any one pay for their hiftory.

SECT.

SECT. V.

As once, ('twas in *Astræa*'s reign)
The vernal powers renew'd their train,
It happened that immortal *Love*
Was ranging thro' the spheres above,
And downward hither cast his eye
The year's returning pomp to spy;
He saw the radiant God of day
Lead round the globe the rosy *May*;
The fragrant *airs* and genial hours
Were shedding round him dews and flow'rs;
Before his wheels *Aurora* past,
And *Hesper*'s golden lamp was last.
But, fairest of the blooming throng,
When HEALTH majestic mov'd along,
All gay with smiles, to see below
The joys which from her presence flow,
While earth inliven'd hears her voice,
And fields, and flocks, and swains rejoice;
Then mighty *Love* her charms confess'd,
And soon his vows inclin'd her breast;
And known from that auspicious morn,
The pleasing CHEARFULNESS was born.

    Thou, CHEARFULNESS, by heav'n design'd
To rule the pulse, that moves the mind,
Whatever fretful passion springs,
Whatever chance or nature brings
To strain the tuneful poize within,
And disarrange the sweet machine,
Thou, *Goddess*, with a master-hand,
Dost each attemper'd key command,
Refine the soft, and swell the strong,
'Till all is concord, all is song.

The author goes to Harrogate. §. 1. IN the year 1731, I arrived at *Harrogate*, in the West-riding of *Yorkshire*,

in

in order to amuſe my mind with the diverſions and company of the place. It is a ſmall ſtraggling village on a heath, two miles from *Knareſborough*, which is thirteen miles from *York*, and 175 from *London.* The ſulphur wells are three, on the north ſide of the town, about 500 yards eaſt of the bog. They riſe out of a little dry hill. The ſecond is a yard from the firſt, and the third is five yards and a half from the ſecond. The water riſes into ſtone-baſons, which are each incloſed in a ſmall neat building of ſtone and lime a yard ſquare on the inſides, and two yards high, covered over with thick flag-ſtones laid ſhelving.

An account of the place, the wells, and company.

The ſoil out of which theſe ſprings riſe is, firſt, corn-mould, then a marle lime-ſtone, and a ſtratum of plaiſter: the lime-ſtone is ſo abraded by the ſalt in the water, that when dried, it ſwims: and where the water ſtagnates between the baſons and the brook, the earth is ink black, and has a dry white ſcum, which ſmells like ſulphur, and burns with a blue flame. The water does likewiſe throw up much candied ſea-ſalts, that is, ſalts to which ſulphur adheres, and the pidgeons reſort from all parts to pick them up. In moiſt or rainy

H 5

weather,

weather, thefe waters fend forth a ftrong fmell at a diftance, and before rain they bubble up with an impetuous force; yet neither rain nor drought increafes or de-creafes the fprings.

From the large quantities of fine flower of brimftone which thefe waters throw off, it is plain, that fulphur is the principal thing in them; but experiment likewife proves, that befides fulphur, the ftinking well has vitriol, nitre, copper, and falt: Thefe lie *in folutis principiis* in earth from which the water comes, and may be fepa-rated by operation: fome, I know, deny there is any copper in thefe waters; but they do not confider, that the glittering glebes of a gold colour found here, can be nothing elfe than glebes gilt with cop-per.

As to the difeafes wherein this ftrong *fulphur-water* is proper, it is good for every thing, except a confumption. For this I recommend the *Scarborough purging-chaly-beate* above all waters. But if, reader, you have obftructions in your liver and other vifcera, and are tormented with vif-cous humours in your inteftines; if your bowels are full of worms, the afcarides, or the broad round worm, or the worms call-ed

ed the dog and the wolf, from their likenefs to thefe animals; or if, from a vene-
real caufe, (the malady of many a prieft
and layman) you have an ulcer in the *anus*,
or in the neck of your bladder, go to *Harrogate*; drink the ftinking-water, live
temperate, and you will be cured. For
the fcurvy, that univerfal difeafe, it is better than all other medicines. It is excellent in the jaundice, though of many years
ftanding. It cures the afthma, the fcoto-
mia, and palfy, and in many other deplorable cafes gives wonderful relief. Whatever ails you, (the confumption excepted)
fly to *Harrogate*, and the water will do
you good, if your hour be not come: and
if you are well, the waters will promote
long life, and make you the more able to
dance with the ladies.

Four pints of water are enough for a
patient, to be taken from half an hour to
two hours after fun-rifing, upon an empty
ftomach. You fhould take fome prepara-
tory medicine; and walk drinking the waters to warm the body a little, and make
the paffage the eafier. Some people I have
known drink their dofe in bed, and it does
well enough: but exercife and the thin
open air do better, and contribute not a
little to the patient's recovery: and there

is

is no finer fresher air in *England* than at this place.

In short, these wells are the strongest sulphur-water in *Great Britain*, and, from the superior strength of the impregnating sulphur, it does not lose but retain the sulphureous smell, even when exposed to a scalding, and almost a violent heat; and, in distilling it, when three pints had been taken off from a gallon of it, the last was as strong as the first, and stunk intolerably.

Make haste then to *Harrogate*, if you are sick, and have money, and in all probibility you will find the waters efficacious, unless thy distemper be a *consumption*, or in its nature incurable, which is the case of many, as death is the common fate of mankind.

Some advice to the drinkers of Harrogate *waters.* §. 2. But when you are there, let me advise you to exercise as much as you can bear, without fatiguing yourself,— and in the next place, to be regular in meats and drinks, and as temperate as possible. Without these things, you will lose the benefit of the waters. No good can be expected, if men will indulge during a

course

courfe of drinking, the *fpaw*, and be not only exceffive in quantity, but indifcreet as to the quality, of meats and liquors.

I have known fome worn-out hard drinkers come to the *Wells* for relief, and at the fame time increafe by intemperance what they had contracted by the fame meafure. I have likewife feen fome in a diabetes drink white wine; in a cachexy, ale; in the ftone and gravel, claret. I have known a man in a dropfy eat nothing but cooling, infipid, mucilaginous foods, and drink malt-drink plentifully:—a man in a jaundice, eat nothing but flefh meat and claret—in a fcurvy, prefer the pungent, faline diet:—in obftinate obftructions, and a chronic hyppo, feed on thickening, hardening, and drying meats:—and in a hectic, vomiting, and fpitting of blood, chufe only fuch things as increafe the blood's momentum and velocity. I have known fome gentlemen, who fat up late, never exercifed, could not eat a dinner, and therefore would indulge in a flefh fupper.—All thefe, and many other irregularities, have I known expect furprifing effects from the waters, and when they received no benefit, fay, there were no fanative

Some obfervations on fpaw-waters, and advice to the drinkers in a mineral courfe.

tive principles in them.   Unreasonable,
unhappy men!   Be *temperate: regular:
exercise: keep the passions within bounds:*
and you may expect very astonishing cures;
provided your bodies are not become *irre-
parable,* and *no longer tenantable:* that your
juices are not to the last degree glutinous
and acrimonious: that the corrosiveness of
your blood is not bringing on mortifica-
tions; — nor inflammations, filling, dilat-
ing, and breaking your vessels into suppu-
ration and putrefactions.   Then, live how
you will,   the *waters* can be of no use.
You must pay the debt of nature by an incurable disease.   Neither mineral waters,
nor physic, can create and enliven new
bodies, or make and adapt particular members to the old.   But if you are only hurt
a little, and the disease is curable, the *waters* will certainly be *efficacious,* and recover you, if you use *moderate exercise* (riding
especially) and *diversion,* a *strict regularity,*
and *great temperance.*

*Conclusion of
the author's
advice.*   O temperance! Divine temperance! Thou art the sup-
port of the other virtues, the
preserver and restorer of health, and the
protracter of life! Thou art the main-
tainer of the dignity and liberty of rational beings, from the wretched inhuman
slavery

flavery of fenfuality, tafte, cuftom, and examples; and the brightner of the underftanding and memory! Thou art the fweetner of life and all its comforts, the companion of reafon, and guard of the paffions! Thou art the bountiful rewarder of thy admirers and followers: thine enemies praife thee: and thy friends with rapturous pleafure raife up a panegyric in thy praife.

O hunger, hunger, immortal hunger! Thou art the bleffing of the poor, the regale of the temperate rich, and the delicious guft of the *plaineft morfel*. Curfed is the man that has turned thee out of doors, and at whofe table thou art a ftranger! Yea, thrice curfed is he, who always thirfts, and hungers no more!

§. 3. As to the company at thefe wells, I found it very good, and was pleafed with the manner of living there. *The company and manner of living at Harrogate.* In the day-time we drank the waters, walked or rid about, and lived in feparate parties; lodging in one or other of the three inns that are on the edge of the common: but at night, the company meet at one of the *public-houfes*, (the *inns* having the benefit of the meeting in their turn) and

and fup together between eight and nine
o'clock on the beft fubftantial things, fuch
as hot fhoulders of mutton, rump-ftakes,
hot pidgeon-pies, veal-cutlets, and the
like. For this fupper, ladies and gentlemen pay eight-pence each, and after fitting
an hour, and drinking what wine, punch,
and ale, every one chufes, all who pleafe
get up to country-dances, which generally
laft till one in the morning; thofe that
dance, and thofe who do not, drinking as
they will. The ladies pay nothing for
what liquor is brought in, either at fupper
or after, and it cofts the gentlemen five or
fix fhillings a man. At one the ladies
withdraw, fome to their houfes in the
neighbourhood, and fome to their beds in
the inns. The men who are temperate, do
then likewife go to reft.

In fhort, of all the wells I know, *Harrogate* is in my opinion the moft charming.
The waters are incomparable, no air can
be better: and with the greateft civility,
chearfulnefs, and good-humour, there is a
certain rural plainnefs and freedom mixed,
which are vaftly pleafing. The lady of
pleafure, the well-dreft taylor, and the
gamefter, are not to be found there. Gentlemen of the country, and women of birth
and fortune, their wives, fifters, and daugh-

5   ters,

ters, are for the moſt part the company. There were at leaſt fourſcore ladies in the country-dances every night, while I was there, and among them many fine women.

§. 4. Among the company I found at this agreeable place, were ſix *Iriſh* gentlemen, who had been my contemporaries in Trinity-College, *Dublin*, and were right glad to ſee me, as *The author meets at Harrogate fix gentlemen of his acquaintance from Dublin.* we had been *Sociorums*, (a word of *Swift*'s) at the conniving-houſe at *Ring's-end*, for many a ſummer's evening, and their regard for me was great. They thought I had been long numbered with the dead, as they could not get any account of me for ſo many years; and when they ſaw me, at their entering the public room, fitting by a beauty, in deep diſcourſe, God-zounds, (ſays one of them), there he is, making love to the fineſt woman in the world. Theſe gentlemen were Mr. *Gollogher*, Mr. *Gallaſpy*, Mr. *Dunkley*, Mr. *Makins*, Mr. *Monaghan*, and Mr. *O'Keefe*, deſcended from the *Iriſh* kings, and firſt couſin to the great *O'Keefe*, who was buried not long ago in *Weſtminſter* Abbey. They were all men of large fortunes, and, Mr. *Makins* excepted, were as handſome fine fellows

as

as could be picked out in all the world.
Makins was a very low, thin man, not four
feet high, and had but one eye, with
which he fquinted moft fhockingly. He
wore his own hair, which was fhort and
bad, and only dreft by his combing it himfelf in the morning, without oil or powder.
But as he was matchlefs on the fiddle, fung
well, and chatted agreeably, he was a favourite with the ladies. They preferred
ugly *Makins* (as he was called) to many
very handfome men. I will here give the
public the character of thefe *Irifh* gentlemen, for the honour of *Ireland*, and as
they were curiofities of the human kind.

The charac-
ters of fix I
rifh gentle-
men.

O'Keefe's
character.

§. 5. O'Keefe was as diftin-
guifhed a character as I have
ever known. He had read
and thought, travelled and converfed, was a man of fenfe,
and a fcholar. He had a greatnefs of foul,
which fhewed a pre-eminence of dignity,
and by conduct and behaviour, the faithful interpreters of the heart, always atteft-
ed the nobleft and moft generous fentiments. He had an extreme abhorrence of
meannefs of all kinds, treachery, revenge,
envy, littlenefs of mind, and fhewed in all
his actions the qualities that adorn a man.
—His learning was of the genteel and ufeful

ful kind; a fort of agreeable knowledge, which he acquired rather from a found tafte and good judgment than from the books he had read. He had a right eftimation of things, and had gathered up almoft every thing that is amufing or inftructive. This rendered him a mafter in the art of pleafing: and as he had added to thefe improvements the fashionable ornaments of life, languages, and bodily exercifes, he was the delight of all that knew him.

Makins was poffeffed of all the excellent qualities and perfections that are within the reach of human abilities. *Character of Mr. Makins.* He had received from nature the happieft talents, and he made fingular improvements of them by a fuccefsful application to the moft ufeful and moft ornamental ftudies. Mufic, as before obferved, he excelled in. His intellectual faculties were fine, and, to his honour I can affirm, that he moftly employed them, as he did his great eftate, to the good of mankind, the advancement of morality, and the fpread of *pure theifm*, the worfhip of God *our Saviour*, who raifed and fent Chrift to be a Redeemer. This gentleman was a zealous *Unitarian*, and, though but five and twenty, (when we met at *Harrogate*)

a religious man : but his religion was without any melancholy ; nor had it any thing
of that feverity of temper, which diffufes
too often into the hearts of the religious a
morofe contempt of the world, and an an-
tipathy to the pleafures of it. He avoided
the affemblies of fools, knaves, and block-
heads, but was fond of good company,
and condemned that doctrine which taught
men to retire from human fociety to feek
God in the horrors of folitude. He thought
the Almighty may be beft found among
men, where his goodnefs is moft active,
and his providence moft employed.

Character of
Mr. Gallaf-
py.
Gallafpy was the talleft and
ftrongeft man I have ever feen,
well made, and very hand-
fome. He had wit and abilities, fung
well, and talked with great fweetnefs and
fluency, but was fo extremely wicked, that
it were better for him, if he had been a
natural fool. By his vaft ftrength and activity, his riches and eloquence, few things
could withftand him. He was the moft
prophane fwearer I have known : fought
every thing, whored every thing, and drank
feven in a hand ; that is, feven glaffes fo
placed between the fingers of his right
hand, that in drinking, the liquor fell into
the next glaffes, and thereby he drank out
of

of the firſt glaſs ſeven glaſſes at once. This was a common thing, I find from a book in my poſſeſſion, in the reign of *Charles* the Second, in the madneſs that followed the reſtoration of that profligate and worthleſs prince. But this gentleman was the only man I ever ſaw who could or would attempt to do it; and he made but one gulp of whatever he drank; he did not ſwallow a fluid like other people, but if it was a quart, poured it in as from pitcher to pitcher. When he ſmoaked tobacco, he always blew two pipes at once, one at each corner of his mouth, and threw the ſmoak of both out of his noſtrils. He had killed two men in duels before I left *Ireland*, and would have been hanged, but that it was his good fortune to be tried before a Judge, who never let any man ſuffer for killing another in this manner. (This was the late Sir *John St. Leger.*) He debauched all the women he could, and many whom he could not corrupt, he raviſhed. I went with him once in the ſtage-coach to *Kilkenny*, and ſeeing two pretty ladies paſs by in their own chariot, he ſwore in his horrible way, having drank very hard after dinner, that he would immediately ſtop them, and raviſh them: nor was it without great difficulty that I hindered him from attempting the thing; by aſſuring

him

him 1 would be their *protector*, and he muſt paſs through my heart before he could proceed to offer them the leaſt rudeneſs. In ſum, I never ſaw his equal in impiety, eſpecially when inflamed with liquor, as he was every day of his life, though it was not in the power of wine to make him drunk, weak, or ſenſeleſs. He ſet no bounds or reſtrictions to mirth and revels. He only ſlept every third night, and that often in his cloaths in a chair, where he would ſweat ſo prodigiouſly as to be wet quite through; as wet as if come from a pond, or a pail of water had been thrown on him. While all the world was at reſt, he was either drinking or dancing, ſcouring the bawdy-houſes, or riding as hard as he could drive his horſe on ſome iniquitous project. And yet, he never was ſick, nor did he ever receive any hurt or miſchief. In health, joy, and plenty, he paſſed life away, and died about a year ago at his houſe in the county of *Galway*, without a pang or any kind of pain. This was *Jack Gallaſpy*. There are however ſome things to be ſaid in his favour, and as he had more regard for me than any of his acquaintance, I ſhould be ungrateful if I did not do him all the juſtice in my power.

He

He was in the firſt place far from being quarrelſome, and if he fought a gentleman at the ſmall ſword, or boxed with a porter or coachman, it was becauſe he had in ſome degree been ill uſed, or fancied that the laws of honour required him to call an equal to an account, for a tranſaction. His temper was naturally ſweet.

In the next place, he was the moſt generous of mankind. His purſe of gold was ever at his friend's ſervice: he was kind and good to his tenants: to the poor a very great benefactor. He would give more money away to the ſick and diſtreſſed in one year, than I believe many rich pious people do in ſeven. He had the bleſſings of thouſands, for his charities, and, perhaps, this procured him the protection of heaven.

As to *ſwearing*, he thought it was only criminal, when it was falſe, or men lyed in their affirmations: and for *whoring*, he hoped there would be mercy, ſince men will be men while there are women. *Raviſhing* he did not pretend to juſtify, as the laws of his country were againſt it; but he could not think the woman was a ſufferer by it, as ſhe enjoyed without ſinning the higheſt felicity. He intended her happineſs;

nefs; and her faying *No*, kept her an *innocent.*

How far all this can excufe Mr. *Gallafpy*,
I pretend not to determine: but as I
thought it proper to give the world the
picture of fo extraordinary a man, it was
incumbent on me, as his friend, to fay all
I could, with truth, in his vindication.

Character of   *Dunkley* had an extenfive
Mr. Dunk-   capacity, an exquifite tafte,
ley.   and a fine genius. Befides an
erudition which denominates what we call
a man of learning, he happily poffeffed a
focial knowledge, which rendered him a-
greeable to every body. He was one of
the men that are capable of touching every
note. To all the variety of topics for converfation, the diverfity of occurrences and
incidents, the feveral diftinctions of perfons, he could adapt himfelf. He would
laugh like *Democritus:* weep like *Heracli-
tus.* He had the fhort, pert trip of the affected; the haughty, tragic ftalk of the
folemn; and the free, genteel gait of the
fine gentleman. He was qualified to pleafe
all taftes, and capable of acting every part.
He was grave, gay, a philofopher, and a
trifler. He had a time for all things, relative to fociety, and his own true happinefs,

nefs, but none for any thing repugnant to honour and confcience. He was a furprifing and admirable man.

Monaghan had genius and knowledge, had read many books, but knew more of mankind. He laughed at the men who loft among their books the elegancy of mind fo neceffary in civil fociety. He had no relifh but for nice ftudies and fine literature, and defpifed too ferious and abftrufe fciences. This was reckoned a fault in him by feveral judges: but with me it is a *quere*, if he was much to blame. Politenefs is certainly preferable to dry knowledge and thorny enquiries. This gentleman's was fuch as rendered him for ever agreeable and engaging. He was continually an improving friend, and a gay companion. In the qualities of his foul, he was generous without prodigality, humane without weaknefs, juft without feverity, and fond without folly. He was an honeft and charming fellow. This gentleman and Mr. *Dunkley* married ladies they fell in love with at *Harrogate* Wells: *Dunkley* had the fair *Alcmena*, Mifs *Cox* of *Northumberland*; and *Monaghan*, *Antiope* with haughty charms, Mifs *Pearfon* of *Cumberland*:

Character of Mr. Monaghan.

VOL. III.   I   They

They lived very happy many years, and their children I hear are settled in *Ireland*.

Character of Mr. Gollogher.   *Gollogher* was a man of learning and extraordinary abilities. He had read very hard for several years, and during that time, had collected and extracted from the best books more than any man I ever was acquainted with. He had four vast volumes of commonplace, royal paper, bound in rough calf, and had filled them with what is most curious and beautiful in works of literature, most refined in eloquent discourses, most poignant in books of criticism, most instructive in history, most touching and affecting in news, catastrophes, and stories; and with aphorisms, sayings, and epigrams. A prodigious memory made all this his own, and a great judgment enabled him to reduce every thing to the most exact point of truth and accuracy. A rare man! Till he was five and twenty, he continued this studious life, and but seldom went into the mixed and fashionable circles of the world. Then, all at once, he sold every book he had, and determined to read no more. He spent his every day in the best company of every kind; and as he had the happy talent of manner, and possessed that great power which strikes and awakens fancy, by giving
every

every subject the new dress and decoration it requires;—could make the most common thing no longer trivial, when in his hand, and render a good thing most exquisitely pleasing;—as he told a story beyond most men, and had, in short, a universal means towards a universal success, it was but natural that he should be every where liked and wished for. He charmed wherever he came. The specific I have mentioned made every one fond of him. With the ladies especially he was a great favourite, and more fortunate in his amours than any man I knew. Had he wanted the fine talents he was blest with, yet his being an extremely handsome man, and a master on the fiddle, could not but recommend him to the sex. He might, if he had pleased, have married any one of the most illustrious and richest women in the kingdom. But he had an aversion to matrimony, and could not bear the thought of a wife. Love and a bottle were his taste. He was however the most honourable of men in his amours, and never abandoned any woman to distress, as too many men of fortune do, when they have gratified desire. All the distressed were ever sharers in Mr. *Gollogher*'s fine estate, and especially the girls he had taken to his breast. He provided happily for them all, and left nine-

I 2   teen

teen daughters he had by feveral women a thoufand pounds each. This was acting with a temper worthy of a man; and to the memory of the *benevolent Tom Gollogher* I devote this memorandum.

Having faid above, that too many men of fortune abandon the girls they have ruined, I will here relate a very remarkable ftory, in hopes it may make an impreffion on fome rake of fortune, if fuch a man fhould ever take this book in his hand.

The hiftory of the unfortunate Mifs Hunt. §. 6. As I travelled once in the county of *Kildare* in *Ireland*, in the fummer-time, I came into a land of flowers and bloffoms, hills, woods, and fhades: I faw upon an eminence a houfe, furrounded with the moft agreeable images of rural beauties, and which appeared to be on purpofe placed in that decorated fpot for retirement and contemplation. It is in fuch filent receffes of life, that we can beft enjoy the *noble* and *felicitous* ideas, which more immediately concern the attention of man; and in the *cool hours* of reflection, fecreted from the fancies and follies, the bufinefs, the faction, and the pleafures of an engaged world, thoroughly confider

fider

fider the wifdom and harmony of the works
of nature, the important purpofes of providence, and the various reafons we have
to adore that ever glorious *Being*, who
formed us for rational happinefs here, and
after we have paffed a few years on this
fphere, in a *life* of *virtue* and *charity*, to
tranflate us to the realms of endlefs blifs,
Happy they who have a tafte for thefe filent retreats, and when they pleafe, can
withdraw for a time from the world.

The owner of this fweet
place was Mr. *Charles Hunt*, a
gentleman of a fmall eftate and good
fenfe, whom I knew many years before
fortune led me to his houfe. His wife was
then dead, and he had but one child left,
his daughter *Elizabeth*. The beauties of
this young lady were very extraordinary.
She had the fineft eyes in the world, and
fhe looked, fhe fmiled, fhe talked with
fuch diffufive charms, as were fufficient to
fire the heart of the morofeft woman-hater
that ever lived, and give his foul a foftnefs
it never felt before. Her father took all
poffible pains to educate her mind, and
had the fuccefs to render her underftanding
a wonder, when fhe was but twenty years
old. She fung likewife beyond moft women, danced to perfection, and had every

The picture of Mifs Hunt.

accom-

accomplishment of soul and body that a man of the best taste could wish for in a wife or a mistress. She was all beauty, life, and softness.

Mr. *Hunt* thought to have had great happiness in this daughter, though it was not in his power to give her more than five hundred pounds for a fortune, and she would have been married to a country-gentleman in his neighbourhood of a good estate, had not death carried off both her father and lover in a few days, just as the match was agreed on. This was a sad misfortune, and opened a door to a long train of sorrows. For two years however after the decease of her father, she lived very happily with an old lady, her near relation, and was universally admired and respected. I saw her many times during that term, at the old lady's villa within a few miles of *Dublin*, and took great delight in her company. If I had not been then engaged to another, I would most certainly have married her.

In this way I left *Eliza* in *Ireland*, and for several years could not hear what was become of her. No one could give me any information: but, about a twelve-month

month ago, as I was walking in *Fleet-street*, I saw a woman who cleaned shoes, and seemed to be an object of great distress. She was in rags and dirt beyond all I had ever seen of the profession, and was truly skin and bone. Her face was almost a skull, and the only remaining expression to be seen was despair and anguish. The object engaged my attention, not only on account of the uncommon misery that was visible; but, as her eyes, though sunk, were still extraordinary, and there were some remains of beauty to be traced, I thought I had somewhere seen that face in better condition. This kept me looking at her, unnoticed, for near a quarter of an hour; and as I found she turned her head from me, when she saw me, with a kind of consciousness, as if she knew me, I then asked her name, and if she had any where seen me before? —— The tears immediately ran plentifully from her eyes, and when she could speak, she said, I am *Elizabeth Hunt.*—What, Mr. *Hunt*'s daughter of *Rafarlin!* I replied with amazement, and a concern that brought the tears into my eyes. I called a coach immediately, and took her to the house of a good woman, who lodges and attends sick people: ordered her clean cloaths, and gave the woman a charge to take the greatest care of her,

and

and let her want for nothing proper, till I called next day.

When I saw her again, she was lean and whole, and seemed to have recovered a little, tho' very little, of what she once was : but a more miserable spectacle my eyes have not often seen. She told me, that soon after I went to *England*, Mr. *R.* a gentleman of my acquaintance of great fortune, got acquainted with her, courted her, and swore in the most solemn manner, by the supreme power, and the everlasting gospel, that he would be her husband, and marry her as soon as a rich dying uncle had breathed his last, if she would consent, in the mean while, to their living in secret as man and wife; for his uncle hated matrimony, and would not leave him his vast fortune, if he heard he had a wife; and he was sure, if he was married by any of the church, some whisperer would find it out, and bring it to his ear. But notwithstanding this plausible story, and that he acted the part of the fondest and tenderest man that ever lived, yet, for several months, she would not comply with his proposal. She refused to see him any more, and for several weeks he did not come in her sight.

The fatal night however at last arrived, and from the Lord Mayor's ball, he prevailed

vailed on her, by repeated vows of sincerity and truth, to come with him to his
lodgings. She was undone, with child,
and at the end of two months she never
saw him more. When her relations saw
her big belly, they turned her out of
doors; her friends and acquaintance would
not look at her, and she was so despised,
and ashamed to be seen, that she went to
England with her little one. It fortunately
died on the road to *London*, and as her five
hundred pounds were going fast by the
time she had been a year in the capital, she
accepted an offer made her by a great man
to go into keeping. Three years she lived
with him in splendor, and when he died,
she was with several in high life, 'till she
got a cancer in her breast; and after it was
cut off, an incurable abscess appeared.
This struck her out of society; and as she
grew worse and worse every day, what money she had, and cloaths, were all gone in
four years time, in the relief she wanted,
and in support. She came the fifth year to
a garret and rags, and at last to clean
shoes, or perish for want. She then unco-
vered the upper part of her body, which
was half eaten away, so as to see into the
trunk, and rendered her, in the emaciated
condition she was in, an object shocking
to behold. She lived in torment, and had

no

no kind of eafe or peace, but in reflecting that her mifery and diftrefs might procure her the mercy of heaven hereafter, and in conjunction with her true repentance bring her to reft, when fhe had paffed through the grave and gate of death.

Such was the cafe of that *Venus* of her fex, Mifs *Hunt*.—When firft I faw her, it was rapture to be in her company: her perfon matchlefs, and her converfation as charming as her perfon: both eafy, unconftrained, and beautiful to perfection.—When laft I faw her, fhe was grim as the fkeleton, horrid, loathfome, and finking faft into the grave by the laws of corruption. What a change was there! She lived but three months from the time I put her into a lodging, and died as *happy a penitent* as fhe had lived an *unhappy woman*. I gave her a decent private funeral; a *hearfe*, and one *mourning-coach*, in which I alone attended her *remains* to the *earth*; the great *charnel-houfe*, where all the *human race* muft be *depofited*. Here ends the ftory of Mifs *Hunt*.

A word or two to Mr. R. who debauched Mifs Hunt. And now a word or two to the man who ruined her. *Bob R.* is ftill living, the mafter of thoufands, and has thought

no

no more of the *wretched Eliza*, than if her
ruin and mifery were a trifle. He fancies
his riches and power will fkreen him from
the hand of juftice, and afford him lafting
fatisfaction : but, *cruel man*, after this fhort
day, the prefent life, the night of death
cometh, and your unrelenting, foul muft
then appear before a judge infinitely knowing and righteous ; who is not to be im-
pofed upon, and cannot be biaffed. The
fighs and groans of *Eliza* will then be remembered, and *confound* and *abafh* you for
your *falfhood* and *inhumanity* to this *unhappy woman*. In your laft agony, her
ghoft will haunt you, and at the feffions of
righteoufnefs appear againft you, execrable
R. R.

§. 7. But to return to *Harrogate.* While I was there, it
was my fortune to dance with
a lady who had the *head* of
Ariftotle, the *heart* of a *primitive Chriftian*,
and the *form* of *Venus de Medicis*. This
was Mifs *Spence*, of *Weftmoreland*. I was
not many hours in her company, before I
became moft paffionately in love with her.
I did all I could to win her heart, and at
laft afked her the queftion. But before I
inform my readers what the confequence
of this was, I muft take fome notice of

*The author
falls in love
with Mifs
Spence.*

what

what I expect from the critical reviewers.
These gentlemen will attempt to raise the
laugh.   Our *moralist* (they will say) has
buried three wives running, and they are
hardly cold in their graves, before he is
dancing like a buck at the Wells, and
plighting vows to a fourth girl, the beauty, Miss *Spence*.   An *honest fellow*, this
Suarez, as *Pascal* says of that *Jesuit*, in his
provincial letters.

An apology for the author's marrying so often.   To this I reply, that I think
it unreasonable and impious to
grieve immoderately for the
dead.   A decent and proper
tribute of tears and sorrow, humanity requires; but when that duty has been paid,
we must remember, that to lament a dead
woman is not to lament a wife. A wife
must be a living woman. The wife we lose
by death is no more than a sad and empty
object, formed by the imagination, and to
be still devoted to her, is to be in love with
an idea.   It is a mere chimerical passion,
as the deceased has no more to do with
this world, than if she had existed before
the flood.   As we cannot restore what nature has destroyed, it is foolish to be faithful to affliction.——Nor is this all.   If the
woman we marry has the seven qualifications which every man would wish to find
in

in a wife, beauty, difcretion, fweetnefs of temper, a fprightly wit, fertility, wealth, and noble extraction, yet death's fnatching fo amiable a wife from our arms can be no reafon for accufing fate of cruelty, that is, providence of injuftice; nor can it authorize us to fink into infenfibility, and neglect the duty and bufinefs of life. This wife was born to die, and we receive her under the condition of mortality. She is lent but for a term, the limits of which we are not made acquainted with; and when this term is expired, there can be no injuftice in taking her back: nor are we to indulge the tranfports of grief to diftraction, but fhould look out for another with the feven qualifications, as it is not good for man to be alone, and as he is by the *Abrahamic* covenant bound to carry on the *fucceffion*, in a regular way, if it be in his power.— Nor is this all; if the woman adorned with every natural and acquired excellence is tranflated from this gloomy planet to fome better world, to be a fharer of the *divine favour*, in that peaceful and happy ftate which God hath prepared for the *virtuous* and *faithful*, muft it not be fenfelefs for me to indulge melancholy and continue a mourner on her account, while fhe is breathing the balmy air of paradife, enjoy-

ing

ing pure and radiant vifion, and beyond defcription happy?

In the next place, as I had forfeited my father's favour and eftate, for the fake of *Chriftian Deifm*, and had nothing but my own honeft induftry to fecure me daily bread, it was neceffary for me to lay hold of every opportunity to improve my fortune, and of confequence do my beft to gain the heart of the firft rich young woman who came in my way after I had buried a wife. It was not fit for me to fit fnivelling for months, becaufe my wife died before me, which was, at leaft, as probable as that fhe fhould be the furvivor; but inftead of folemn affliction, and the inconfolable part, for an event I forefaw, it was incumbent on me, after a little decent mourning, to confecrate myfelf to virtue and good fortune united in the form of a woman. Whenever fhe appeared, it was my bufinefs to get her if I could. This made me fometimes a dancer at the Wells, in the days of my youth.

Mifs Spence's reply to my addreffes.

§. 8. As to Mifs *Spence*, fhe was not cruel, but told me at laft, after I had tired her with my addreffes and petitions, that fhe would confider my cafe, and

and give me an anfwer, when I called at
her houfe in *Weftmoreland*, to which fhe
was then going: at prefent however, to
tell me the truth, fhe had very little inclination to change her condition: fhe was
as happy as fhe could wifh to be, and fhe .
had obferved, that many ladies of her acquaintance had been made unhappy by
becoming wives. The hufband generally
proves a very different man from the cour-
tier, and it is luck indeed if a young woman, by marrying, is not undone.—During the *mollia tempora fandi*, as the poet
calls it, the man may charm, when, like
the god of eloquence, he pleads, and every
word is foft as flakes of falling fnow; but
when the man is pleafed to take off the
mafk, and play the domeftic hero, Gods!
what miferies have I feen in families enfue!
If this were my cafe, I fhould run ftark
mad.

Mifs *Spence's* mentioning the memorable
line from *Virgil*, furprifed me not a little,
as fhe never gave the leaft hint before,
(though we had converfed then a fortnight)
of her having any notion of the Latin
tongue, and I looked at her with a raifed
admiration, before I replied in the following manner.——What you fay, Mifs *Spence*,
is true. But this is far from being the cafe

of

of all gentlemen. If there be something stronger than virtue in too many of them, something that masters or subdues it; a passion, or passions, rebellious and lawless, which makes them neglect some high relations, and take the throne from God and reason; gaming, drinking, keeping; yet there are very many exceptions, I am sure. I know several, who have an *equal affection* to goodness, and were my acquaintance in the world larger than it is, I believe I could name a large number, who would not prefer indulgence to virtue, or resign her for any consideration. There are men, madam, and young men, who would allow a partial regard to rectitude is inconsistent and absurd, and are sensible, it is not certain, that there is absolutely nothing *at all* in the evidences of religion: that if there was but even a chance for obtaining blessings of *inestimable worth*, yet a chance for *eternal* bliss is worth securing, by acting as the spotless holiness of the Deity requires from us, and the reason and fitness of things makes necessary, in respect of every kind of relation and neighbour. This is the case of many men. They are not so generally bad as you seem to think.

On the other hand, I would ask, if there are no unhappy marriages by the faults of women?

women? Are all the married ladies *con-siftently* and *thoroughly* good, that is, *effec-tually* fo? Do they all yield themfelves *intirely* and *univerfally* to the government of confcience, fubdue every thing to it, and conquer every adverfe paffion and in-clination? Has reafon always the fove-reignty, and nothing wrong to be feen? Are truth, piety, and goodnefs, the fettled *prevailing* regard in the hearts and lives of all the married ladies you know? Have you heard of no unhappy marriages by the paffions and vices of women, as well as by the faults of men? I am afraid there are too many wives as fubject to ill habits as the men can be. It is poffible to name not a few ladies who find their vir-tuous exercifes, the duties of piety, and the various offices of love and goodnefs, as diftafteful and irkfome to them as they can be to a libertine or a cruel man. I could tell fome fad ftories to this purpofe: but all I fhall fay more is, that there are faults on both fides, and that it is not only the ladies run a hazard of being ruined by marrying. I am fure there are as many men of fortune miferable by the manners and con-duct of their wives, as you can name ladies who are fufferers by the temper and prac-tice of their hufbands. This is the truth of the cafe, and the bufinefs is, in order to

avoid

avoid the miseries we both have seen among married people, to resolve to act well and wisely. This is the thing, to be sure, Miss *Spence* replied. This will prevent faults on either side. Such a course as virtue and piety require must have a continued tendency to render life a scene of the greatest happiness; and it may gain infinitely hereafter.——Call upon me then at *Cleator* as soon as you can, (Miss *Spence* concluded, with her face in smiles) and we will talk over this affair again. Thus we chatted as we dined together in private; and early the next morning Miss *Spence* left the *Wells*.

May 12, a remove to Oldfield-Spaw, for a week, on account of an indisposition. §. 9. Miss *Spence* being gone from *Harrogate*, and finding myself very ill from having drank too hard the preceding night, I mounted my horse, and rid to *Oldfield-Spaw*, a few miles off, as I had heard an extraordinary account of its usefulness after a debauch. There is not so much as a little ale-house there to rest at; and for six days I lodged at the cottage of a poor labouring man, to which my informer directed me. I lived on such plain fare as he had for himself. Bread and roots, and milk and water, were

my

my chief fupport; and, for the time, I was as happy as I could wifh.

O nature! nature! would man be fatisfied with thee, and follow thy wife dictates, he would conftantly enjoy that true pleafure, which advances his real happinefs, and very *A reflection at folitary Oldfield-Spaw, after a night's hard drinking.* rarely be tormented with thofe evils which obftruct and deftroy it: but, alas! inftead of liftening to the voice of reafon, keeping the mind free of paffions, and living as temperance and difcretion direct, the man of pleafure will have all the gratifications of fenfe to as high a pitch, as an imagination and fortune devoted to them can raife them, and difeafes and calamities are the confequence. Fears and anxieties and difappointments are often the attendants, and too frequently the ruin of health and eftate, of reputation and honour, and the lafting wound of remorfe in reflection follows. This is generally the cafe of the voluptuary. Dreadful cafe! He runs the courfe of pleafure firft, and then the courfe of produced evils fucceed. He paffes from pleafure to a ftate of pain, and the pleafure paft gives a double fenfe of that pain. We ought then furely, as rea-fonable sonable beings, to confine our pleasure within the bounds of just and right.

A description of Oldfield-Spaw. ·§. 10. As to the place called *Oldfield-Spaw*, it is seven miles from *Harrogate*, and four from *Rippon*, lies on a rising ground between two high hills, near an old abbey, about five yards from a running stream, and in a most romantic delightful situation, which resembles *Matlock* in *Derbyshire* (ten miles beyond *Derby*, in the *Peak*) so very much, that one might almost take it for the same place, if conveyed there in a long deep sleep. The same kind of charms and various beauties are every where to be seen; rocks and mountains, groves and vallies, tender shrubs and purling currents, at once surprize and please the wandering eye.

An account of Oldfield-Spaw-water. As to the mineral water at *Oldfield-Spaw*, it is an impetuous spring, that throws out a vast quantity of water, and is always of the same height, neither affected by the rain or drought. It is bright and sparkling, and when poured into a glass, rises up in rows, like strings of little beads. It has an uncommon taste, quite different from all other mineral waters that

ever

ever came in my way; but it is not difa-
greeable. What impregnates it I know
not. Dr. *Rutty* I fuppofe never heard of
this water, for it is not in his valuable
quarto lately publifhed; and Dr. *Short*, in
his excellent hiftory of mineral waters,
(2 vols. 4to. *London*, 1734) fays little more
than that there is a *medicinal fpring* there.
What I found upon trial is, that two quarts
of it, fwallowed as faft as I could drink it
in a morning, vomits to great advantage;
and that four quarts of it, drank by degrees, at invervals, works off by fiêge or
ftool, and urine, in a very beneficial manner.
I was apprehenfive of a high fever from a
night's hard drinking at *Harrogate*, (which I
could not avoid) and the *Oldfield-water*, ope-
rating as related, carried off the bad fymp-
toms, and reftored me to fanity in two days
time. This is all I can fay of this fine water.
It is very little, in refpect of what it deferves
to have faid of it.

§. 11. By the way, it is to
me a matter of great admiration, that fo many of our rich
and noble not only endure the
fatigues and hazards of fail-
ing and travelling to remote
*An obferva-
tion on our
people of for-
tune going to
other countries
to drink mi-
neral waters.*
countries, but wafte their money, to drink
fpaw-waters abroad, when they can have as
good

good of every kind in *England*, by riding a few miles to the moſt delightful places in the world, in ſummer time. Our own country has healing waters equal to the beſt in *France, Italy*, and *Weſtphalia. Harrowgate-water*, in particular, has all the virtues of the famous baths of *Aponus*, within a mile of *Padua* in *Italy*, and is in every reſpect exactly alike. See the *analyſis* of *Aponus-water* by *Fallopius* and *Baccius*, and the *analyſis* of the *Engliſh ſulphur-ſpaw* by Dr. *Rutty*. It is injuſtice then to our country to viſit foreign nations upon this account.—*Moffat-waters* likewiſe are as good as any in all the world.

Of Moffat-Wells. N. B. *Moffat* is a village in *Annandale*, 35 miles S. W. of *Edinburgh*. The mineral waters, called *Moffat-waters*, lie at the diſtance of a long mile northward from the village, and are 36 miles from *Edinburgh*. The ſprings are ſituated on the declivity of a hill, and on the brow of a precipice, with high mountains at a diſtance, and almoſt on every ſide of them. The hill is the ſecond from *Hartfield*, adjoining the higheſt hill in *Scotland*.

A vein of ſpar runs for ſeveral miles on this range of hills, and forms the bottom and

and lower fides of the wells. It is a greyifh fpar, having polifhed and fhining furfaces of regular figures, interfperfed with glittering particles of a golden colour, which are very copious and large.

There are two medicinal fprings or wells, which are feparated from one another by a fmall rock: the *higher well* lies with its mouth fouth-eaft. 'Tis of an irregular fquare figure, and is about a foot and a half deep. The *lower well* is furrounded with naked rocks: it forms a fmall arch of a circle. Its depth is four feet and a half, and by a moderate computation, the two fprings yield 40 loads of water in 24 hours, each load containing 64 or 68 *Scotch* pints; a *Scotch* pint is two *Englifh* quarts. —The higher fhallow well is ufed for bathing, as it is not capable of being kept fo clean as the lower well, on account of the fhallownefs and the loofenefs of its parts.

Thefe waters are ftrongly fulphureous, and refemble the fcourings of a foul gun, or rotten eggs, or a weak folution of *fal polychreftum*, or *hepar fulphuris*. The colour of the water fomewhat milky or bluifh.

5   N. B.

N. B. The foil on every fide of the wells is thin; and the hills rocky, only juft below the wells there is a fmall mofs, caufed by the falling of water from the hill above it.

Virtues of thefe waters. Great is the medicinal virtue of thefe waters, in relieving, inwardly, colics, pains in the ftomach, griping of the guts, bilious and nephritic colics; nervous and hyfteric colics; the gravel, by carrying off the quantities of fand, (but does not diffolve the flimy gravel) clearing the urinary paffages in a wonderful manner; in curing ifchuries, and ulcerated kidneys; the gout, the palfy, obftructions of the menfes, old gleets, and barrennefs: it is a fovereign remedy in rheumatic and fcorbutic pains, even when the limbs are monftroufly fwelled, ufelefs, and covered with fcales.—Outwardly, ulcers, tumors, itch, St. *Anthony*'s fire, and king's evil.

The waters are ufed by bathing and drinking: to drink in the morning three chopins, fix pints or a *Scotch* quart, four *Englifh* quarts, at moft, between the hours of fix and eleven. After dinner to drink gradually.

Medicines

Medicines commonly ufed during the drinking of the waters are, an emetic or two at firft, and a few cathartic dofes. The dofes *fal Glauberi* and *polychreftum:* fyrup of buckthorn, and fulphur, is ufed along with the water.

But the cathartic prefcription moft in ufe, which was given by an eminent phyfician, for a general recipe, to be taken by all who fhould at any time ufe the water, is, pills that are a compofition of gambozia, refin of jalop, aloes, and fcammony: thefe to all intents are a ftrong hydragogue.

The large vein of fpar three feet thick runs in one direction for fix miles to the wells, and croffes obliquely the rivulet at the bottom of the precipice, and afcends the hill on the oppofite fide. Small veins of the fame fpar which appears on the precipices, are on the fide of the rivulet, and fix fmall gufhes of water of the mineral kind proceed from them. The rocks and ftones about the tops of the wells, and in other parts of the hill and precipices, differ not from common ftones, no more than the water of the fmall fprings in the neighbourhood with the common water.

The virtue of this water was difcovered by Mifs *Whiteford*, daughter of Bifhop *Whiteford*, in 1632. She was married in 1633. She had been abroad, and all over *England*, drinking mineral waters for the recovery of her health, but found little benefit, till by accident fhe tafted thefe waters in her neighbourhood, and finding they refembled thofe fhe had ufed elfewhere, made a trial of them, and was cured of all her diforders.

Upon this fhe recommended the ufe of them to others, and employed workmen to clear the ground about the fprings, (their overflowing having made a fmall morafs) that the poor and the rich might come, and make ufe of a medicine, which nature had fo bounteoufly offered to them.

The author leaves Old-field-Spaw, and fets out for Knaref-borough, but arrives at another place, May 19, 1731.

§. 12. The 19th of *May*, at that hour, when a fine daybreak offers the moft magnificent fight to the eyes of men, (though few who have eyes will deign to view it), I mounted my horfe again, and intended to breakfaft at *Knaref-borough*, in order to my being at *Harrogate* by dinner time, with my friends again; but the land I went over

3   was

was fo inchantingly romantic, and the morning fo extremely beautiful, that I had a mind to fee more of the country, and let my horfe trot on where he pleafed. For a couple of hours, he went flowly over the hills as his inclination directed him, and I was delightfully entertained with the various fine fcenes, till I arrived at a fweet pretty country feat.

The rifing fun, which I had directly before me, ftruck me very ftrongly, in the fine fitu- *A morning thought on the rifing fun.* ation I was in for obferving it, with the power and wifdom of the author of nature, and gave me fuch a charming degree of evidence for the Deity, that I could not, but offer up, in filence, on the altar of my heart, praife and adoration to that *fovereign* and *univerfal mind*, who produced this glorious creature, as the bright image of his benignity, and makes it travel unweariedly round; not only to illuftrate fuccefsively the oppofite fides of this globe, and thereby enliven the animal world, fupport the vegetable, and ripen and prepare matter for all the purpofes of life and vegetation; but, to enlighten and cheer furrounding worlds, by a perpetual diffufion of bounties, to difpel darknefs and forrow, and like the prefence of the deity,

K 2 infufe

infufe fecret ravifhment into the heart. This cannot be the production of *chance*. It muft be the work of an *infinitely wife and good Being*. The nature, fituation, and motion of this fun, bring the *Deity* even within the reach of the methods of fenfe affifted by reafon, and fhews fuch conftant operations of his power and good-nefs, that it is impoffible to confider the prefent difpofition of the fyftem, without being full of a fenfe of love and gratitude to the almighty creator; — *the Parent of Being and of Beauty!* By this returning minifter of his beneficence, all things are recalled into life, from corruption and de-cay; and by its, and all the other heavenly motions, the whole frame of nature is ftill kept in repair. His name then alone is excellent, and his glory above the earth and heaven. It becomes the whole fyftem of rationals to fay, *Hallelujah.*

SECTION

SECTION VI.

Come, CHEARFULNESS, triumphant Fair,
Shine thro' the painful cloud of care.
O sweet of language, mild of mien,
O virtue's friend, and pleasure's queen!
Fair guardian of domestic life,
Best banisher of home-bred strife;
Nor sullen lip, nor taunting eye
Deform the scene where thou art by:
No sick'ning husband damns the hour,
That bound his joys to female power;
No pining mother weeps the cares,
That parents waste on hopeless heirs:
Th' officious daughters pleas'd attend;
The brother rises to the friend:
By thee our board with flowers is crown'd,
By thee with songs our walks resound:
By thee the sprightly mornings shine,
And evening hours in peace decline.

§. 1. WHILE I was thinking in this manner of the sun, and the author of it, I came into a silent unfrequented glade, that was finely adorned with streams and trees. Nature there seemed to be lulled into a kind of pleasing repose, and conspired as it were to soften a speculative genius into solid and awful contemplations. The woods,

May 19, 1731. A description of a beautiful spot of ground, and a sweet pretty country seat in the west-riding of Yorkshire.

K 3

woods, the meadows, and the water, formed the moſt delightful ſcenes, and the
charms of diſtant proſpects multiplied as I
travelled on : but at laſt I came to a ſeat
which had all the beauties that proportion,
regularity, and convenience, can give a
thing.   The pretty manſion was ſituated in
the midſt of meadows, and ſurrounded
with gardens, trees, and various ſhades.
A fountain played to a great height before
the door, and fell into a circular reſervoir
of water, that had foreign wild-fowl ſwim-
ing on its ſurface.   The whole was very
fine.

Here I walked for ſome time, and after
roaming about, went up to the houſe, to
admire the beauties of the thing.   I found
the windows open, and could ſee ſeveral
ladies in one of the apartments.   How to
gain admittance was the queſtion, and I
began to contrive many ways ; but while
I was buſied in this kind of ſpeculation, a
genteel footman came up to me, and let
me know, his lady ſent him to inform me
I might walk in and look at the houſe, if
I pleaſed.   So in I went, and paſſed thro'
ſeveral grand rooms, all finely furniſhed,
and filled with paintings of great price.
In one of thoſe chambers the ſervant left
me, and told me, he would wait upon me
again

again in a little time. This furprized me, and my aftonifhment was doubled, when I had remained alone for almoft an hour. No footman returned: nor could I hear the found of any feet. But I was charmingly entertained all *An account of* the while. In the apartment *two wonder-* I was left in, were two figures, *ful figures,* dreffed like a fhepherd and *which played* fhepherdefs, which amazed me *on the* Ger- *man flute.* very much. They fat on a rich couch, in a gay alcove, and both played on the *German* flute. They moved their heads, their arms, their eyes, their fingers, and feemed to look with a con-fcioufnefs at each other, while they breath-ed, at my entering the room, that fine piece of mufic, the mafquerade minuet; and afterwards, feveral excellent pieces. I thought, at firft, they were living crea-tures; but on examination, finding they were only wood, my admiration increafed, and became exceeding great, when I faw, by fhutting their mouths, and ftopping their fingers, that the mufic did not pro-ceed from an organ within the figures. It was an extraordinary piece of clock-work, invented and made by one *John Nixon*, a poor man.

§. 2. At length, however, a door was opened, and a lady entered, who was vaftly pretty, and richly dreffed beyond what I had ever feen. She had diamonds enough for a queen. I was amazed at the fight of her, and wondered ftill more, when, after being honoured with a low courtefy, on my bowing to her, fhe afked me in *Irifh*, how I did, and how long I had been in *England*. My furprize was fo great I could not fpeak, and upon this, fhe faid, in the fame language, I fee, Sir, you have no remembrance of me. You cannot recollect the leaft idea of me. You have quite forgot young *Imoinda*, of the county of *Gallway* in *Ireland*, who was your partner in country dances, when you paffed the Chriftmas of the year 1715, at her father's houfe. What (I faid) Mifs *Wolf* of *Balinefkay? O my Imoinda!* And fnatching her to my arms, I almoft ftifled her with kiffes. I was fo glad to fee her again, and in the fituation fhe appeared in, that I could not help expreffing my joys in that tumultuous manner, and hoped fhe would excufe her *Valentine*, as I then remembered I had had that honour when we were both very young.

This lady, who was good humour itfelf
in

in flesh and blood, was so far from being angry at this strange flight of mine, that she only laughed excessively at the oddness of the thing; but some ladies who came into the apartment with her seemed frightened; and at a loss what to think, till she cleared up the affair to them, by letting them know who I was, and how near her father and mine lived to each other in the country of *Ireland*. She was indeed extremely glad to see me, and from her heart bid me welcome to *Clankford*. Our meeting was a vast surprize to both of us. She thought I had been in the *Elysian* fields, as she had heard nothing of me for several years: and I little imagined, I should ever find her in *England*, in the rich condition she was in. She asked me by what destiny I was brought to *Yorkshire*; and in return for my short story, gave me an account of herself at large. Till the bell rung for dinner, we sat talking together, and then went down to as elegant a one as I had ever seen. There were twelve at table; six young ladies, all very handsome, and six gentlemen. Good humour presided, and in a rational delightful chearfulness, we passed some hours away. After coffee, we went to cards, and from them to country dances, as two of the footmen played well on the fiddle. The charming *Imoinda* was

K 5 my

my partner, and as they all did the dances extremely well, we were as happy a little fet as ever footed it to country meafure. Two weeks I paffed in this fine felicity. Then we all feparated, and went different ways. What became of Mifs *Wolf* after this—the extraordinary events of her life —and the ftories of the five ladies with her,—I fhall relate in the fecond volume of my *Memoirs of feveral ladies of Great Britain.* Four of them were Mrs. *Cheolin*, Mrs. *Fanfhaw*, Mrs. *Chadley*, and Mrs. *Biffel*; the fifth was Mifs *Farmor*; all mentioned in the Preface to the firft volume of my Memoirs aforefaid.

May 25, 1731. *An account of* Oliver Wincup, *Efq*; §. 3. A fortnight, as faid, I ftayed with Mifs *Wolf*, that was; but, at the time I am fpeaking of, the relict of Sir *Loghlin Fitzgibbons*, an old *Irifh* knight, who was immenfely rich, and married her when he was creeping upon all-fours, with fnow on his head, and froft in his bones, that he might lie by a naked beauty, and gaze at that awful fpot he had no power to enjoy. I did intend, on leaving this lady, to be at *Knarefborough* at night; but the fates, for a while, took me another way. At the inn where I dined, I became acquainted with a gentleman, much

of

of my own age, who was an ingenious a-
greeable man. This was *Oliver Wincup*,
Efq; who had lately married Mifs *Horner*
of *Northumberland*, a fine young creature,
and a great fortune. This gentleman, by
his good humour, and feveral good fongs,
pleafed me fo much, that I drank more
than I intended, and was eafily prevailed
on to go with him, in the evening, to
Woodcefter, the name of his feat, which
was but ten miles from the houfe we had
dined at. We came in juft as they were
going to tea. There was a great deal of
company, at leaft a dozen ladies, befides
half a fcore gentlemen, and all of them as
gay and engaging as the beft-bred young
mortals could be.

§. 4. The vill here was very *A defcription*
odd, but a charming pretty *of* Woodcef-
thing. The houfe confifted *ter Houfe.*
of feveral ground rooms, (ten I think),
detached from one another, and feparated
by trees and banks of flowers. They were
intirely of wood, but finely put together,
and all difpofed with the greateft fymmetry
and beauty. They were very handfome
without fide, and the infide furnifhed and
adorned with the fineft things the owner
could get for money. Eafy hills, little
vallies, and pretty groves, furrounded the
fweet retreat, and the vallies were watered
K 6 with

with clear ſtreams. The whole had a fine appearance. The varied ſcenes for ever pleaſed.

The manner of living at Woodceſter. §. 5. At this delightful place I ſtayed ten days, and was very happy indeed. We drank, we laughed, we danced, we ſung, and chatted; and when that was done, 'twas night. But country dances were the chief diverſion; and I had a partner, who was not only a wonder in face and perſon, (divinely pretty), but did wonders in every motion. This was Miſs *Veyſſiere* of *Cumberland:* the dear creature! Reader, when I was a young fellow, there were few could equal me in dancing. The famous *Paddy Murphy,* an *Iriſh* member of the houſe of commons, commonly called the *Little Beau,* well known at *Lucas*'s coffeehouſe, *Dublin:* (He danced one night, in 1734, that I was at the caſtle, before the late Duke of *Dorſet* and his Ducheſs, at their grace's requeſt:) this gentleman, and *Langham,* the miller, who danced every night at the renowned *Stretch*'s puppetſhew, before the curtain was drawn up, were both deſervedly admired for their performance in the hornpipe; yet were nothing to me in this particular: but Miſs *Veyſſiere* outdid me far: her ſteps were infinite, and ſhe did them with that amazing

agility,

agility, that she seemed like a dancing angel in the air. Eight nights we footed it together, and all the company said, we were born for each other. She did charm me, and I should have asked her the question, to try her temper, if *Wincup* had not told me, her father intended to sacrifice her to a man old enough to be her grandfather, for the sake of a great jointure; and in a week or two she was to dance the *reel of Bogee* with an *old monk*.—— Poor Miss *Veyssiere!* I said, what connection can there be between the *hoary churl* and you,

> *While side by side the blushing maid*
> *Shrinks from his visage, half afraid?*

I do not wish you may feather him; but may you bury him very quickly, and be happy.

§. 6. Another of our diversions at *Woodcester*, was a little company of singers and dancers Mr. *Wincup* had hired, to perform in a sylvan theatre he had in his gardens. These people did the *mime*, the *dance*, the *song*, extremely well. There was among them one Miss *Hinxworth*, a charming young creature, who excelled in every thing; but in singing especially,

An account of a company of strolling players at Woodcester.

especially, had no equal I believe in the world. She was a gentleman's daughter, and had been carried off by one *O Regan*, an *Irishman*, and dancing-master, the head of this company. He was the most active fellow upon earth, and the best harlequin I have ever seen. Every evening we had something or other extraordinary from these performers. He gave us two pieces which so nearly resembled the two favourite entertainments called *Harlequin Sorcerer*, and the *Genii*, (tho' in several particulars better) that I cannot help thinking Mr. *Rich* owed his *Harlequin Sorcerer* to *O Regan*: and that the *Genii* of *Drury-Lane* was the invention of this *Irishman*.

You know, reader, that in the first scene of *Harlequin Sorcerer*, there is a group of witches at their orgies in a wilderness by moon-light, and that harlequin comes riding in the air between two witches, upon a long pole: Here *O Regan* did what was never attempted at *Covent-Garden* house, and what no other man in the world I believe did ever do. As the witches danced round and round, hand in hand, as swift as they could move, *O Regan* leaped upon the shoulder of one of them, and for near a quarter of an hour, jumped the contrary way as fast as they went, round all their shoulders.

shoulders. This was a fine piece of activity. I think it much more wonderful, than to keep at the top of the outwheel 'of a water-mill, by jumping there, as it goes with the greatest rapidity round. This *Mun. Hawley*, of *Loch-Gur* in the county of *Tipperary*, could do. He was a charming fellow in body and mind, and fell unfortunately in the 22d *An account of Mr.* Hawley *of* Loch-Gur. year of his age. In a plain field, by a trip of his horse, he came down, and fractured his skull. He did not think he was hurt: but at night, as soon as he began to eat, it came up. A surgeon was sent for to look at his head. It was cracked in several places, and he died the next day. He and I were near friends.

§. 7. The first of *June*, 1731, at five in the morning, I took my leave of honest *Wincup*, as chearful and worthy a fellow as ever lived, and set out for *Knaresborough*; but lost my way, went quite wrong, *June 1, 1731. The author leaves* Woodcester, *and rides to a lone silent place called* Lasco. and in three hours time came to a little blind alehouse the sign of the Cat and Bagpipe, in a lone silent place. The master of this small inn was one *Tom Clancy*, brother to the well-known *Martin Clancy* in *Dublin.*

Dublin. He came to *England* to try his fortune, as he told me, and married an old woman, who kept this public houfe, the fign of the Cat, to which *Tom* added the Bagpipe. As he had been a waiter at his. brother's houfe, he remembered to have feen me often there, and was rejoiced at my arrival at the Cat and Bagpipe. He got me a good fupper of trouts, fine ale, and a fquib of punch, and after he had done talking of all the gallant feHows that ufed to refort to his brother *Martin*'s, fuch as the heroes of Trinity-college, *Dublin*, Captain *Maccan* of the county of *Kerry*, and many more, he let me go to fleep.

The hiftory of the two beauties in the wood.

§. 8. The next morning, betimes, I was up, and walked into a wood adjoining to. *Clancy*'s houfe. I fauntered on for about an hour eafily enough, but at laft came to a part of the foreft that was almoft impenetrable. Curiofity incited me to ftruggle onwards, if poffible, that I might fee what country was before me, or if any houfe was to be found in this gloomy place : this coft me a couple of hours, much toil, and many fcratches ; but at length, I arrived at the edge of a barren moor, and beyond it, about a quarter of a mile off, faw another wood. Proud to be daring,

daring, on I went, and foon came to the wood in view, which I found cut into walks, and arrived at a circular fpace furrounded with a foreft, that was above a hundred yards every way. In the center of this was a houfe, enclofed within a very broad deep moat, full of water, and the banks on the infide, all round, were fo thick planted with trees, that there was no feeing any thing of the manfion but the roof and the chimnies. Over the water was one narrow draw-bridge, lifted up, and a ftrong door on the garden fide of the mote. Round I walked feveral times, but no foul could I fee: not the leaft noife could I hear; nor was there a cottage any where in view. I wondered much at the whole; and if I had had my lad *O Finn* with me, and my pole, I would moft certainly have attempted to leap the fofs, broad as it was, and if it was poffible, have known who were the occupants of this ftrange place. But as nothing could be done, nor any information be had, I returned again to the Cat and Bagpipe.

It was ten by the time I got back, and at breakfaft I told *Clancy*, my landlord, where I had been, and afked him, if he knew who lived in that wonderful place.

Charaƈter of Mr. Jeremiah Cock, an old lawyer.

His

His name (he replied) is *Cock*, an old lawyer and limb of the devil, and the moſt
hideous man to behold that is upon the face
of the earth. Every thing that is bad and
ſhocking is in his compound : he is to outward appearance a monſter : and within,
the miſer, the oppreſſor, the villain. He
is deſpiſed and abhorred, but ſo immenſely
rich, that he can do any thing, and no one
is able to contend with him. I could relate, ſays *Tom*, a thouſand inſtances of his
injuſtice and cruelty; but one alone is ſufficient to render his memory for ever curſ-
ed. Two gentlemen of fortune, who had
employed him ſeveral years in their affairs,
and had a good opinion of him, on account
of a canted uprightneſs and ſeeming piety,
left him ſole guardian of a daughter each
of them had, and the management of fifty
thouſand pounds a-piece, the fortune of
theſe girls, with power to do as he pleaſed,
without being ſubje&ct to any controul, till
they are of age. Theſe ladies, as fine
creatures as ever the eye of man beheld, he
has had now a year in confinement in that
priſon you ſaw in the wood; and while he
lives, will keep them there to be ſure, on
account of the hundred thouſand pounds,
or till he diſpoſe of them to his own advantage, ſome way or other. He intends
them, it is ſaid, for two ugly nephews he
has,

has, who are now at school, about fourteen years old, and for this purpose, or some other as bad, never suffers them to stir out of the garden surrounded by the mote, nor lets any human creature visit them. They are greatly to be pitied, but bear the severe usage wonderfully well. One of them, Miss *Martha Tilston*, is in her twentieth year; and the other, Miss *Alithea Llansoy*, in her nineteenth. They are girls of great sense, and would, if any kind of opportunity offered, make a brave attempt to escape: but that seems impossible. They are not only so strictly confined, and he for ever at home with them, except he rides a few miles; but are attended continually in the garden, when they walk, by a servant who is well paid, and devoted to the old man her master. This makes them think their state is fixed for life, and to get rid of melancholy, they read, and practise music. They both play on the fiddle, and do it extremely fine.

Here *Clancy* had done, and I was much more surprised at his relation than at the place of their residence which I had seen. I became very thoughtful, and continued for some time with my eyes fixed on the table, while I revolved the case of these unfortunate young ladies. But is all this true?

true ? (at laſt I ſaid): Or only report ? How did you get ſuch particular
information ?—I will tell you, *Tom* anſwered. Old *Cock* is my landlord, and
buſineſs often brings me to his houſe in the
wood, to pay my rent, or aſk for ſome-
thing I want. Beſides, I ſometimes bring
a fat pig there, and other things to ſell.
My daughter likewiſe has ſometimes a
piece of work in hand for the ladies, and
ſhe and I take a walk with it there by a
better and ſhorter way than you went. You
cannot think how glad they are to ſee us,
and they let me into all their perplexities
and diſtreſs.

On hearing this, a ſudden thought of
being ſerviceable to theſe ladies came into
my head, and I was going to aſk a queſtion in relation to it, when two horſemen
rode up to the door, and one of them
called *Houſe!* This, ſays my landlord, is
old *Cock* and his man; and immediately
went out to him, to know his will. He
told him, he came for the ride-ſake himſelf, to ſee if any letters were left for him
by that day's poſt at his houſe, and would
dine with him, if he had any thing to eat:
That I have, (the man replied), as fine
a fowl, bacon and greens, as ever was
ſerved up to any table, and only one gentleman,

man, a stranger and traveller, to sit down to it. *Cock* upon this came into the room I was sitting in, and after looking very earnestly at me, said, Your servant, Sir. I told him I was his most humble, and right glad to meet with a gentleman for society in that lone place. I immediately began a story of a cock and a bull, and made the old fellow grin now and then. I informed him among other things, that I was travelling to *Westmoreland*, to look after some estates I had there, but must hurry back to *London* very soon, for my wife was within a few weeks of her time. You are a married man then, Sir, he replied. Yes, indeed, and so supremely blest with the charms and perfections, the fondness and obedience of a wife, that I would not be unmarried for all the world: few men living so happy as I am in the nuptial state.— Here dinner was brought in, and to save the old gentleman trouble, I would cut up the fowl. I helped him plentifully to a slice of the breast, and the tips of the wings, and picked out for him the tenderest greens. I was as complaisant as it was possible, and drank his health many times. The bottle after dinner I put about pretty quick, and told my old gentleman, if affairs ever brought him up to *London*, I should be glad to see him at my house in

Golden-

Golden-Square, the very next door to Sir
John Heir's; or, if I could be of any fervice to him there, he would oblige me very
much by letting me know in what way.
In fhort, I fo buttered him with words,
and filled him with fowl and wine, that he
feemed well pleafed, efpecially when he
found there was nothing to pay, as I informed him it was my own dinner I had
befpoke, and dined with double pleafure
in having the fatisfaction of his moft agreeable company. He was a fine politician,
I faid, and talked extremely well of the
government and the times: that I had received more true knowledge from his juft
notions, than from all I had read of men
and things, or from converfing with any
one. The glafs during this time was not
long ftill, but in fuch toafts as I found
were grateful to his Jacobite heart, drank
brimmers as faft as opportunity ferved;
and he pledged me and cottoned in a
very diverting way. He grew very fond
of me at laft, and hoped 1 would fpare fo
much time, as to come and dine with him
the next day. This honour I affured him
I would do myfelf, and punctually be with
him at his hour. He then rid off, brim-
full, and I walked out to confider of this
affair. But before I proceed any farther

in

in my ſtory, I muſt give a deſcription of this man.

Cock, the old lawyer and guardian, was a low man, about four feet eight inches, *A deſcription of old* Cock *the lawyer.* very broad, and near ſeventy years old. He was humped behind to an enormous' degree, and his belly as a vaſt flaſket of garbage projected monſtrouſly before.' He had the moſt hanging look I have ever ſeen. His brows were prodigious, and frowning in a ſhocking manner; his eyes' very little, and above an inch within his head; his noſe hooked like a buzzard, wide noſtrils like a horſe, and his mouth' ſparrow. In this caſe was a mind quite cunning, in the worſt ſenſe of the word, acute, artful, deſigning, and baſe. There was not a ſpark of honour or generoſity in his ſoul.

How to circumvent this able one, and deliver the two beauties from his oppreſſive power, was the queſtion: it ſeemed almoſt impoſſible; but I reſolved to do my beſt. This I told *Clancy*, and requeſted, as I was to dine with *Cock* the next day, that he would be there in the morning, on ſome pretence or other, and let the ladies know, I offered them my ſervice,

without

without any other view than to do them
good; and if they accepted it, to inform
me by a note, flipt into my hand when
they faw me, that if they could direct me
what to do, I would execute it at any hazard, or let them hint the leaft particular
that might have any tendency to their freedom in fome time to come, though it were
three months off, and I would wait for the
moment, and ftudy to improve the fcheme.
This my landlord very carefully acquainted them with, at the time I mentioned;
and by two o'clock I was at *Cock*'s houfe
to fee thefe beauties, and know what they
thought of the fervice offered them. The
old man received me much civiler than I
thought he would do when he was fober,
and had, what my landlord told me was
a very rare thing in his houfe, to wit, a
good dinner that day. Juft as it was
brought in, the ladies entered, (two charming creatures indeed), and made me very
low courtefies, while their eyes declared
the fenfe they had of the good I intended
them. *Cock* faid, thefe are my nieces, Sir,
and as foon as I had faluted them, we fat
down to table. The eldeft carved, and
helped me to the beft the board afforded,
and young as they were, they both fhewed
by their manner, and the little they faid,
that they were women of fenfe and breeding.

ing. They retired, a few minutes after dinner, and the youngeſt contrived, in going off, to give me a billet in an inviſible manner. I then turned to *Cock* intirely, heard him abuſe the government in nonſenſe and falſhoods, as all *Jacobites* do; and after we had drank and talked for better than an hour, took my leave of him very willingly, to read the following note.

    " S I R,

  " As you can have nothing in view but
" our happineſs in your moſt generous
" offer of aſſiſtance, we have not words
" to expreſs our grateful ſenſe of the in-
" tended favour. What is to be done upon
" the occaſion, as yet we cannot imagine,
" as we are ſo confined and watched, and
" the doors of the houſe locked and barred
" in ſuch a manner every night, that a cat
" could not get out at any part of them.
" You ſhall hear from us however ſoon,
" if poſſible, to ſome purpoſe; and in the
" mean time we are,

    " S I R,
      " Your ever obliged ſervants,
          " *M. T.*
          " *A. L.*"

What to do then I could not tell; but as I rid back I confulted with my lad *O Fin*, who was a very extraordinary young man, and afked him what obfervations he had made on the fervants and place. He faid, he had tried the depth of the water in the mote all round, and found it fordable, at one angle, waift high, and about two feet broad the rock he trod on. He had ftripped, and walked it over, to be fure of the thing. As to the people, he fancied there was one young man, a labourer by the year under the gardener, who would, for a rea- fonable reward for lofing his place, be aid- ing in the efcape of the ladies; for he talked with pity of them, and with great feverity of his mafter: that if I pleafed, he would found this man, and let me know more in relation to him: that if he would be concerned, he could very eafily carry the ladies on his back acrofs the water, as he was a tall man, and then we might take them behind us to what place we pleafed: or, if it was not fafe trufting this man, for fear of his telling his mafter, in hopes of more money on that fide, then he would himfelf engage to bring the la- dies and their cloaths over, on his own back, with wetting only their legs, if they could be at the water-fide fome hour in the night. This was not bad to be fure; but I was afraid to truft the man; for, if he

fhould

should inform old *Cock* of the thing, they would be confined to their chambers, and made close prisoners for the time to come. It was better therefore to rely entirely upon *O Fin*, if they could get into the garden in the night.

In answer then to another letter I had from the ladies by my landlord's daughter the next morning, in which they lamented the appearing impossibility of an escape, I let them know immediately the state of the water, and desired to be informed what they thought of the gardener's man; or, if he would not do, could they at any particular hour get to that angle of the mote I named, to be brought over on my man's back, and then immediately ride off behind us on pillions, which should be prepared.—Their answer was, that they dared not trust any of Mr. *Cock*'s men, but thought my own servant would do, and the scheme reasonable and seemingly safe, if they could get out. They gave me a million of thanks for my amazing care of them, and called the immortal powers to witness the high sense they had of their unutterable obligation to me.

Waiting then for them, I staid at the little inn three days longer, and at last received

ceived

ceived a billet to let me know, that at
twelve o'clock that night, which was the
fixth of *June*, they could, by an accident
that had happened, be at the appointed
place, and ready to go wherever I pleafed.
To a minute my man and I were there,
and in a few moments, *O Fin* brought them
and their cloaths over fafe. In an inftant
after they were behind us, and we rid away
as faft as we could. Six hours we travelled without ftopping, and in that time had
gone about thirty miles. We breakfafted
very gaily at our inn, and when the horfes
had refted a couple of hours, we fet out
again, and rid till three in the afternoon,
when we baited at a lone houfe in a valley,
called *Straveret Vale*, which had every rural
charm that can be found in the fineft part
of *Juan Fernandes*. A young couple, vaftly civil, kept here a fmall clean public
houfe, the fign of the pilgrim, on the very
margin of a pretty river, and the plain
things they had were as good as we could
defire. Their bread, their drink, their
fowl, their eggs, their butter, cheefe, vegetables, and bacon, were excellent, and
as they had good beds, I thought we could
not do better than lie by for two or three
days in this fweet place, till it was determined where the ladies fhould fix. We
were at leaft fixty miles from old *Cock*'s

houfe,

houfe, and in an obfcurity that would con-
ceal us from any purfuers ; for we had kept
the crofs-roads and by-ways, and were on
the confines of *Weftmoreland*. Here then
we agreed to reft for a little time. In reality, it was juft as I pleafed. The ladies
were all acknowledgment for what I did
to deliver them, and all fubmiffion to my
direction. They had each of them thirty
guineas in their purfes, as they fhewed me,
but what to do after that was gone, or
where to go while it lafted, to be in fafety,
they could not tell.

The affair perplexed me very much, and
I turned it a thoufand ways, without being able to fettle it as I would. I had two
young heireffes on my hands, who wanted
more than a year of being at age, and I
muft fupport them, and place them in fome
fpot of decency, fecurity, and peace, fince
I had gone thus far, or I had injured them
greatly, inftead of ferving them, in bringing them from their guardian's houfe.
This took up all my thoughts for three
days. I concealed however my uneafinefs
from them, and endeavoured to make the
houfe and place quite pleafing to them.
I kept up a chearfulnefs and gaiety, and
we fat down with joy and pleafure to
breakfaft, dinner, and fupper. Within

L 3   doors,

doors, we played at cards, we fung, and I entertained them with my *German* flute. Abroad, we walked, fifhed, and fometimes I rowed them up the river in a boat the man of the houfe had. The whole fcheme was really delightful, and as the girls had great quicknefs and vivacity, and were far from being ignorant, confidering their few years, I could have wifhed it was poffible to ftay there much longer: but it was no place for them, and I was obliged to call at *Claytor* in a little time. I could not forget my promife to the lovely Mifs *Spence*. My honour was engaged, and there was no time to lofe. It is true, if I had not been engaged, I might immediately have married either the beautiful Mifs *Tilfton*, or the more beautiful Mifs *Llandfoy*, then become my wards; but as they were minors, if fuch a wife died under age, I could be no gainer, and might have children to maintain without any fortune. All thefe things fat powerfully on my fpirits, and I was obliged at laft to make the following declaration to the ladies, which I did the third day after dinner.

Mifs *Tilfton*, Mifs *Llandfoy*, I am fenfible you have too high an opinion of what I have done to ferve you, and think there is

more

'more merit in it than there really is; for a man of any generofity and ability would, I imagine, do all that was poffible to deliver two young ladies of your charms and per-fections from the flavery and mifery your guardian kept you in. I am likewife fure you believe I would do every thing in my power to fecure your happinefs, and give you the poffeffion of every bleffing of time. I honour, I admire, I regard you both to a high degree; and if I were fome power-ful *genie*, I would crown your lives with ftable felicity and glory. But nature, la-dies, has irrevocably fixed limits, beyond which we cannot pafs, and my fphere of action is far from being large. My for-tune is not very great, and thereby pre-vents my being fo ufeful a friend to you as I would willingly be. However, though it is not in my power to do according to my inclination, in regard to your cafe, and with fecurity place you in fome ftation fit for your rank and worth, yet I can bring you to a fpot of tranquillity, and in ftill life enable you to live without perplexity or care of any kind. You fhall have peace and little, and may perhaps hereafter fay, you have enjoyed more real happinefs, for the time you had occafion to refide there, than you could find in the tumult, pomp, and grandeur of the world.

L 4

Here

Here I gave the ladies an account of *Orton-Lodge*, in the northern extremity of *Weftmoreland*, where I had lived a confiderable time, told them the condition it was in, the goods, the books, the liquors, and other neceffaries and conveniencies that were there, and if, in that charming romantic fpot, where no mortal could come to hurt them, they could bear to live for a while, I would fettle them there, and get a man-fervant to work in the garden, and a couple of maids. I would likewife procure for them two cows, a few lambs, fome poultry, and corn, and feeds for the ground: in fhort, that they fhould have every thing requifite in fuch a place: I would return to them as foon as poffible; I would write to them often, directing my letters to the neareft town, to be called for by their man. What do you fay, ladies, to this propofal? In *London* it is not poffible for you to be; at a farm-houfe you might have no fatisfaction; and any where that was known and frequented, you may be liable to difcovery, as *Cock*, your guardian, will enquire every where; and if he hears of you, you will be carried home moft certainly to his difmal habitation, and be ufed ten times worfe than before. What do you think then of this fcheme?

Sir,

Sir, (they both replied) you are to us a fubaltern power, by heaven fent to deliver us from mifery, and fecure our happinefs in this world. We have not words to exprefs the gratitude of our fouls for this further inftance of your goodnefs in the offer you make us; nor can it ever be in our power to make you the return it deferves. You will be pleafed to accept our grateful thanks, and all we have to add at prefent, our prayers for your prefervation and health. Conduct us, we befeech you, immediately to that fweet fpot of peace you have defcribed.

This being agreed on, the next thing to be done was to get two horfes for the ladies, for mine were not able to carry double any further, if there had been a turnpike road before us; then up the mountains we were to go, where no double horfe could travel; and when they were at the Lodge, they would want horfes to ride fometimes, or to remove, if the neceffity of their cafe fhould happen to require it: to my landlord therefore I applied upon the occafion, and he very quickly got for me not only two pretty beafts, but a young labouring man, and two country girls to wait upon the ladies. I then fent to the next town for a couple of fide-faddles, gave

the

the fervants directions to go to the Rev.
Mr. *Fleming*'s houfe, to wait there till they
heard from me, and then we fet out for
Orton-Lodge. Two days we fpent in travelling there, feeding on cold provifions
we had with us, and lying a night on the
fern of the mountains. The fecond evening we arrived at the Lodge. There I
found every thing fafe, and the place as I
had left it. I opened my various ftore-
houfes, to the furprize of the young ladies,
and brought them many good things; bif-
cuits, potted char, potted black-cocks,
fweetmeats, and liquors of various kinds:
O Fin likewife got us a difh of trouts for
fupper, and the two beauties and I fat
down with chearfulnefs to our table.———
Vaftly amazed they were at all they faw.
Every thing was fo good, and the wild
charms of the place fo pleafing, that they
could not but exprefs the tranfports they
were in at their prefent fituation. The
whole they faid, was charming as inchant-
ment, and in language there was not a
force fufficient to exprefs their grateful fentiments upon the occafion. This gave me
much pleafure, and till the end of *June*, I
lived a very happy life with thefe fine
young creatures. They did all that was
poffible to fhew their efteem and gratitude.
Exclufive of their amazing fine faces and
perfons,

perfons, they were ingenious, gay, and engaging, and made every minute of time delightful. If I had not been engaged to Mifs *Spence*, I fhould certainly have fat down in peace with thefe two young ladies, and with them connected, have looked upon *Orton-Lodge* as the Garden of *Eden*. They were both moft charming women. Mifs *Llandfoy* was a perfect divinity!

S E C T. VII.

Come all, O come, ye family of joy;
Ye children of the chearful hour, begot
By wifdom on the virtuous mind; O come!
Come innocence, in confcious ftrength fecure;
Come courage, foremoft in the manly train;
Come all, and in the honeft heart abide,
Your native refidence, your fortrefs ftill,
From real or from fancied evils free:
Let's drive far off, for ever drive that bane,
That hideous peft, engender'd deep in hell,
Horrid to fight, and by the frighted furies
In their dread panic *Superftition* nam'd.

Let refcu'd fancy turn aloft her eye,
And view yon wide extended arch; behold
Yon cryftal concave, ftudded with the gems,
The radiant gems of heaven, that nightly burn,
In golden lamps, and gild th' ætherial fpace;
That fmiling vault, that canopy of ftars.
Or eaftward turn, and fee, ferenely bright,
The full orb'd moon begins her filent round:
The mountain tops, the rocks, the vales, the lawns,
By her fet off, adorn'd, and made delightful.
On earth, benign, fhe fheds her borrowed ray,
And onward leads along her fparkling train.

Behold yon blazing fun in glory rife:
Oceans of light he pours upon the world,
And night with all her train before him fly.
All nature fmiles, rejoicing in his beams.
The feather'd kinds their morning anthem fing:
The fifh fkim fportive o'er the gilded lakes:
Their tow'ring tops the waving forefts fhew;
And op'ning flowers their various dyes difplay,
Perfume the air, and grateful incenfe yield.
It is a glorious and charming fcene.

What

What fhould we fear then ? this grand profpect
　　　brings
No dreadful phantom to the frighted eye,
No terror to the foul; 'tis tranfport all!
Here fancy roves in fweet variety.
All thefe, in their eternal round, rejoice ;
All thefe, with univerfal praife, proclaim
Their great Creator; bountiful, benign,
Immenfely good, rejoicing in his creatures.
They wake new raptures in the heart of man;
And fill his foul with gratitude immenfe.

§. 1. **THE** firft of July, *July 1, 1731.* juft as the day was *My departure from* Orton-breaking, I mounted my horfe, Lodge *a fe-* and went again from *Orton-* *cond time:* *Lodge.* The morning being *miffed my* extremely fine, and every thing *road: the* appearing as in the above lines, *country de-* I rid foftly on for three or *fcribed.* four hours, and was fo delighted with the beauties, and an infinite variety of lovely objects my eyes were feafted with, that I did not mind the way; and inftead of coming to the turning that was my road, I got into a bending valley, which ended at a range of rocky mountains. For half an hour I travelled by the bottom of thefe frightful hills, and came at length to a pafs through them, but fo narrow, that the beafts had not above an inch or two to fpare on each fide. It was dark as the blackeft night in this opening, and a ftream came
　　　　　　　　　　　　　　from

from it, by the waters falling in feveral places from the top of the high inclofing precipices. It was as fhocking a foot-way as I had ever feen.

Finn, (I faid to my young man) as the bottom is hard, and you can only be wet a little, will you try where this pafs ends, and let me know what kind of country and inhabitants are beyond it? That I will, faid *O Finn*, and immediately entered the cleft or crevice between the mountains. A couple of hours I allowed my adventurer to explore this dark way; but if in that time he could make nothing of it, then his orders were to return: but there was no fign of him at the end of fix hours, and I began to fear he had got into fome pound. After him then I went, about one o'clock, and for near half a mile the narrow way was directly forward, a rough bottom, and ancle deep in water; but it ended in a fine flowery green of about twenty acres, furrounded with fteep rocky hills it was impoffible to afcend. Walking up to the precipice before me, I found many caverns in it, which extended on either hand, and onwards, into a vaft variety of caves; fome of them having high arched openings for entrance, and others only holes to creep in at; but all

5   of

of them fpacious within, and high enough
for the talleft man to walk in.

In these difmal chambers I apprehended
my fellow had loft himfelf, and therefore went into them as far as I could ven-
ture, that is, without lofing fight of the
day, and cried out *Finn! Finn!* but could
hear no found in return. This was a great
trouble to me, and I knew not what to do.
Back however I muft go to my horfes,
and after I had fpent two hours in fearching, fhouting, and expecting my lad's return, by fome means or other, I was juft
going to walk towards the crevice, or dark
narrow pafs I had come through to this
place, when cafting my eyes once more towards the caverns in the mountains, I faw
my boy come out, leaping and finging for
joy. He told me, he never expected to
fee the day-light more: for after he had
foolifhly gone too far into the caves, till
he was quite in the dark, in hopes of finding a paffage through the mountain to
fome open country, he was obliged to
wander from chamber to chamber he knew
not where for many hours, without one
ray of light, and with very little expectation of deliverance; that he did nothing but cry and roar, and was hardly
able to ftand on his legs any longer, when

by

by a chance turn into a cave, he faw fome light again, and then foon found his way out. Poor fellow! he was in a fad condition, and very wonderful was his efcape.

After this, we made what hafte we could to our horfes, which we had left feeding in the vale, and *Finn* brought me fome cold provifions from his wallet for my dinner. I dined with great pleafure, on account of the recovery of my lad; and when we had both recruited and refted fufficiently, on we went again. We found the valley winded about the mountains for three miles, and then ended at the higheft hill I had ever feen, but which it was poffible to afcend. With great difficulty we and our horfes got to the top of it, and down on the other fide. Six mountains of the fame height, whofe tops were above the clouds, we had to crofs, and then arrived at a bottom, which formed a moft delightful fcene.

Mrs. Thurlowe's *feat in* Weftmoreland.   §. 2. The *Vale of Kefwick*, and *Lake of Derwentwater*, in *Cumberland*, are thought, by thofe who have been there, to be the fineft point of view in *England*; and extremely beautiful they are, far more fo than the Rev. Dr. *Dalton* has been able to make

make them appear in his Defcriptive Poem; (addreffed to two ladies, at their return from viewing the coal-mines, near *Whitehaven*, that is, the late excellent Lord *Lonfdale*'s charming daughters;) or than the Doctor's brother, Mr. *Dalton*, has painted them in his fine drawings; and yet they are inferior in charms to the vale, the lake, the brooks, the fhaded fides of the furrounding mountains, and the tuneful falls of water, to which we came in *Weftmoreland*. In all the world, I believe, there is not a more glorious rural fcene to be feen, in the fine time of the year.

In this fine vale, I found one pretty little houfe, which had gardens very beautifully laid out, and ufefully filled with the fineft dwarf fruit trees and ever-greens, vegetables, herbs, and fhrubs. The manfion, and the improved fpot of ground, were at the end of the beautiful lake, fo as to have the whole charming piece of water before the door. The projecting fhaded fells feemed to nod or hang over the habitation, and on either hand, a few yards from the front of the houfe, cafcades much higher than that of dread *Lodore*, in *Cumberland*, fell into the lake. There is not any thing fo beautiful and ftriking as the whole in any part of the globe that I have feen: and

I.

I have been in higher latitudes, north and
fouth, than moſt men living. I have converfed with nations who live many degrees
beyond the poor frozen Laplander. I have
travelled among the barbarians who fcorch
beneath the burning zone.

An account of §. 3. Who lived in this de-
the two Miſs lightful valley, was, in the
Thurloe's. next place, my enquiry, after
I had admired for an hour the amazing
beauties of the place. I walked up to
the houfe, and in one of the parlour windows, that had a view up the loch, I
faw a young beauty fitting with a muſic-
book in her hand, and heard her fing in a
maſterly manner. She could not fee me,
but I had a full view of her fine face, and
as I remembered to have feen her fomewhere, I ſtood gazing at her with wonder
and delight, and was ſtriving to recollect
where I had been in her company, when
another young one came into the room,
whom I had reafon to remember very well,
on account of an accident, and then I knew
they were the two young ladies I had feen
at Mr. *Harcourt's*, (fee p. 374. of *Memoirs
of ſeveral Ladies of Great Britain,)* and admired very greatly for the charms of their
perfons, and the beauties of their minds.
Upon this I walked up to the window,
and

and after a little aftonifhment at feeing me, they behaved with the greateft civility, and feemed to be highly pleafed with the accidental meeting. While we were talking, their mamma came into the apartment, and on their letting her know who I was, and where they had been acquainted with me, the old lady was pleafed to afk me to ftay at her houfe that night, and to affure me fhe was glad to fee me, as fhe had often heard her daughters fpeak of me. Three days I paffed with great pleafure in this fweet place, and then with regret took my leave. Thefe two fine young creatures were the Mifs *Thurloe*'s, and are Mrs. *Lowman* and Mrs. *Munkley*, in the *Memoirs of feveral Ladies of Great Britain*. In the 2d volume of that work, the reader will find their lives.

§. 4. The 5th of *July* I left Mrs. *Thurloe*'s, and by the affiftance of a guide, had a fine ride to the houfe of Friar *Fleming*, in *Richmondfhire*, where *Account of a Carthufian monaftery in Richmondfhire.* I arrived by noon. I dined with this good *Francifcan*, and fhould have lain there that night, but that I could not help being melancholy, on miffing my dear friend *Tom*, the Monk's brother, who died of a fever, as before related. From him then I parted

in

in the evening, and rid to a *Carthusian monastery*, which confisted of seven monks, men of some estate, who had agreed to live together in this remote place, and pass their lives in piety, study, and gardening. I had a letter from *Fleming* to one of these gentlemen, the superior, letting him know I was his near friend, and desiring he would receive me as himself; that, although a protestant, I was of no party, but in charity with all mankind. This letter procured me all the kindness and honours these gentlemen could shew me. They behaved with great civility and tenderness, and gave me the best they had, good fish, good bread, good wine, excellent fruit, and fine vegetables; for as to flesh, they never eat any, by their rule.

They were all learned and devout men, very grave and silent for the most part, except when visited, but without any thing stiff or morose in their manner. They had a large collection of books, and seemed to understand them well. What time they had to spare from the hours of divine service, and working in their gardens, according to the rule of St. *Bruno*, which they follow, they give to study, and had many volumes of their own writing; being mostly old MSS. they had transcribed, *Greek*, *Latin*,

Latin, and *French*. Making such copies was their principal work in the closet.

§. 5. I stayed two days with these gentlemen, and had a good deal of useful conversation with them, on various subjects. On looking into the writings of the *Rabbies*, which *Reasons for reading the works of the Rabbies, fictitious and extravagant as they are.* I saw in their library, I told one of these *Chartreux*, that it was a wonder to me, that any one read such extravagant fabulous relations and despicable fictions as these books contained, and should be glad to know what good could be extracted from them.

The *Friar* replied, that notwithstanding their being fictitious and extravagant to a high degree, yet great use may be made of the *works* of the *Rabbies*, and especially of the *Talmud of Babylon* (11.) We obtain

---

(11) Reader, that you may the better understand the conversation I had *An account of the Talmuds.* with this learned *Carthusian*, I must inform you what the *Talmud*, and other writings of the *Rabbies*, are.——

The *Talmud* is a celebrated piece of *Jewish* literature, that is full of *Rabinical* domination and enthusiasm. The *Rabbins* pretend, this book contains the *Oral*

obtain from thence a knowledge of the cuftoms and opinions of the *Jews*, which afford fome benefit.   In the next place,
they ferve to the confirmation of the hiftory
of *Jefus Chrift*; for it appears by the *Baby-
lonifh Talmud*, that there was one *Jefus*,
who had difciples, lived in fuch and fuch
a place, and did and faid divers things;
and in the Bible many texts relating to the
Meffias are confirmed and explained by
thefe

Oral laws, and other fecrets, which God communi-
cated to *Mofes*. It confifts of two parts, each of which
is divided into feveral books.   In the firft part, which
they call *Mifhna*, is the *text*.   In the other, is a
fort of *comment* on the text, and this is ftiled the *Gemara*.

This oral law, or tradition of the *Jews*, was collected after the deftruction of the Temple, A. D.
150, by *Rabbi Judah*, and is by them preferred before the fcripture.   They fuppofe it was orally delivered by *Mofes* to *Ifrael*, and unlawful to be written;
but when *Jerufalem* was deftroyed, they were con-
ftrained to write it, left it fhould be loft; but yet it was
fo written, as that none but themfelves might underftand it.——This *Mifhna* and *Gemara* complete the
two *Talmuds*:—that of *Jerufalem*, A. D. 230;—and
that of *Babylon*, 500 years after Chrift.   Many parts
of thefe *Talmuds* are tranflated by feveral learned
men, who have endeavoured to render them intelli-
gible: but in order to underftand them fully, you
muft read the *Jad Chafka*, or *Mifhna Torah* of *Mofes
Maimonides*, who was phyfician to the king of *Egypt*
about 600 years ago.   This *Rabbi* hath comprized
the fubftance of the *Mifhna* and *Gemara* of the *Talmud*,

these books of the *Rabbies*, though not by them intended. This I have since found to be the truth of the case. I have read the works of the *Rabbins* since, and find it to be as the *Carthusian* said. For example,

It is said in *Gen.* iii. 15. *I will put enmity between thy feed and her feed. It shall bruise thy head, and thou shalt bruise his heel.* Now the *Targum* of *Onkelos* gives the sense thus: The man shall be mindful of, or

---

mud, in his books, and enabled us to understand all the *Mishna* with ease and pleasure. See likewise the *Clavis Talmudica, Cook's Excerpta,* and the works of the excellent *Ludivicus de Campeigne du Veil,* who had been a *Jew,* but became a *Roman Catholic;* from *Rome* went over to the Church of *England,* where he was for several years in the character of a great divine: but at last turned *Baptist,* and died a member of that christian church; which lost him all his friends and interest. He died the beginning of this century, with the reputation of an upright Christian and a most learned man. There is no tolerable account given of him in any of the Biographical Dictionaries. What they say is short, and next to nothing. And the *Popish* accounts are not only short, but false, and mere calumny.——I took a great deal of pains some years ago, to collect among the *Baptists,* and from others who knew this great man, every thing I could get relating to him and his works, and formed what I had got into a life of him, which I did intend to insert in this place: but by some accident or other, it is gone. I cannot find it any where.

remember,

remember, what thou (Satan) haft done to him in times paft, and thou fhalt obferve, *watch* or *haunt* him till the end of days; that is, the ferpent or devil fhould purfue and have dominion over the world till the *laft days*, and then the *prince of this world fhould be caft out*, and the *works of the devil* deftroyed. *Beacherith Heyamim*, the *end of days*, or *laft days*, is, by a general rule given by the moft learned *Rabbins*, meant of the *Meffias*. So *Kimchi* on *Ifa.* ii. 2.— and *Abarbriel* and *R. Mofes Nachm* on *Gen.* xlix. 1. inform us.

It is likewife very remarkable, that the *Targum* of *Jerufalem*, and that of *Jonathan Ben Uziel*, apply this place to the coming of the *Meffias*. They give the words the following fenfe.—I will put enmity between thy feed and her feed: when the fons of the woman keep my law, they fhall bruife thy head, and when they break my law, thou fhalt bruife their heel; but the wound given to the feed of the woman fhall be healed, but thine fhall be incurable; they fhall be healed in the *laft days*, in the days of the *Meffias*.——Such is the opinion of the moft learned *Jews*:—and from thence it follows, that the *Chriftians* have not put their fenfe upon the text I have cited to ferve their own turn; the

Rabbins,

Rabbins, we fee, give the very fame meaning to the place.

Again, in *Numb.* xxiv. 17. we have the famous prophecy of *Balaam*: *There shall come a star out of Jacob, and a sceptre shall rife out of Israel.* — In *Isaiah* xi. 1. it is written, *And there shall come forth a rod out of the stem of Jesse, and a branch shall grow out of his roots, and the spirit of the Lord shall rest upon him.* And in *Jeremiah* xxiii. 5. 6. *Behold the days shall come, saith the Lord, that I will raise unto David a righteous branch,—and this is his name whereby he shall be called, The Lord our Righteousness.* That the *Christians* apply thefe *texts* to the Meffias, I need not inform the reader: but it muft be grateful to obferve, that the paraphrafes of *Onkelos, Jonathan,* and *Jerufalem,* all of them expressly attribute the *prophecy* of *Balaam* to the *Meffias.* And *Rabbi Mofes Hadarfan* and *Maimon,* fay, he is here called a *Star,* (which fignifies what *Malachi* expreffes by the *Sun* of *Righteoufnefs. Mal.* iv. 2. and *Zechariah* by the *Eaft. I will bring forth my fervant the Eaft,* Zech. iii. 8. as it is tranflated in the *Vulgar, Septuagint, Arabic,* and *Syriac)* is here, fay thefe *Rabbins,* called a *Star,* becaufe he fhould come and deftroy *idolatry,* among the heathen nations, by becoming *a light to the gentiles*, and *the glory of Ifrael.*

As to the other two texts, the Jews do likewife attribute them to the *Meffias*. *Rabbi Jofeph Albo*, fpeaking of the words, *The Lord our Righteoufnefs*, in particular, fays exprefsly, that this is one name given to the *Meffias*; *Albo, Sep. ikker.* lib. 2. c. 28. Thus do the *Jews* concur with us in the application of *texts* to the *Meffias*. But what is become of this *Meffias*, they cannot tell. They are amazed, perplexed, and confounded about him. They difpute on the article, and have the wildeft fancies in relation to it. Whereas the Chriftians give a clear and confiftent account of the *Meffias*, and by every argument that can be defired by a rational, prove the truth of chriftianity.

Again, in *Ifa.* ix. 6. we have thefe words: *Unto us a child is born, unto us a fon is given, and the government fhall be upon his fhoulders: and his name fhall be called Wonderful, Counfellor, the Mighty God, the Everlafting Father, the Prince of Peace.* Or as the Alexandrian MSS. hath it, *He fhall call his name the Angel, Wonderful, Counfellor, Mighty, the Governor, the Prince of Peace, the Father of the age to come.* This
is

is thought by all *Chriſtians* to be a plain declaration of the *Meſſias*; for to apply it to any mere mortal, as to *Hezekiah*, or *Iſaiah*'s ſon, cannot be done without the greateſt abſurdity: and therefore *Ben Maimon (epiſt. ad Afric.)* fairly yields that theſe words belong to the *Meſſias*, and ſo doth *Jonathan Ben Uziel* in his *Chaldee* paraphraſe. The *Talmud* itſelf allows it. *Tract. Sanhedrim.* that it relates to a perſon not come in the time of the *prophets*, but to the man, whoſe name is *the Branch which was to come forth out of the ſtem of Jeſſe, and to grow out of his roots. My Servant the Branch. Behold the man whoſe name is the Branch*; Zech. iii. 8. and ch. xii. and Iſa. iv. 1. *Even the perſon that ſhall be ſent; Shilo,* that *remarkable perſon* God had promiſed to his people. So ſays the *Talmud*.

But further, as to the birth of the *Meſſias*, in reſpect of the manner and the place, it is thus ſet down by the prophet *Micah*, v. 2. *And thou Bethlehem Ephrata, though thou be little among the thouſands of Judah, yet out of thee ſhall come forth unto me, that is to be ruler in Iſrael; whoſe goings forth have been of old, even from everlaſting.—* And in *Iſa.* vii. 14. are theſe words, *Behold a virgin ſhall conceive, and bring forth a ſon, and call his name Immanuel.* In theſe two

texts,

texts, (the *Chriftians* fay), the *place* of the
birth of the *Meffias*, and the *manner* of it,
are as plainly defcribed as words can do;
and if they cannot, without abfurdity, be
explained as relating to any other perfon,
then it muft be perverting the meaning of
the records to oppofe this explication : but
this the *Jews* are far from doing. The
place is acknowledged in the *Talmud*, in the
Chaldee paraphrafe of *Jonathan*, and all
their moft famous *mafters* declare with one
voice, that *Bethlehem* indifputably belongs
to the *Meffias*. *Exte Bethlehem coram me
prodilit Meffias, ut fit dominium exercens in
Ifrael, cujus nomen dictum eft ab æternitate.
a Diebus feculi. (Talmud. lib. Sanhedrim, et
Midrafch. The hillinic Rabbi Selemoh. pa-
raph. Jonath. in Loc. Rabbi David Kimchi.)*
——And as to the *manner*, though it be
true that fome *Jews* fay, the *Hebrew* word
Gnalma fignifies a *young woman* as well as
a *virgin*; yet *Kimchi*, *Jarchi*, and *Selemoh*,
three of their greateft *Rabbins*, confefs that
here is fomething wonderful prefaged in
the birth and generation of this perfon, and
that he was not to be born as other men
and women are born. What can we defire
more, in the cafe, from an enemy ? And
in truth, the *behold*, or wonder, with which
the text begins, would be nothing, if it
was only that a young woman fhould have

a

a child:—And as to the *Hebrew* word *Gnalmah*, if it ever does signify a young woman, which I very much doubt, yet in the translation of the *Seventy*, who well understood the original surely, they render the word by *parthenos*, παρθίνΘ in *Græc*; which always signifies a virgin in the strict propriety of the phrase. And in the *Punic* language, which is much the same as the *Hebrew*, the word *Alma* signifies a *virgin*, *virgo intacta*, and never means a young woman.

Such are the advantages we may gain by reading the books of the *Rabbins*; and to me it is pleasing to see these great *Hebrew masters* granting so much to us for our *Messias*, while they hate our holy religion beyond every thing. Even the *gay* among the *Jews*, (if I have been truly informed by one who danced a night with them) have, in contempt and abhorrence of our faith, a country dance, called *The Little Jesus*.

§. 6. The eighth of *July*, I left the little *Chartreuse*, and went from thence to *Knaresborough*, where I arrived that night, and resided three days. It is a fine old town, and borough by prescription, in

An account of Knaresborough and its waters.

M 3   the

the weft-riding of *Yorkfhire*, and wapen-take of *Claro*. The vaft hills of *Craven* look beautifully wild in its neighbourhood, and the rapid river *Nid*, which iffues from the bottom of thofe mountains, almoft encompaffes - the town. It is 175 meafured miles from *London*, and the beft way to it is from *Ferrybridge* to *Wetherby*, the left hand road, where there is an excellent inn, and from that to *Knarefborough*.

When this very ancient town paffed from the pofterity of *Surlo de Burgh*, the founder of it, we know not, but we find that Henry III. Reg. 13. granted the honour, caftle, and manor, to the Earl of *Kent*, *Margaret* his wife, and their iffue and heirs, and that on failure of iffue and right heirs, it returned again to the crown : for *Edward* the Second, among other lands, gave this lordfhip of *Knarefborough* to his favourite *Pierfe de Gavefton*, Earl of *Cornwall*, and his heirs. *Gavefton* was taken not long after by the *Barons*, in *Scarborough* caftle, after a fhort fiege, and on *Gaverfly-heath*, near *Warwick*, was beheaded by order of the Earl of *Warwick*, *June* 20, 1312.

By the fall of the *infolent Gavefton*, who had been banifhed by the great *Edward* the Firft, but recalled and received into favour

vour by *Edward* the Second, before his
father's funeral was performed; by the
death of this favourite, who had involved
his master's interest with his own, and rendered any displeasure against himself, the
want of duty to the prince (just as Lord
*B***, and the now *Outs* did the other
day) which ruined the miserable King;
Knaresborough came again to the crown, and
so continued till the 44th of *Edward* the
Third, when this king made a grant of the
honour, castle, and manor of this town,
and the cell of St. *Roberts*, to *John of
Gaunt*, the king's fourth son, who was Earl
of *Richmond*, and created Duke of *Lancafter*, on his having married one of the co-
heiresses of *Henry* Duke of *Lancafter*. O-
ther great estates were likewise given at the
same time to this fourth son of *Edward*,
that he might maintain his grandeur: and
ever since, this town has belonged to the
dutchy of *Lancafter*. It is an appendage to
the crown.

Not far from this town are two wells, as
strong of sulphur as *Harrogate-water*, and
as valuable, though no one takes any notice of them. One lies in the way to *Harrogate*, in a low ground by a brook-side.
The other is *Bitton-fpaw*, in a park by
Mr. *Staughton*'s house.

As

Description of a dropping well. As to the famous *dropping-well* or *petrifying water*, it lies on the weft fide of the town and river, about 26 yards from the bank of the *Nid*. It rifes 15 yards below the top of a mountain of marle ftone, and in four falls, of about two yards each fall, comes to an eafy afcent, where it fpreads upon the top of an *ifthmus* of a *petrified rock*, generated out of the water, which falls down round it. This *ifthmus* or rock is ten yards high, and hangs over its bafe or bottom about 5 yards. It is near 16 yards long and 13 broad, and as it ftarted from the bank about fifty years ago, leaves a chafm between them, that is about three yards wide. In this chafm, you will find petrified twigs of trees, fhrubs, and grafs-roots, hanging in moft beautiful pillars, all interwoven, and forming many charming figures; and on the common fide are whole banks like *Stalactilites*, hard and infeparable from the rock, where the water trickles down. Thefe *petrefactions,* the *falling water*, and the little *ifthmus* or ifland being beautifully cloathed with afh, ofier, elm, fambucus, fervicana major, geraniums, wood-mercury, hart's-tongue, fage, ladies mantle, cowflips, wild angelica, &c. form all together a delightful fcene.—The firft fpring of this water is out of a fmall hole

hole on the little mountain, in the middle of a thick-fet of fhrubs It fends out 20 gallons in a minute of the fweeteft water in the world, and it is 24 grains in a pint heavier than common water.

Moft people are of opinion, that *petrifying water* is dangerous drink, and may produce abundance of mifchief, in caufing the ftone and gravel in the body: the original particles or principles of the ftony fubftance called *fpar*, which are in abundance fufpended in this kind of water, muft get into the flood-gates of the kidneys and ureters, (as they opine), and create great mifery in a little time.

Obfervations on petrifying waters.

But this fear of *petrefaffions* in living animal bodies is grounded upon neither reafon nor experience; for the *fpar* in thefe waters forms no *petrefaffions*, whilft in a brifk motion, or in a temperate feafon, or on vegetables while they preferve their vegetating life. While there is warmth and circulation of juices, there can be no *incruftation* or *petrefaffion* from the fufpended ftony particles. Befides, if the *minims* of *fpar* are not within the fpheres of fenfible attraction, whilft in motion; much lefs are they fo when mingled with the fluids of the human

M 5   man

man body: you may therefore very safely drink these limpid petrifying waters at all times, as a common fluid, if they come in your way, as the best, and most grateful or pleasant water in the world, on account of the infinitesimals, or original leasts, of spar that are in them, in vast quantities, but infinitely small particles: and if you are sick, in many cases sure I am, they are the best of medicines. Human invention has nothing equal to them for fluxes of any part of the body, or colliquations from an acid salt. So far are they from being in the least dangerous, that in all unnatural discharges, by spitting, stool, or urine; by excessive menstrual or hæmorrhoidal fluxes, in the fluor albus, diabetes, profuse sweatings; in the diarrhœa, dysentery, or lienteria (where the springs are not quite worn out:) in ulcers of the viscera, hectic fevers, atrophy, and colliquations or night sweats, there is not any thing in physic more profitable or pleasant, to recover a patient. Let your dose, in such cases, be three half-pints of *Knaresborough dropping-well* in the forenoon; and before you begin to drink this water, remember to take two doses of rhubarb, to cleanse off the excrements of the first viscera. You must not drink ale, drams, or punch, during a course of these waters: and take but very little red port.

You.

You muft likewife have a ftrict regard to diet. Let it be milk, eggs, jellies, barley-broth, chickens, kid, lamb, and the like. You muft avoid all falt, fharp, ftimulating things, day-fleep, and night-air: but a-greeable converfation, and diverfions that require very little exercife, conduce to the fuccefs of this kind of water, in the dif-tempers I have mentioned. If fuch difeafes are curable, you may expect a reftoration of health.

But, in the dropfy, jaundice, diminifh-ed or irregular menfes; in hyppo, melan-choly, ftuffings of the lungs, obftructions of the vifcera, ftoppages of the lacteals and mefentery, glandular fwellings, king's-evil, or any cafe, where thinning, relaxing, o-pening, deterging, attenuation or ftimula-tion are wanting, fuch water is death.

Note, reader, there is another excellent *petrifying-water* at *Newton-Dale in York-fhire*, N. R. thirteen miles from *Scarbo-rough*.——Another near *Caftle-Howard*, the fine feat of the Earl of *Carlifle*, ten miles from *York*.——Another, near *Skipton*, in that rough, romantic, wild and filent country, called *Craven*, in the Weft-riding of *York-fhire*.——And one, called *Bandwell*, at *Stone-field* in *Lincolnfhire*, weft of *Horncaftle*, which

M 6   is

is 122 miles from *London*. Thefe fprings, and many that are not to be come at among the vaft fells of *Weftmoreland*, and the high mountains of *Stanemore*, have· all the virtues of *Knarefborough dropping-well* ; tho' *Knarefborough-water* is the only one reforted to by company : and as to this fpring, I can affirm from my own knowledge, that it is as excellent, and truly medicinal, as the famous *petrifying water* at *Clermont*. There is no manner of need for *Britons* going to the mountain *Gregoire* in *Baffe-Auvergne.*

A P.O S T I L L A, (12)

Containing an account of *Wardrew Sulphur-water*, — the *Life of Claudius Hobart*, — and *A Differtation on Reafon and Revelation.*

In my account of fulphur-waters, I forgot to mention one very extraordinary
fpring

---

(12) A *Poftilla*, reader, is a *barbarous word* made up of the words *poft illa*, and was brought into ufe in the twelfth century, when the marginal explicators of the bible left the margins, and under their text writ fhort and literal notes, before which they put the word *poftilla*, inftead of the words *poft illa*, meaning the particular words in the text, from whence, by a
letter,

ſpring of this kind, and therefore make a *poſtilla* of it here, that the reader may find in one ſection all I have to ſay on mineral waters.—And as I found by the ſide of this water, a man as extraordinary as the ſpring, I ſhall add his life to my account of the water, and a couple of little pieces written by him.

In *Northumberland*, on the borders of *Cumberland*, there is a place called *Wardrew*, to the north-weſt of *Thirlwall-caſtle*, which ſtands on that part of the Picts-wall, where it croſſes the *Tippel*, and is known by the name of *Murus Perforatus*, (in *Saxon*, *Thirl-wall*) on account of the gaps made in the wall at this place for the *Scots* paſſage. Here, as I wandered about this wild, un-travelled country, in ſearch of *Roman* an-

Of Wardrew ſulphur-wa-ter.

letter, they referred to the little note below: but in the 13th century, the barbarous word took ſo much, that all the commentators following, appropriated the name to their moſt copious commentaries, con-trary to the firſt practice in the uſe of the word, and for three centuries after, the biblial learning was all *poſtilla*, till at length the word diſappeared, accord-ing to the wonted inconſtancy and agitation of all human things, and gave place to a new and fifth in-vention, called *tractatus*, or *homily*. This is the hiſ-tory of a *poſtilla*.

tiquities,

tiquities, I arrived at a *fulphur-fpring*, which I found to be the ftrongeft and moft excellent of the kind in all the world. It rifes out of a vaft cliff, called *Arden-Rock*, over the bank of the river *Arde* or *Irthing*, fix feet above the furface of the water, and comes out of a chink in the cliff by a fmall fpout. The difcharge is fifty gallons in a minute from a mixture of limeftone and ironftone. And the water is fo very fœtid, that it is difficult to fwallow it. The way to it is not eafy, for there is no other paffage than along a very narrow ledge, about nine inches broad, which has been cut off the rock over the deep river, and if you flip, (as you may eafily do, having nothing to hold by), down you go into a water that looks very black and fhocking, by the fhade of the hanging precipice, and fome aged trees which project from the vaft cliff.

This dangerous fituation, and its remotenefs, will prevent its being ever much vifited, admirable as the fpaw is; yet the country-people thereabout make nothing of the ledge, and drink plentifully of the water, to their fure relief, in many dangerous diftempers.—It is to them a bleffed fpring.

The

The land all round here was one of the finest rural scenes I have seen, and made a ·pensive traveller with for *A description of* Wardrew *in* Northumberland. some small public house there, to pass a few delightful days. Its lawns and groves, its waters, vales, and hills, are charming, and form the sweetest softest region of silence and ease. Whichever way I turned, the various beauties of nature appeared, and nightingales from the thicket inchantingly warbled their loves. The fountains were bordered with violets and moss, and near them were clumps of pine and beech, bound with sweet-briar, and the tendrils of woodbine. It is a delightful spot: a paradise of blooming joys, in the fine season of the year.

§. 8. One inhabitant only I found in this fine solitude, who lived on the margin of *The history of* Claudius Hobart. the river, in a small neat cottage, that was almost hid with trees. This was *Claudius Hobart*, a man of letters, and a gentleman, who had been unfortunate in the world, and retired to these elysian fields, to devote the remainder of his time to religion, and enjoy the calm felicities of contemplative life. He was obliged by law to resign his estate to a claimant, and death had

had robbed him of a matchless mistress of great fortune, to whom he was to have been married. The men who had called themselves his friends, and as *Timon* says in *Lucian*, honoured him, worshipped him, and seemed to depend on his nod, ἐμῶ νεύματ Ꙍ ανηϱ τημῷοι, no longer knew him; jam ne agnoscor quidem ab illis, nec aspici ne dignantur me, perinde ut eversum hominis jam olim defuncti cippum, ac temporis longitudine collapsum pretereunt quasi ne norint quidem ; μηδ'ὲ ἀναγνόντες: so true, (continued Mr. *Hobart)* are the beautiful lines of *Petronius* ;

> Nomen amicitiæ si quatenus expedit, hæret,
>   Calculus in tabula mobile ducit opus.
> Quum fortuna manet, vultum servatis amici :
>   Cum cecidit, turpi vertitis ora fugâ.

And so sweet *Ovid* says was his case,

> Eandem cum Timone nostro sortem
>   Expertus naso, qui sic de seipso :
> En ego non paucis quondam munitus amicis :
>   Dum flavit velis aura secunda meis :
> Ut fera terribili tumuerunt æquora vento,
>   In mediis lacera puppe relinquor aquis.

So *Hobart* found it, and as his health was declining from various causes, and he had nothing in view before him while he appeared,

peared, but mifery: therefore he retired to *Wardrew*, while he had fome money, built the little houfe I faw on a piece of ground he purchafed, and provided fuch neceffaries and comforts as he imagined might be wanting: he had a few good books, the bible, fome hiftory, and mathematics, to make him wifer and better, and abroad he diverted himfelf moftly in his garden, and with fifhing: for fifteen years paft he had not been in any town, nor in any one's houfe, but converfed often with fiveral of the country people, who came to drink the mineral water: what he had frefh occafion for, one or other of them brought him, according to his written directions, and the money he gave them, and once or twice a week he was fure of feeing fomebody: as the people knew he was not rich, and lived a harmlefs life, they were far from being his enemies, and would do any thing in their power to ferve the hermit, as they called him: but he feldom gave them any trouble. His food was bifcuit, honey, roots, fifh, and oil; and his drink, water, with a little rum fometimes. He was never fick nor melancholy; but by a life of temperance and action, and a religion of truft and refignation, enjoyed perpetual health and peace, and run his latent courfe in the pleafing expectation of a remove, when his days

were

were paſt, to the bright manſions of the
bleſt.

Such was the account Mr. *Hobart* gave
me of himſelf, (which made me admire
him much, as he was but fifty then) and to
convince me his temper had nothing Timo-
nean or unſocial in it from his ſolitary life,
he requeſted I would dine with him. He
entertained me with an excellent pickled
trout and biſcuit, fine fruit, and a pot of
extraordinary honey : with as much cream
of tartar as lay on a ſixpence, fuſed in warm
water, he made half a pint of rum into good
punch, and he talked over it like a man
of ſenſe, breeding, and good humour.
We parted when the bowl was out, and at
my going away, he made me a preſent of
the following MS. and told me I might
print it, if I could think it would be of any
uſe to mankind. It was called, *The Rule
of Reaſon, with a few Thoughts on Revelation.*

A tract.   §. 9. The throne of God
reſts upon reaſon, and his *prerogative* is *ſupported* by it. It is the *ſole
rule* of the *Deity*, the *Mind* which preſides
in the univerſe, and therefore is *venerable*,
ſacred, and *divine*. Every ray of reaſon
participates of the majeſty of that Being

to whom it belongs, and whofe attribute it is; and being thereby *awful*, and invefted with a *fupreme* and *abfolute authority*, it is rebellion to refufe fubjection to *right reafon*, and a violation of the great and fundamental law of heaven and earth.

To this *beft*, and *fitteft*, and *nobleft* rule, the *rule of truth*, we ought to fubmit, and in obedience to the *facred voice* of *reafon*, refift the importunities of fenfe, and the ufurpations of appetite. Since the *will* of that Being, who is infinitely pure and per-fect, rational and righteous, is *obliged* and *governed* by his unerring underftanding; our wills fhould be guided and directed by our reafon. In imitation of the wifeft and beft of Beings, we muft perpetually adhere to truth, and ever act righteoufly for righ-teoufnefs fake. By acting in conformity to moral truths, which are really and ftrict-ly divine, we act in conformity to ourfelves, and it is not poffible to conceive any thing fo glorious, or godlike. We are thereby taught the duties of piety, our duties to-ward our fellows, and that felf-culture which is fubfervient to piety and huma-nity.

Reafon informs us there is a *fuperior Mind*, endued with knowledge and great
power,

Difcourfe on the rule of reafon. power, prefiding over human affairs; fome original, independent Being, complete in all poffible perfection, of boundlefs power, wifdom, and goodnefs, the Contriver, Creator, and Governor of this world, and the inexhauftible fource of all good. A vaft collection of evidence demonftrates this. Defign, intention, art, and power, as great as our imagination can conceive, every where occur. As far as we can make obfervations, original intelligence and power appear to refide in a Spirit, diftinct from all divifible, changeable, or moveable fubftance; and if we can reafon at all, it muft be clear, that an original omnipotent Mind is a *good Deity*, and efpoufes the caufe of virtue, and of the univerfal happinefs; will glorioufly compenfate the *worthy* in a future ftate, and then make the vicious and oppreffive have caufe to repent of their contradicting his will. It follows then moft certainly, that with this great fource of our being, and of all perfection, every rational mind ought to correfpond, and with internal and external worfhip adore the divine power and goodnefs. His divine perfections, creation and providence, muft excite all poffible efteem, love, and admiration, if we think at all; muft beget truft and refignation; and raife the higheft fenfations of gratitude.

gratitude. All our happiness and excellency is from his bounty, and therefore not unto us, not unto us, but to his name be the praise. And can there be a joy on earth so stable and transporting as that which rises from living with an habitual sense of the Divine Presence, a just persuasion of being approved, beloved, and protected by him who is infinitely perfect and omnipotent?

By *reason* we likewise find, that the excesses of the passions produce misery, and iniquity makes a man completely wretched and despicable: but integrity and moral worth secure us peace and merit, and lead to true happiness and glory. Unless reason and inquiry are banished, vice and oppression must have terrible struggles against the principles of humanity and conscience. Reflection must raise the most torturing suspicions, and all stable satisfaction must be lost: but by cultivating the high powers of our reason, and acquiring moral excellence, so far as human nature is able; by justice and the benevolent affections, virtue and charity, we are connected with, and affixed to the Deity, and with the inward applauses of a good heart, we have the outward enjoyment of all the felicities suitable to our transitory condition. Happy state, surely!

ſurely! There are no horrors here to haunt us. There is no dreadful thing to poiſon all parts of life and all enjoyments.

Let us hearken then to the *original law of reaſon*, and follow God and nature as the ſure guide to happineſs. Let the offices of piety and beneficence be the principal employment of our time; and the chief work of our every day, to ſecure an happy immortality, by equity, benignity, and devotion. By continual attention, and internal diſcipline, reaſon can do great things, and enable us ſo to improve the ſupreme and moſt godlike powers of our conſtitution, and ſo diſcharge the duties impoſed upon us by our Creator, that when we return into that ſilence we were in before we exiſted, and our places ſhall know us no more, we may paſs from the unſtable condition of terreſtrial affairs to that eternal ſtate in the heavens, where everlaſting pleaſures and enjoyments are prepared for thoſe who have lived in the delightful exerciſe of the powers of reaſon, and performed all ſocial and kind offices to others, out of a ſenſe of duty to God. Thus does truth oblige us. It is the baſis of morality, as morality is the baſis of religion.

This,

This, I think, is a juſt account of *moral truth and rectitude*, and ſhews that it is eſſentialy glorious in itſelf, and the ſacred rule to which all things muſt bend, and all agents ſubmit. But then a queſtion may be aſked, What need have we of *revelation*, ſince reaſon can ſo fully inſtruct us, and its bonds alone are ſufficient to hold us; — and in particular, what becomes of the principal part of revelation, called *redemption?*

The *ſyſtem of moral truth and revelation*, (it may be anſwered) are united, and at perfect amity with each other. *Morality* and the *goſpel* ſtand on the *ſame foundation*, and differ only in this, that revealed religion, in reſpect of the corrupt and degenerate ſtate of mankind, has brought freſh light, and additional aſſiſtance, to direct, ſupport, and fix men in their duty. We have hiſtories which relate an early deviation from moral truth, and inform us that this diſeaſe of our rational nature ſpread like a contagion. The caſe became worſe, and more deplorable, in ſucceeding ages; and as evil examples and prejudices added new force to the prevailing paſſions, and reaſon and liberty of will, for want of due exerciſe, grew weaker, and leſs able to regain their

Account of revelation.

loſt

loft dominion, corruption was rendered u-
niverfal. Then did the true God, the Father of the Univerfe, and the moft provi-
dent and beneficent of Beings, interpofe
by a revelation of his will, and by advice
and authority, do all that was poffible, to
prevent the felf-deftructive effects of the .
culpable ignorance and folly of his off-
fpring. He gave the world a *tranfcript* of
the *law of nature* by an extraordinary mef-
fenger, the *Man Chrift Jefus*, who had
power given him to work miracles, to
roufe mankind from their fatal ftupidity,
to fet their thoughts on work, and to con-
ciliate their attention to the heavenly declaration. In this *republication* of the *original law*, he gave them doctrines and
commandments perfectly confonant to the
pureft reafon, and to them annexed *fanctions* that do really bind and *oblige* men, as
they not only guard and ftrengthen religion, but affect our natural *fenfibility* and
felfifhnefs. Religion appears to great dif-
advantage, when divines preach it into a
bond of indemnity, and a *mere contract of intereft*; but exclufive of this, it muft be allowed, that the *fanctions* of the gofpel
have a weight, awfulnefs, and folemnity,
that prove to a great degree effectual.
Safety and *advantage* are reafons for well-
doing.

In fhort, the evidence of the obligation of the duties of natural religion is as *plain* and *ftrong* from *reafon*, as any *revelation* can make it; but yet the means of rendering thefe duties *effectual* in practice, are not fo clear and powerful from mere reafon, as from revelation. The proof of obligation is equally *ftrong* in reafon and infpiration, but the obligation itfelf is rendered *ftronger* by the gofpel, by fuperadded means or motives. The primary obligation of natural religion arifes from the *nature* and *reafon* of things, as being objects of our rational moral faculties, agreeably to which we cannot but be obliged to act; and this obligation is *ftrengthened* by the tendency of natural religion to the final happinefs of every rational agent: but the clear knowledge, and exprefs promifes which we have in the gofpel, of the nature and greatnefs of this final happinefs, being added to the obligation from, and the tendency of reafon or natural religion to the final happinefs of human nature, the obligation of it is thereby ftill more ftrengthened. In this lies the benefit of chriftianity. It is the *old,* uncorrupt religion of *nature* and *reafon,* intirely free from *fuperftition* and *immorality*; delivered and taught in the moft rational and eafy way, and enforced by the moft gracious and powerful *motives.*

N   But

Of the Myste-
ries, Trinity,
and Sacrifice of
the Cross.
But if this be the cafe, it may be afked, Where are our holy myfteries—and what do you think of our Redemption? If natural reafon and confcience can do fo much, and to the gofpel we are obliged only for a little more light and influence, then Trinity in Unity, and the Sacrifice of the Crofs are nothing. What are your fentiments on thefe fubjects?

As to the *Trinity*, it is a word invented by the doctors, and fo far as I can find, was never once thought of by *Jefus Chrift* and his apoftles; unlefs it was to guard againft the fpread of *tritheifm*, by taking the greateft care to inculcate the *fupreme divinity* of *God the Father:* but let it be a trinity, fince the church will have it fo, and by it I underftand one Uncreated, and one Created, and a certain divine virtue of quality. Thefe I find in the Bible, *God, Jefus the Word,* and a *Divine Affiftance* or *Holy Wind,* (not Holy Ghoft, as we have tranflated it): called a *Wind,* becaufe God, *from whom every good and perfect gift cometh,* gave the moft extraordinary inftance of it under the emblem of a *Wind;* and *holy,* becaufe it was fupernatural. This is the fcripture doctrine, in relation to the *Deity,* the *Meffias,* and the *Energy* of God; of-
which

which the *Wind* was promised as a pledge, and was given as an emblem, when the day of *Pentecost* was come; and if these three they will call a Trinity, I shall not dispute about the word. But to say *Jesus Christ* is God, though the apostles tell us, that *God raised from the dead the Man Jesus Christ, whom they killed; that he had exalted him at his right hand, and had made him both Lord and Christ*; and to affirm that this *Ghost* (as they render the word *Wind)* is a person distinct and different from the person of God the Father, and equally supreme;—this I cannot agree to. If the scripture is true, all this appears to me to be false. It is a mere invention of the Monks.

As to *Redemption*, it may be in perfect consistence and agreement with truth and rectitude, if the accomplishment of it be considered as *premial*, and as resulting from a *personal reward:* but to regard the accomplishment as *penal*, and as resulting from a *vicarious punishment*, is a notion that cannot be reconciled to the principle of rectitude. Vicarious punishment or suffering appears an impossibility: but as *Jesus*, by adding the most extensive benevolence to perfect innocence, and by becoming obedient to death, even the death of the cross, was most *meritorious*, and was entitled to the highest

highest honour, and most distinguished reward, *his reward* might be *our deliverance
from the bonds of sin and death*, and the *res-
toration of immortality*. This reward was
worthy of the giver, and tended to the advancement and spread of virtue. It was
likewise most acceptable to the receiver.
It no way interfered with right and truth.
It was in all respects most proper and suitable. These are my sentiments of Redemption. This appears to me to be the truth
on the most attentive and impartial examination I have been capable of making.

To this, perhaps, some people may reply, that though these notions are for the
most part just, and in the case of redemption in particular, as innocence and punishment are inconsistent and incompatible
ideas; that it was not possible Christ's oblation of himself could be more than a *figurative sacrifice*, in respect of *translation of
guilt*, *commutation of persons*, and *vicarious
infliction*; though a *real sacrifice* in the sense
of intending by the oblation to procure the
favour of God, and the *indemnity of sinners*:
yet, as the author appears to be a *Socinian*,
his account is liable to objections. For,
though the *Socinians* acknowledge the truth
and necessity of the revelation of the gospel, yet, in the opinion of some great divines,

vines, they interpret it in such a manner, as no unprejudiced person, who has read the scriptures with any attention, nor any sensible heathen, who should read them, can possibly believe. They make our Redeemer a man, and by this doctrine reflect the greatest dishonour on christianity, and its Divine Author.

This is a hard charge. The *Socinians* are by these divines described as people who read the scriptures with prejudice, and without attention; men more senseless than the Heathens, and as wicked too; for, in the highest degree, they dishonour Christ Jesus and his religion. Astonishing assertion! It puts me in mind of an imputation of the celebrated *Waterland* in his second charge;—" What atheism chiefly aims at, is, to sit loose from present restraints and future reckonings; and these two purposes may be competently served by *deism*, which is a *more refined kind of atheism.*" Groundless and ridiculous calumny. *True and proper deism is a sincere belief of the existence of a God, and of an impartial distribution of rewards and punishments in another world, and a practice that naturally results from, and is consonant to such belief;* and if atheism aims to sit loose from restraints and reckonings, then of consequence, *deism* is

the

the *grand barrier* to the purposes of atheism.
The *true Deist* is so far from breaking
through restraints, that he makes it the great
business of his life *to discharge the obligations
he is under*, because he *believes in God*, and
perceives the *equity* and *reasonableness* of
duties, *restraints*, and *future reckonings.*
The *assertion* therefore demonstrates the
prejudice of Dr. *Waterland*, in relation to
the *Deists.*

And the case is the same in respect of the
charge against the *Socinians.* It is the *divines* that are prejudiced against them; and
not the *Socinians* in studying the New Testament. It is the grand purpose of our
lives to *worship God*, and *form our religious
notions according to the instructions of divine
wisdom.* We examine the sacred writings,
with the utmost desire, and most ardent
prayer, that we may be rightly informed in
the truest sense of the holy authors of those
divine books; and it appears to our plain
understandings, after the most honest labour, and wishes to heaven for a clear conception of holy things, that *the Father is
the supreme God*, that is, the first and chief
Being, and Agent; the first and chief Governor; the Fountain of Being, Agency,
and Authority: that the *Christian Messiah*,
the *Man Christ Jesus, was sent into the*

5   *world*

world to bear witness to the truth, and preach the gospel of the kingdom of God, that kingdom of God which is within you, saith the Lord, *Luke* xvii. 21. not a *kingdom of Monks,* a *sacerdotal empire* of *power, propositions,* and *ceremonies.* He came to *call sinners to repentance* and *amendment of life,* to *teach them the law of love,* and *assure mankind of grace and mercy* and *everlasting glory,* if they kept the commandments, and were obedient to the laws of heaven; laws of *righteousness, peace, giving no offence,* and *unanimity in the worship of the God and Father of our Lord Jesus Christ:* but that, if they did not *repent,* and *cease* to be *hurtful* and *injurious*; if they did not open their eyes, and turn from darkness to light, from the power of satan unto God, and put on such an agreeable and useful temper and behaviour, as would render them a *blessing* in the creation, they would be numbered among the *cursed,* and perish everlastingly, for *want* of *real goodness* and a *general sincerity of heart.* This the *Socinians* think is what *Christ* proposed and recommended, as the only and the sure way to God's favour, through the *worthiness* of the *Lamb that was slain.* We say this is pure religion. It is true, original christianity, and if the glorious design of our Lord is answered by his *miracles* and *preaching,* by his *death,* his *re-*
surrection,

surrection, his *ascension*, and by the *grace of
the holy, blessed, and sanctifying Spirit*, it
could reflect no dishonour on christianity,
and its divine author, if, our Redeemer was
a *meer man*. If by the assistance of God Almighty, a *mere man* performed the whole
work of our redemption, all we had to do
was to be thankful for the mighty blessing.
The love of God in this way had been e-
qually inestimable: The worth of Jesus
would be still invaluable.

But it is not the opinion of the *Socinians*
that Christ was a *mere man*. It is plain from
this assertion, that the Rev. Dr. *Heathcote*,
(in his Remarks on free and candid Disqui-
sitions) knows nothing of them: the account
they give of *Jesus Christ*, is very different.
They say, he was a most glorious agent united to a human body, and so far from being
a *mere man*, that he was superior to angels.
He was the next in character to the neces-
sarily existing Being. He is the brightness
of the Father's glory, and the express image
of his person: he has an excellency transcendent, and to the life represents what
is infinitely great and perfect.

If they do not allow that he made the
worlds, or had an eternal generation; if
they say, he had no existence till he was
formed.

formed by the power of God in the womb, and assert this eminency is proper to the *Man Christ Jesus*; yet they are far from affirming he was therefore a *mere man:* no; they believe he was decreed to be as great and glorious as possible, and that God made the world for him; that he was made the *image* of the *invisible person* of the *Father*; *an image the most express and exact*; as great as God himself could make it; and of consequence, so transcendent in all perfections, that what he says and does is the same thing as if God had spoken and acted. This is not making him a *mere man*. No: they say he is the *first of all*, and the *head of all creatures*, whom the infinite love of God produced, to promote greatness, glory, and happiness among the creatures, by the superlative greatness and glory of Jesus; and that angels, and the spirits of the just made perfect, might have the pleasure of beholding and enjoying the presence of this most glorious Image, that is, of seeing their invisible Creator in his *Image Jesus Christ*. He is not a *mere man*; but the *brightness of the glory of God*, the *express Image of his person*, and raised so much higher than *the angels*, as he has inherited from God a more excellent name than they, to wit, the name of *Son*, and is the *appointed heir of all things.*

Se

So that this *Socinianifm* reflects no dishonour on Christianity, and its Divine Author, It conduces as much to the glory of God, and the benefit of man, as any christianity can do.   There is something vastly beautiful and satisfactory in the notion of *Chrift's* being the *most glorious Image* of the *invisible Father*, whenever his existence began.   The many transcendent excellencies of the *Mes-jias*, in *whom all fullnefs dwells*, are exercised upon men to their happinefs, and to his glory; and we learn from thence, that greatnefs and glory are the refult of the exercife of virtue to the relief and happinefs of others.   The Redeemer of the world is, in this account, the next in dignity and power to the Great God; and the perfections of the Father do most eminently shine forth in him.   We are hereby made meet to be partakers of the inheritance of the faints in light, and delivered from the power of darknefs.   We give thanks unto the Father, who hath tranflated us into the kingdom of the Son of his love.

It is certain then that the divines have *mifreprefented* the people, who are *injurioufly* called *Socinians*, as the religion they profefs is *Scripture-Chriftianity:*   I fay *injurioufly*, becaufe, in the firft place, the word *Socinian* is intended as a term of great reproach

to

to chriftians, who deferve better ufage for the *goodnefs of their manners*, and the *purity of their faith*: and in the next place, that *Socinus* was fo far from being the author of our religion, that he was not even the firft reftorer of it. He did not go to *Poland* to teach the people there his religious notions, but becaufe there was an unitarian congrega-tion there, with whom he might join in the *worfhip of the Father, through Jefus the Mediator*, as his confcience would not fuffer him to affemble with thofe who wor-fhip *a Being compounded of three divine per-fons*.

But it is time to have done, and I fhall conclude in the words of a good author in old *French**. The extract muft be a curi-ous thing to the reader, as the valuable book I take it from is not to be bought.

Noftre confeffion de foy até depuis la premiere predication de l'evangile puifque nous luy donnons la fainte ecriture pour fon-dement, mais il arrive de nous ce qu'il ar-rive des tous ceux qui fe font detachés de l'eglife Romaine aux quels le papiftes don-nent malgré eux pour autheurs de leur re-

---

* Or rather in bad *French*, as the writer was no *Frenchman*.

ligion.

ligion Luther, Calvin, & autres docteurs qui n'ont été que les restorateurs, des dogmes & de verités qui s'etoyent presque perdues sous le gouvernement tyrannique de l'eglise Romaine pendant lequel l'ecriture sainte etoit devenue un livre inconnu a la plufpart de chretiens la lecture en ayant été defendue communement. Mais par un decret de la providence de Dieu le periode de la revolution etant venu chacun a commencé a deterrer la verité la mieux qu'il a pu, & comme dans chaque revolution il y a des chefs & des gens illustres, ainsi dans le retablissement des dogmes etouffés si longtems par le papisme Luther, Calvin, Arminius, & *Socin*, ont été des hommes illustres & dont on a donné le nom aux religions. Vous sçaurez donc s'il vous plaist que *Socin* bien loin d'avoir été autheur de nostre religion n'en a pas été meme la premier restaurateur: car il n'etoit venu en Pologne que parce qu'il avoit appris qu'il s'y etoit deja formée une assemblée de gens qui avoyent des opinions semblables aux siennes : Je vous diray de plus, que la seule chose que le fait un heros dans nostre religion c'est qu'il en a ecrit des livres, mais il ny a presque personne qui les life, car comme *Socin* etoit un bon jurisconsulte il est extremement long & ennuyeux ; & outre que nous ne voulous point avoir d'autre livre de religion

I   gion

gion que le nouveau Teſtament & point
d'autres docteurs que ies apoſtres. C'eſt
pourquoy, c'eſt bien malgré nous qu'on
nous appelle *Sociniens* ou *Arriens:* ce ſont
des noms dont la malignité de nos en-
nemys nous couvre pour nous rendre odieux.
Nous appellons entre nous du ſimple nom
de *Chretiens.* Mais puiſque dans cette deſ-
union de la chretienté, on nous dit qu'il
ne ſuffit pas de porter ce nom univerſel,
mais qu'il encore neceſſairement ſe diſtinguer par quelque appellation particuliere,
nous conſentons donc de porter le nom de
chretiens unitaires pour nous diſtinguer de
chretiens trinitaires. Ce nom de *chretiens
unitaires* nous convient fort bien comme a
ceux qui ne voulant en aucune façon en-
cherye ſur la doctrine de Jeſus Chriſt, n'y
ſubtiliſer plus qu'il ne faut, attachent leur
croyance & leur confeſſion poſitivement a
cette inſtruction de Jeſus Chriſt qui ſe trouve
dans le 17 chap. de l'evangile de St. Jean,
quand il dit----Mon pere l'heure eſt venue,
glorifiez voſtre fils afin que voſtre fils vous
glorifie, comme vous luy avez donné puiſ-
ſance ſur tous les hommes a fin qu'il donne
la vie eternelle a tous ceux que vous luy
avez donné; or la vie eternelle conſiſte a
vous connoiſtre, vous qui eſtes le ſeul Dieu
veritable, & Jeſus Chriſt que vous avez en-
voyé. La meſme leçon nous donne l'apoſtre

St. Paul dans le 8 chap. aux Cor. difant,—— qu'il n'y a pour nous qu'un feul Dieu qui eft la pere duquel font toutes chofes & noûs pour luy, & il n'y a qu'un feul feigneur qui eft Jefus Chrift, par lequel font toutes chofes & nous par luy. C'eft donc a caufe de cette confeffion que nous nous appellons chretiens unitaires par ce que nous croyons qu'il n'y a qu'un feul Dieu, pere & Dieu de noftre feigneur Jefus Chrift, celuy que Jefus Chrift nous a appris d'adorer, & lequel il a auffy adoré luy meme, l'appellent non feulment noftre Dieu mais fon Dieu auffy felon qu'il a dit, je m'en vay a mon pere & voftre pere, a mon Dieu & a voftre Dieu.

Ainfy vous voyez que nous nous tenons aux verités divines. Nous avons la reli- gieufe veneration pour la fainte ecriture. Avec tout cela nous fommes ferviteurs tres humble des meffieurs les *trinitaires,——penes quos mundanæ fabulæ actio eft*, & il ne tient pas a nous que nous ne courrions de tout noftre cœur a leurs autels, s'ils vouloyent nous faire la grace de fouffrir noftre fim- plicité en Jefus Chrift, & de ne pas vou- loir nous obliger a la confeffion de fupple- ments a la fainte ecriture*.

---

* La verité & la religion en vifite. Alamagné 1695.

The

§. 8. The great and ex- *An account of* cellent *Fauſtus Socinus* was Socinus. born at *Sienna*, in the year 1539, and died at *Luclavie*, the third of *March*, 1604, aged 65. His book in defence of the authority of the ſacred ſcriptures is a matchleſs performance; and if he had never written any thing elſe, is alone ſufficient to render his memory glorious, and precious to all true chriſtians. Get this book, if you can. It is the fineſt defence of your Bible that was ever publiſhed. (Steinfurti, A. 1611. edit. Vorſt.) And yet, ſuch is the *malignity* of *orthodoxy*, that a late great prelate, Dr. *Smalbroke*, Bp. of *Litchfield* and *Coventry*, (who died A. D. 1749) could not help blackening the author when he mentioned the work: his words are theſe;—" And if *Grotius* was more eſpecially aſſiſted by the *valuable* performance of a writer, *otherwiſe juſtly of ill fame*, I mean, *Fauſtus Socinus*'s little book *De Auctoritate S. Scripturæ*, this aſſiſtance," &c. *2d charge to the clergy of St. David*'s, p. 34.—Here the admirable *Fauſtus*, a man of as much piety, and as good morals, as hath lived ſince the apoſtles time, who truly and godly ſerved the almighty and everlaſting God, through our Lord and Saviour Jeſus Chriſt, is painted by this eminent hand *a man of ill fame*; and for no other reaſon, but becauſe his heavenly reli

gion.

gion made him oppofe the *orthodox herefy of three Gods*, as taught in the *creed of Athanafius*; and pioufly labour, by the purity of his doctrine and example, to keep the world from corruption.

Let us then be careful to confefs the holy *unitarian faith*. Let us take the advice of *Socinus*, and be *original chriftians*. Let there not be in our religion *a God compounded of three fupreme fpirits, equal in power and all poffible perfections*. Let us worfhip the *Invifible Father*, the *firft and chief Almighty Being*, who is *one fupreme univerfal Spirit*, of *peerlefs Majefty*; and, as the infpired apoftles direct, let us worfhip him through his *moft glorious Image*, the *Man Chrift Jefus*; our *Redeemer* and *Mediator*, our *King* and our *Judge*.

N. B. Though the reverend *Dr. Heathcote* hath been very *unfriendly* in his account of the Chriftians he calls *Socinians*, in his Obfervations before mentioned, yet you are not from thence to conclude that he belongs to the *Orthodox Party*. He is far from it, and therefore I recommend to your perufal not only his *Curfory Animadverfions upon free and candid Difquifitions*, and his finer Boyle-Lecture Sermons on the Being of God, but alfo his *Curfory Animadverfions*
upon

upon *the Controverfy, concerning the miracu-lous Powers,* and his *Remarks on Chapman's Credibility of the Fathers Miracles.* They are three excellent pamphlets. The firft is againft the *fcholaftic Trinity.* And the others on the fide of Doctor *Middleton,* againft the *miracles* of the *Fathers.*

, Note Reader, Dr. *Heathcote*'s two pam-phlets on the fide of Dr. *Middleton,* and the Rev. Mr. *Toll*'s admirable pieces in vindi-cation of the Doctor againft the miracles of the Fathers, will give you a juft and full idea of the late controverfy. Mr. *Toll*'s pieces are called ---- *A Defence of Dr. Middleton's Free Enquiry* --- *Remarks upon Mr. Church's Vindication* --- And his *Sermon and Appendix againft Dr. Church's Appeal.*

And if you would fee all that can be faid in relation to this matter, get likewife *Dr. Syke's Two previous Queftions:* and the *Two previous Queftions impartially confidered*; by the fame author.

, *Remarks on two Pamphlets againft Dr. Middleton's Introductory Difcourfe:* --- *Two Letters to the Rev. Mr. Jackfon, in Anfwer to his Remarks on Middleton's Free Inquiry:* --- And, *A View of the Controverfy, con-cerning the miraculous Powers fuppofed, to*

have

have subsisted in the Christian Church through several successive Centuries.

These pamphlets will bind into two large octavo volumes, and make a valuable collection of critical religious learning.

Note, Reader, of that admirable work, called *Bibliotheca Fratrum Polonorum*, by *Socinus*, *Crellius*, *Sclichtingius*, and *Wolzogenius*, 6 tomes, fol. *Irenopoli* 1656. The first and second volumes are the writings of *Socinus*; the third and fourth by *Crellius*; the fifth by *Sclichtingius*; and the sixth by *Wolzogenius*: they are all well worth your reading, as they contain the most valuable and excellent learning; and especially *Socinus* and *Crellius*. In another place, (where you will find me alone in a solitude) I shall give some curious extracts from the works of these great, injured men, and a summary of their lives.

END OF THE THIRD VOLUME.